Beguiled

KAY GREGORY

Heartline Books

Published by Heartline Books Limited in 2001

Copyright © Kay Gregory 2001

Kay Gregory has asserted her rights under the Copyright, Designs and Patents Act, 1988 to be identified as the author of this work.

This is a work of fiction. Names and characters are the product of the author's imagination and any resemblance to an actual persons, living or dead, is purely coincidental.

All rights reserved. No part of this publication may be reproduced, stored in or introduced into a retrieval system or transmitted by any form, or by any means (electronic, mechanical, photocopying, recording or otherwise) without the prior written permission of the publisher. Any person who commits any unauthorised act in relation to this publication may be liable to criminal prosecution and civil claims for damages.

Heartline Books Limited and Heartline Books logo are trademarks of the publisher.

First published in the United Kingdom in 2001 by Heartline Books Limited.

Heartline Books Limited
PO Box 22598, London W8 7GB

Heartline Books Ltd. Reg No: 03986653

ISBN 1-903867-04-5

Designed by Oxford Designers & Illustrators

Printed and bound in Great Britain by
Cox & Wyman, Reading, Berkshire

KAY GREGORY

When Kay was a child growing up in England, she was convinced that a passion for Bonnie Prince Charlie was all the qualification she needed to write romantic stories about boys in kilts – who were always called Bruce, Duncan or Alistair. She had never actually visited Scotland, which must have been obvious to the publishers who kept returning her masterpieces and wishing her luck in placing her work elsewhere!

Now that Kay has grown up she writes about men called Greg, Max or Luke and none of them wear kilts – though Kay has now visited Scotland and found it even more romantic than she'd imagined.

Kay's first romance novel was published in 1986 and she still feels lucky to have the best job in the world – writing books that people actually want to read.

To NATHAN, my favourite biologist with love
and thanks for all his help and expertise

To LORRAINE, friend beyond compare, without
whose powers of observation this book would
have been one scene short – and, of course, to
SARAH and MICHELLE

prologue

Mrs Crump had a voice like a foghorn. Olivia laughed when it boomed up to the gallery where she stood peeking over the railing above the hall. Phantom, who sat panting beside her, lowered his soft, black Labrador ears and scuttled out of sight. Phantom always ran away from Mrs Crump.

Abruptly the foghorn lowered its volume to the growly rumble that was Mrs Crump's idea of a whisper, and after that, no matter how hard she tried, Olivia could only make out an extra loud word here and there. It was very disappointing.

Still straining to hear, she abandoned her post on the gallery and edged down to the bend in the stairs. Oh, this was better. Now she could hear everything.

'...So tragic. Poor Joe and Charlotte. Devoted to Raymond, naturally...'

'Yes, yes. Tragic. Bright young fellow, Raymond. Thank heaven they still have little Olivia...'

That was Dr Crump's voice, as powerful as his wife's but less penetrating.

Olivia slipped the rest of the way down and came to a stop outside the partially-opened door to the sitting room. If they were going to talk about her instead of Raymond, she meant to hear every single word.

Raymond was her brother. He was twenty, ten years older than she was, and he'd been killed three days ago when the plane he'd been learning to fly had crashed on to a dike near Vancouver Airport.

Olivia's mother hadn't stopped crying since. Even her father, who usually paid attention to her and called her his

'Little Moonbeam' had been different. He blew his nose a lot and said they were all going through a difficult time and must try to help each other and 'Not Bother Mother'.

What that really meant, Olivia had discovered, was that she was left almost entirely to the care of Inez, her nanny, who came from the Philippines and who wouldn't stop crying either. Inez called Raymond, 'That so beautiful young man.'

Olivia didn't think he was beautiful. He was just her older brother who never had much time for little girls. People kept saying he was cut out for a brilliant career as something called a diplomat. She wasn't sure what a diplomat was, but it sounded important. Now Raymond was dead – and he was still the one people talked about. Except for Dr Crump. He wanted to talk about *her*.

She put her ear against the wall and listened.

'Oh, Olivia,' Mrs Crump was saying, as if she'd quite forgotten Raymond had a sister. 'Yes, I suppose it is a blessing they have her. But I can't help feeling Joe and Charlotte would cope better if they'd lost their daughter instead of their only son. That boy always was the apple of their eye.'

'Now, now, Dora. You mustn't say things like that.' Dr Crump sounded gruff and uncomfortable. 'God's will, you know. God's will.'

'Yes, of course it is. But Olivia's such a funny, shy little thing...'

'Pretty though, with all that dark hair and those great big eyes of hers. Bet she'll be a knockout when she's older.'

'Oh, perhaps. But Raymond was the one with the future.'

Dr Crump cleared his throat and didn't answer.

As the silence continued, Olivia closed her eyes and tried to understand what she'd just heard. Mother and Dad wanted *her* dead instead of Raymond? Was that why they kept telling her to run away and play with Inez? Dr Crump said she was pretty, but he hadn't told Mrs Crump she had everything all wrong...

A cold feeling was creeping into Olivia's arms and legs, and a kind of hardness was pushing at her chest. For a moment she wanted to cry, but the need passed quickly and, after a while, she opened her eyes to look around the big galleried hall of the house she had always called home.

It didn't feel like home any longer. Raymond had lived here, and *he* wasn't the one who ought to be dead. Mrs Crump said her parents would have coped better if they'd lost their daughter...

Was coped the same as not minded?

'Olivia! What are you doing listening at doors?'

Olivia jumped as her mother swept down the stairs in a flurry of black silk and disapproval.

'Really, Olivia! You've been brought up to know better than that. Where's Inez?'

'I don't know.'

'Well, go and find her.' Her mother's shoulders drooped and she seemed to lose interest. Her face was all blotchy too as she went into the sitting room to join Dr and Mrs Crump.

Olivia heard Dr Crump say, 'There, there, Charlotte. Try to remember all the happiness Raymond brought you.'

As she fled up the stairs with her knuckles pressed against her eyes, Olivia heard her mother's tearful voice answer, 'That's just it, Doctor. I can't bear it that all the happiness is over.'

Over? Happiness? Because Raymond was dead?

She pushed open the door to her bedroom and stamped across the carpet to stare out of the window at the sunlight making shapes on the lawn. Beyond the smoothly-cut grass rose her private copse of fir trees where only yesterday she had seen a racoon.

Olivia loved the garden. She knew their big house on Marine Drive called The Cedars was one of the nicest in Vancouver, but she wasn't supposed to run in the house. The garden was different. She could run there, and there were flowers and a cherry tree and butterflies, and sometimes even a humming-bird or two.

Today the butterflies and flowers didn't make her feel at all happy inside the way they usually did.

Her parents didn't love her as they'd loved Raymond. For a moment, until natural obstinacy came to her rescue, Olivia wished that she *was* dead instead of him.

But she wasn't dead. She, Olivia Elizabeth Franklyn, was alive, and if her parents didn't love her as much as Raymond, then she wouldn't love them either. She wouldn't love anyone. From now on she would only care about herself. She kicked her black patent shoe at the wall and was glad when a chip of paint flaked on to the carpet. She might be second best to Mother and Dad, but she would always be first best to herself. And to Phantom.

Phantom loved her. She knew he did, because he always wagged his long black tail and jumped up to lick her on the nose.

Frowning, Olivia sat down on the pink-flowered chair that matched her bedspread and gazed round her pretty pink-and-cream room. Pink wasn't her favourite colour today. Blue was cleaner and nicer. She'd make Mother change it. That would be as good a way as any to start being the kind of person who didn't care at all about other people.

By the time Inez came in a few minutes later, Olivia had all her bedclothes on the floor and was snipping away with nail scissors at the frill around the bottom of her chair.

Inez screamed. 'Olivia! You are a bad, bad girl. Your mother will be very angry.'

'Don't care,' Olivia said.

In the end though, Mother didn't seem to mind much. She surveyed the devastation with listless eyes, sighed, and told Olivia to leave the chair alone.

Two weeks later the pink bedroom was redecorated in blue.

chapter one

Luke was halfway up a mountain and chest-deep in prickly, shrub-like weeds, when his mobile phone rang. Swearing, he shoved his notebook into a pocket, wrenched himself from the thorny embrace of his least favourite plants and straddled the trunk of a fallen spruce tree. Only when he was as comfortable as was possible in this unwelcoming terrain did he reach into his pocket for the phone.

The voice on the other end, which sounded efficient, female and prepared to soothe, instantly put him on alert.

'Is this Mr Luke Harriman? Rosemary Harriman's brother?'

'It is. What about Rosemary?'

'She's had an accident…'

'An accident? What kind of accident? Is she all right?'

'Don't worry, Mr Harriman. We're looking after her.'

'That's what *I* do, Ms Whoever-you-are. Look after Rosemary. What's the matter with her?'

He heard the sound of indignant breath being sucked in. 'If we could talk to you in person, Mr Harriman…'

'I asked you what's the matter with her,' Luke interrupted. When it came to Rosemary, he had no time for the polite mouthing of bureaucracy. Even well-meaning bureaucracy.

'I'm afraid it's not usually our policy…'

'Damn your policy. Just tell me what's happened.'

'Very well.' The woman's voice was maddeningly calm. 'Your sister took too many pills.'

'She *what*?' Luke leapt to his feet, overbalanced and landed on his back in a pile of thorny weeds with the phone still pressed against his ear.

'Mr Harriman? Are you there?'

'Of course I'm here.' He struggled painfully back on to the tree trunk, restraining his language with an effort. 'What was that you said about pills?'

'Your sister took too many. We've pumped her stomach and she's resting nicely now. But, Mr Harriman, it *would* help if we could talk to you...'

'Of course you'll talk to me. Which hospital are you calling from?'

She told him, and within seconds he had hoisted his backpack and was hurling himself down the steep slope. A routine biological inventory of government-listed species was unimportant compared to his sister's welfare. Rosemary came first, as she had done since the day, fourteen years ago now, when he'd become her only anchor in a world turned upside down.

Rosemary needed him, and all that mattered now was to get to her side by the fastest means possible – in this case, the seat of his pants. Later, when he was sure she was all right, he would deal with whatever, or whoever, had put her in this state.

Rosemary wrinkled her nose, as Luke touched her wrist. 'Oh-h,' she moaned.

Luke growled, 'Rosie, for God's sake...' He broke off, shaking his dark head because he couldn't find the words to tell her how he felt. Luke felt a lot, but he rarely expressed his feelings to her or to anyone else.

'What...?' she asked vaguely. 'Luke, why am I here? This is a hospital, isn't it?'

'Of course it's a hospital. Don't you remember why you're here?'

'Not really. I know I didn't have any classes this morning – it was this morning, wasn't it? – and I was studying for my English exam when... Oh.' She put a hand to her head.

'When...?' Luke pushed. 'What happened then, Rosie?'

Rosemary lowered her eyelids. 'Michael phoned. He said we were finished. That he preferred Olivia Franklyn to me...'

'Who in the Hell is Olivia Franklyn?'

'Joe Franklyn's daughter. You know, the one with all the money. He's some sort of financial wizard, I think. Olivia lives in a big, expensive townhouse in Point Grey.' Rosemary raised her eyelids. 'She's in some of my classes at UBC.'

'OK. So what did you do after Michael phoned?'

'I phoned Olivia. But I shouldn't have. She just laughed and said I was too mousy.'

Luke made an explosive noise 'Mousy? Rosie, you can't believe that. You're pretty and kind and...'

'You're my brother. Most men don't like freckles and beige-looking hair. And Olivia's gorgeous. Like Scarlett O'Hara in *Gone With The Wind*.'

Luke made a rude comment, and Rosemary added hastily, 'Anyway, Olivia got Michael and now she doesn't even want him any more.'

'Rosie...' Luke's big hand closed around her wrist, pulling her hand from her eyes. 'You're crying.'

'I'm all right.'

'No.' Luke shook his head. 'You're not all right. Do you mean to tell me you took all those – what were they? The pills you took?'

'Pills? Did I ...? Oh. Yes, I did, didn't I? They were tranquillisers. I haven't been sleeping well.'

'Why, Rosie? Why did you have tranquillisers?' Luke's eyes were dark with a pain she deeply regretted causing. 'Surely you didn't believe the rat was worth it?'

'No. No, I didn't. But I got them because I couldn't sleep and then took some more because I forgot...' She curled her fingers around his reassuring palm. 'I'm sorry. Truly I am. As soon as I realised what I'd done, I called the Emergency Services.'

Luke gazed down at her white, sweet face on the pillow and felt as if a band of iron had tightened around his chest. He could have lost her in that minute. All because of a little creep, and a dark-eyed beauty without a heart.

'Rosie,' he said, sitting on the edge of the bed and taking her thin hands in his. 'Rosie, you love me, don't you?'

'Of course I do. More than anyone in the world.'

'Then will you promise me something?'

'If I can.'

'You can. Promise me you'll never ever do anything like this again. No matter what happens.'

The blue of her eyes darkened to smoke, and her eyebrows drew together in a small, familiar frown. 'All right,' she agreed. 'I promise. I'll throw the wretched pills away!'

The band around Luke's chest tightened until he wanted to roar his fury at the sterile hospital walls. How dare that miserable creature who called himself a man do this to his vulnerable little sister? As for Olivia Franklyn — that little tramp needed a damn good kick in the butt...

Once Luke was outside in the damp spring air, his head cleared quickly. Dammit, this Michael had no right to sleep peacefully tonight. Luke glanced up at Rosemary's window. 'I'll fix him for you, Rosie,' he said out loud.

Visions of bruised chins and bloody noses kept Luke going nicely until he reached Michael's home on West Third. There his dreams of revenge met with a setback when he was informed by Michael's mother that her son had left with his basketball team for points north.

Luke, balked of his prey, managed to murmur semi-polite thanks. He slouched back to his truck, the black ball of anger curling inside him still in dire need of a target.

The solution came to him as he was crossing the Burrard Street Bridge. Olivia Franklyn. She was the witch behind his sister's pain.

Luke had no clear idea of what he meant to do as he turned the truck around and headed back the way he had come. But he damn well meant to do something.

A phone book, that was what he needed. As it turned out, there was only one Franklyn listed in the area. O.E. Franklyn sounded like a man but probably wasn't.

Luke knew he had come to the right place, the moment he pulled up in front of a converted brick mansion with tree-shaded lawns and beds full of daffodils and heather.

He knocked on the first door he came to.

It opened after a brief pause during which he guessed he was being assessed through a peephole, and when he saw the woman standing in the entrance, for a few seconds he felt as if the sky had exchanged places with the earth beneath his feet. He shut his eyes. When he opened them again he realised that the slim, dark-eyed woman framed by the ivy-covered doorway was merely a beautiful mortal, not some siren sent to lure him to destruction.

'Hi,' she said, in a low voice that made the hairs on the back of his neck stand on end. 'Come in.'

Luke swiped an arm across a forehead that was inexplicably damp, as well as stinging from his brief encounter with the nettles. 'You don't know me,' he said.

'No, but I know your sister.' She smiled, and again the earth seemed to lurch beneath his feet. 'I've seen you once or twice when you came to pick her up after class.'

His sister. Rosemary. The reason he was here. This goddess in the skin-tight black slacks and red silk shirt, whose slightest movement made him want to forget that he was a civilised, twenty-first-century man who treated women with respect, was the witch responsible for putting Rosemary in hospital.

'I see,' he said, wondering why his voice sounded cracked.

The witch raised her eyebrows. 'Won't you come in?'

14   *Kay Gregory*

Feeling as clumsy and self-conscious as any libidinous fourteen-year-old, Luke edged past her into a narrow hall with a polished hardwood floor and an oak staircase leading, presumably, to the bedrooms. He noted several good watercolours on the walls painted by artists whose names even *he* recognised. Most of the paintings were of animals. Beyond the hall was a bright, comfortable sitting-room decorated in warm shades of yellow and brown – an old-fashioned room that didn't quite match the 'modern miss' who owned it.

Only when he heard the front door close behind him did it occur to Luke to ask, 'Are you Olivia Elizabeth Franklyn?'

'Yes, but most people call me Olivia.'

Luke, still feeling as if he'd been winded, said over his shoulder, 'So you're the bitch who put my sister in the hospital.'

If he'd been facing her, he wouldn't have been able to say it. She looked too angelic to be a bitch.

'What?' Olivia moved round to stand in front of him, her big eyes wide and reproachful. 'Of course I didn't. *Is* she in hospital.'

'Yes, she is.'

'Oh. What's the matter with her?'

So innocent, as if butter wouldn't melt in her mouth. And yet he could see she didn't really care. Her beautiful, heart-shaped face was merely curious.

'She took some pills after you stole her boyfriend.' Luke shoved his hands deep into the pockets of his jeans. Olivia's eyes followed the movement, and he saw her moisten her lower lip.

'Oh dear. How dramatic of her. She shouldn't have. He really isn't worth it.'

Luke's hands curled into fists. Had he really thought this woman was a goddess? 'You don't give a damn, do you?' he said.

'About Rosemary? No. But don't take it personally. I don't give a damn about anybody much.'

'Except yourself.'

Her full mouth curved in a smile that made him want to throttle her. It was the sweetest, phoniest smile he had ever had the misfortune to behold on the face of a beautiful woman.

'Of course,' she said. 'If I didn't care about me, who would?'

'Not many people, I guess. Not if you usually treat your friends the way you treated Rosemary.'

She shrugged. 'I do, I suppose. Although, if it makes any difference, your sister isn't really my friend. Why did you come?'

He took a step forward so that he was standing almost on top of her. She smelled of something sinful and exotic with an oddly intriguing hint of lemon. 'Why do you think?'

Olivia didn't flinch. 'I don't know. I hoped it was because you'd noticed me noticing you.'

Luke released his breath in a snort of outrage. 'Sorry to disappoint you. I didn't.'

'Oh. Too bad.' She ran manicured nails through her smooth, shoulder-length hair. 'What have you done to your face? It looked better the last time I saw it.'

Luke's fingers bit into his palms. So help him, if he didn't get out of here soon, he was likely to do something they'd both regret. What in the *hell* had possessed him to come?

'I don't doubt it did,' he replied. 'The last time you saw me, I hadn't been forced to slide down a mountain because some cruel little witch had broken my sister's heart.'

'Hearts mend,' Olivia said. 'Besides, I didn't do it on my own. Michael had a say in the matter. Why don't you take it up with him?'

'I tried. He's away.'

'Oh. So that leaves me.' She put her hands on her hips and raised her chin defiantly. 'What are you going to do about it?'

Lord, she was gorgeous. And what he would like to do didn't bear thinking about. 'I don't know,' he snapped. 'But I'll think of something. What would you have done if Rosemary had died?'

'Done? I couldn't have done anything.'

'You wouldn't have cared either, would you?' It was hard to believe such beauty could be so callous.

'I think I would. It's hard to say.' She tipped her head to one side. 'Do you want to know what your sister really needs?'

'What does my sister need?' He raised his hands, meaning to grasp her by the shoulders, then thought better of it and shoved them back into his pockets.

'To develop some spine, of course, instead of relying on you to fight her battles for her. No one can hurt her unless she lets them.'

Luke shook his head in disbelief. It was clear this beautiful creature without a heart didn't know the meaning of hurt.

'And what *you* need,' he replied, 'is something else entirely.' Inside his pockets, his fingers flexed.

Olivia laughed. 'Cave-man stuff? I'd like to see you try.'

'I wouldn't,' Luke said. 'I might not know when to stop.'

For the first time since he'd entered her townhouse, he saw a flicker of something that wasn't indifference in her eyes. He wasn't sure if it was fear or excitement, but what he did know was that he had to leave at once, before he inflicted the kind of damage that made titillating headlines in the tabloids.

He lowered his head and brought his face close to hers. 'So help me, Ms Franklyn,' he said. 'If you ever come near my sister or anyone she cares about again, I promise you'll regret it. Do you understand me?'

'Perfectly,' Olivia replied. Smiling coolly, she raised an arm and plucked a leaf out of his hair. 'Don't you think you ought to clean yourself up?' Her hand brushed lightly across his chest.

Luke swore silently, stepped backwards, and stalked into the hall and out the door.

It had started to rain. Breathing hard, he lifted his face to the sodden skies and allowed the cool, heavy drops to bathe his heated skin.

Olivia stood at the window watching Luke slouch down the driveway to the battered truck parked beneath the trees.

He was certainly one glorious specimen of manhood – even covered as he was in dirt and bruises. But she'd got off to a bad start with Luke Harriman. He wasn't immune to her though, she'd seen that at once. The problem was that at present he was far too angry about that weak-boned sister of his, to give in to his natural inclinations.

Olivia shook her head and twisted a lock of hair around her thumb. No, she hadn't handled him well – which was odd, because she usually knew exactly how to get what she wanted from a man. Of course what she should have done was bat her eyelashes and smile, and pretend to be overcome with horror that silly Rosemary had tried to take her own life.

Olivia continued to watch the dark shape of Luke's body in the moonlight until he climbed into the cab of his truck. Yes, he was definitely worth working on, though what she would do with him once she got him, she wasn't sure. Probably send him packing like all the rest. But Luke, at least, would offer her a challenge.

She smoothed her hands down her hips, nodding approvingly as he bent forward to switch on the engine. She liked a man who moved as though he knew what he was doing... Right now, of course, he thought of her as not much better than the slime the owners of Athington Woods occasionally dredged up from the ditch at the bottom of the garden.

It would be fun to change his mind.

Luke had made an impression on her the very first time she saw him sitting in his truck outside the campus bookstore. His thick, dark hair, square jaw and attractively crooked mouth formed an irresistibly masculine combination. She had envied the smile he gave his sister when she clambered up beside him. No one had smiled at *her* like that since – oh, she couldn't even remember when. Phantom would have smiled if he'd known how, but poor Phantom had died of old age only a few months after she turned twelve.

Olivia frowned, as she always did when she made the mistake of remembering that particular birthday.

Raymond had been dead for more than a year then, and her parents were over the first sharp agony of loss. Life went on, and her father said that although the pain would always be with them, they must learn to accept what could never be changed.

Olivia supposed that was true, although she hadn't, for a moment, forgotten the vow she had made following Raymond's death. She had done her best not to reach out for the love and warmth she often missed. But as the months passed her resolve began to weaken. Maybe Mrs Crump had been wrong...

A few weeks before her birthday, Olivia decided to ask if she could have an extra-special party to celebrate being twelve, and her parents immediately agreed.

Olivia, older now and convinced she was a lot smarter, began to believe she had misjudged her parents' feelings. Mrs Crump thought she knew everything, but that didn't mean she did – and surely people didn't give big parties for daughters they didn't love. Filled with excitement, she made a list of the friends she wanted to invite – all her classmates from her exclusive private school, plus her second-cousin, Margaret.

Then, four days before the party, Joe Franklyn announced that he had to leave at once for New York.

'But you'll miss my party,' Olivia wailed.

'Party?' Joe frowned. 'Ah. Yes, of course. Don't worry, Moonbeam, I'll do my best to get back for it.'

Olivia believed him and was satisfied, even though Mother spent half the time in bed after he left, and didn't seem to want to talk to anyone.

On the morning of her birthday she awoke with a wriggly, excited feeling in her tummy, and jumped up to get dressed right away before Mother could come in and tell her not to put on her pretty blue dress until the afternoon.

She needn't have worried. Her mother didn't come, and when Olivia went to find her she was told by Mrs Cavendish, the cook-housekeeper, that Mrs Franklyn had gone shopping with Mrs Crump. No party was, or ever had been planned. At least Olivia was spared the humiliation of her friends turning up to the non-existent party. According to Mrs Cavendish, Mrs Franklyn hadn't even glanced at the guest list and certainly hadn't asked for any invitations to be sent out.

That night Olivia didn't go down to dinner, and when Mrs Cavendish was sent to fetch her, she said she felt sick and wasn't hungry – which was more or less true.

Later Mother came to ask how she was, but she looked more irritated than worried, so Olivia said she was fine. When her father hadn't come home by midnight, she went to bed and cried until her pillow was sodden and her eyes so sore and puffy that they hurt.

Hearing her sobs, Phantom pushed open the door with his snout and heaved himself on to the bed. Olivia spent the rest of the night with her arms around his neck.

It was years before she cried again, and even then it was only on the stage.

Olivia squared her shoulders. Luke didn't have to *like* her, that wasn't the point. She had long ago given up trying to win the approval of others. It was safer, less painful, to suit herself.

With a small sigh, she sank into her favourite yellow wingback. The rain was steady now, pelting against the windows in a grey, monotonous stream. She tilted her head back to gaze pensively at the white, coved ceiling.

Somehow she *had* to make Luke change his mind about seeing her again – and clearly, the first thing she must do was apologise. That part was easy enough.

She waited twenty minutes, checked the telephone book, then picked up the phone and began to dial.

'Yup?' snapped a man's deep voice.

'Luke?'

'Yup.'

Obviously he was not in a communicative mood. 'Luke, this is Olivia Franklyn…'

The line went dead.

Damn. He wouldn't talk to her. Now what?

Olivia thought some more, and after a while she made another phone call. It proved a lot more satisfactory than the first.

An hour and a half later she called a taxi.

Hmm! Luke's lodgings weren't particularly impressive. Vancouver's West End had some smart and exclusive apartment blocks, but this square five-storey box wasn't one of them. Never mind, at least his address had been listed in the phone book.

Olivia pressed the buzzer.

The moment Luke answered, she said, 'It's Olivia here. May I come up?'

'No. Go away.' The connection was severed without further conversation.

Olivia pressed again and went on pressing.

'I said "go away",' Luke repeated.

'Don't hang up,' she pleaded.

'Give me one reason why not?'

'I've come to apologise. And I've brought you something.'

'Apology not accepted. And I don't want anything.' Once again the connection was shut down.

Olivia narrowed her eyes and was about to press a third time, when a thin young man ran up the steps and inserted his key in the lock.

'Oh, excuse me,' she said. 'Would you mind letting me in? I seem to have forgotten my key.' She gave him her best winning smile.

He was down for the count within seconds.

'Sure.' He blinked very fast. 'What number are you?'

'311,' Olivia replied, giving Luke's number.

'I'm 210,' he informed her.

Did he expect her to care? 'Great,' she said, wishing he would stop blinking and open up.

Eventually he shook his head bemusedly and turned the key.

When the elevator door slid open, Olivia hesitated. Lone man, confined space, no way out. Oh, never mind. Who cared? The building was only five stories high, and he didn't *look* dangerous. Just stunned. Besides, she'd never been afraid to take risks.

Her confidence proved justified. The young man made no attempt to touch her, and waved politely when he got off at the second floor.

Luke had the television on and didn't hear her knock. She rapped again, sharply and, this time after a short pause, the door was flung open.

Olivia inserted a neat black shoe in the opening.

'How the hell did *you* get in?' Luke growled. 'No, don't tell me. I can guess.'

'May I come in?' Olivia noted approvingly that he'd had a shower and changed into clean jeans and a casual black sweatshirt.

'You may not. Get your foot out of my door.'

'I will not. I want to talk to you.'

'Stalemate. OK.' Luke shrugged and conceded defeat with suspicious alacrity. He draped his long body against the doorframe. 'Talk away.'

Olivia removed her foot. 'I'm sorry I hurt Rosemary,' she said. 'I didn't mean to.'

'You expect me to believe that?'

'Yes, because it's true. I didn't know how much she cared about Michael. And then, when you told me she was in hospital, I was so shocked I didn't know what to say.'

'Hadn't had time to think about what to say, you mean.'

Olivia judged it the right moment to turn on the smile. 'That too. Please...I really am sorry – and I *would* like to make it up to you...'

'To me? It's Rosemary you should make it up to.'

Oh. She hadn't thought of that complication. 'I will, of course,' Olivia said hastily. 'As soon as she's out of hospital. But I'd like to do something for you too. I...um...bought tickets to the play at the Playhouse. It's a comedy. We've still time to get there if we hurry. I thought it might help to...well, you know...take your mind off things.'

'My mind is just fine where it is, thank you. With my sister.'

Ouch! This wasn't going well. Time to change tactics. 'Oh, please,' Olivia said, willing a suitable amount of moisture into her eyes, a manoeuvre she had perfected long ago in her drama class at school. Whenever she wanted to cry she thought of Phantom. 'Please. I do feel so awful about what happened...'

She allowed a single tear to trickle down her cheek.

Luke said something she didn't catch.

Olivia sniffed, and sent two more teardrops chasing after the first.

Luke said, 'Hell! For heaven's sake, what are you crying about?'

'You're so angry with me,' she whimpered. She wasn't the star of her theatre class for nothing.

'Of course I'm angry, you little... Listen, stop that snivelling – right this minute!'

'I c-can't stop.' Olivia fumbled in her purse and pulled out the tickets. 'Here, you have them. Take someone else if you don't want to take me.'

'Don't be an idiot. And for heaven's sake stop crying.'

Ah. The weak link. He was one of those men who couldn't stand to see a woman cry. Those were usually the first to succumb.

'I told you, I c-can't,' she repeated, thinking hard about darling Phantom.

The trickle became a flood. While Luke continued to glare, she sobbed with gentle pathos until the moment he started to close the door.

She gazed up at him piteously, then raised a hand to brush ineffectually at her eyes.

'For Pete's sake,' Luke muttered. He hesitated. 'All right, all right, if I take the damn tickets, will you cut it out?'

She nodded, head bowed, and held them out to him. He took them, and again made to close the door.

Olivia sniffed noisily.

'Now what's the matter?' he demanded.

'I can understand that you don't want my company,' she said, blinking rapidly.

Luke growled something that sounded like a curse – an unusual one she hadn't heard before.

Judging her timing to the second, Olivia dashed a hand across her eyes, stumbled, and reached out to clutch at his arm. He stiffened, and immediately she moved her hand to his shoulder.

'Enjoy the play,' she said, her voice trembling.

Luke groaned and held up his hands. 'OK, I give up,' he said, sounding a lot like a martyr surrendering his body to the stake. 'We'll go to your damn play. And after that you will stay the hell out of my life. And Rosemary's. Is that the deal?'

It wasn't, but it would do for a start.

Olivia lowered her eyelids so he wouldn't see the triumph behind her tears. 'Yes,' she said, smiling seraphically. 'Of course.'

Luke, looking as though he'd been hit on the head with a chunk of moon rock, told her to wait while he put on a jacket.

Olivia leaned against the doorframe, raised her fists above her head, and whispered, '*Yes*!'

chapter two

Luke tightened his grip on the wheel of the Ranger. The play had, he supposed, been amusing, but he hadn't been in any mood to laugh.

This was twice in one day he'd made the same idiotic mistake. He had allowed his actions to be dictated by the whims of the beautiful, self-centred, empty-hearted harpy who was currently seated beside him – masquerading as a cross between an angel and a temptress.

He knew why he'd gone to her house in the first place. Sheer rage had driven him to her door. But why, against all his saner instincts, had he agreed to go to the damn play with her? All right, perhaps he knew the answer to that too in some more honest recess of his mind, but it was an answer he didn't care to dwell on. Besides, he had never been proof against a woman's tears.

Olivia leaned forward, and from the corner of his eye he noted the outline of her breasts in the moonlight. A shudder rippled down his spine and he returned his gaze forcibly to the road.

Rosemary. He had to think of Rosemary, who had cried so many rivers when their mother died of an aneurysm when he was thirteen and she was only eight, that it had become second nature to him to react to tears with instant reassurance. Two weeks after their mother's death, their grief-stricken father had shot himself, and Rosemary's rivers had turned into waterfalls. From then on, Luke had been kept so busy trying to stem the flow that he'd had no time left to cry for himself.

The two of them had been sent to live on their aunt and

uncle's farm in the Fraser Valley, though Aunt Lily and Uncle Peter already had four children of their own and had practically lost touch with Luke's parents.

He remembered the day he and Rosemary arrived at the farm: wary, lost and still stunned by the blow life had dealt them. Uncle Peter was the taciturn type. But Aunt Lily, to give her credit, had tried to be kind and make them welcome. The cousins had frankly resented them, and Luke and the oldest boy had come to blows even before his one suitcase was unpacked.

Soon it had become obvious that the addition of two confused and unhappy little orphans into the household, was a burden his aunt and uncle were ill-equipped to handle.

Luke and Rosemary had been fed, clothed and tolerated, but they hadn't received the extra love and support that Rosemary, in particular, had needed. Thus the care and protection of his sister had fallen primarily to Luke.

He hadn't minded, had even welcomed her dependence in a way – which made it doubly difficult for him to accept that he couldn't continue to protect her now that she was a grown woman of twenty-two.

He slanted a glance at Olivia, the cause of Rosemary's current distress. What had made her into the cold, selfish creature she was? Had she been born that way? He'd heard it happened sometimes...

'Right, and maybe you've always been a damn fool about women, Luke Harriman,' a voice in his head responded bluntly. He tried to ignore it. Yet it was true his relationships never lasted long. His last two girlfriends had waved him goodbye when he refused to move in with them and...

'What are you thinking about?' Olivia's low voice penetrated his private thoughts like a knife sliding into butter. Which, so far, was exactly what he'd been in her hands. Butter. And it had to stop. He would drop her at her door, and that would be the last she'd see of Luke Harriman.

'I'm thinking about Rosemary,' he said.

'Oh. I'm sure she'll be all right.'

'I know she'll be all right. That doesn't stop me from worrying about her.'

Olivia sighed. 'I wish there was something I could do.'

'There is. Stay away from her. And from me.'

'Of course, if you think that's best.' She folded her hands demurely in her lap.

'I do.'

Olivia sighed again, and they drove the rest of the way to her home in an atmosphere of restrained and silent tension.

'Aren't you going to see me to my door?' she asked, when Luke didn't move.

'If you like. But that's as far as I'm going.' With a shrug, Luke swung himself to the ground and strolled round to open up her side.

She was gazing down at him, all sweet and big-eyed, as if the drop to the ground was too much for her – which he knew damn well it wasn't.

'Jump,' he ordered.

Olivia jumped, missed her footing, and ended up clamped against his chest.

'That was quite a manoeuvre,' Luke remarked, holding her away – and furious at the way his body had reacted to the feel of her softness in his arms. 'Come on, let's go. Where's your umbrella?'

'I must have left it in your truck. By mistake.'

Mistake, my eye, Luke thought as he retrieved and hoisted the umbrella. This lady had more tricks up her sleeve than a magician.

When they reached the front door he waited until she'd inserted her key, then wished her a brusque, 'Goodnight,' and turned swiftly back into the rain.

Behind him, Olivia screamed.

He paused. What game was she playing at now? That it

was a game he hadn't the slightest doubt, and he waited only a few seconds before continuing on his way down the driveway.

Olivia screamed again. 'Luke, Luke, come back. Please. There's a mouse...'

'A mouse can't hurt you,' he replied without turning around.

'But I'll never be able to get to sleep knowing it's here.' Her voice rose higher with each pleading word. '*Please* won't you help me catch it?'

Luke groaned. Even Rosemary, who worried about a lot of things, wasn't likely to be spooked by a mouse. And he wouldn't have expected Olivia to be spooked by anything less than a grizzly bear charging straight at her. Even then, he'd give odds on the grizzly turning tail first. Still...his mother hadn't liked mice, either.

'Where did you see it?' he asked, returning reluctantly and looking round the small, empty hall.

'I think it ran into my bedroom.'

Oh-oh. Luke glanced at her with instant suspicion, but her eyes were wide and terrified and she was clutching the red silk of her blouse so tightly he could see...

Right. He turned away hastily and began to climb the stairs. 'OK, let's take a look. Which way is your bedroom?'

'The door on the right.'

Luke pushed open the door and looked around the very feminine bedroom with its blue-and-white flowered curtains, antique dressing table with silver-backed brushes and abundance of silver-topped crystal. When he realised he was deliberately ignoring the bed, Luke made himself take in the flowered bedspread that matched the curtains and the white velvet cushions piled on top of big, downy pillows. He also noted the subtle smell of Olivia's sinful perfume.

There was no mouse.

'Maybe you imagined it,' he said, after peering under the bed and checking an enormous wardrobe filled with more clothes than he could remember Rosemary possessing in her entire lifetime.

'No, no, I didn't. Oh, please...'

'Look,' Luke said, 'I've done my best, and you know as well as I do that there isn't, and never was, a mouse.' He wasn't sure why he was so certain. Olivia hadn't dropped her terrified pose for a second, and she was damn good at it. All the same, he knew she was lying.

'But...' she began.

'There *are* no "Buts". Goodnight, Ms Franklyn, and thank you for the play.'

This time when she called after him, he ignored her.

He was half way out the door when a blast of rain hit him in the face. At the same moment, a pair of arms locked like silken steel around his waist.

Hell. Didn't the woman ever give up? He unclasped the fingers scrabbling at his belt and swung around.

Immediately she reached for his shoulders, but he grabbed her hands before they found their mark and held them firmly at her sides.

'Stop it,' he ordered. 'The answer is no. Not now, not ever.'

She lowered her amazing eyelashes as if to hide her hurt and, to his fury, Luke felt as if he'd just kicked a kitten. He knew Olivia Franklyn was no kitten, but that didn't prevent him from reacting to her act as if she were.

He hesitated a fraction too long. Just as he was turning away for the third time, Olivia wrapped her arms around his waist, inserted a leg between his thighs and began to rotate her hips in a way calculated to drive a man made of iron and ice to measures of savage desperation.

Luke wasn't made of iron and ice. And Olivia was the sexiest, most seductive little temptress ever put on earth to make a mockery of his efforts to reject her.

'If you don't cut that out this instant...' he threatened, knowing his desperation showed.

'What will you do?' Olivia smiled up at him, her small teeth gleaming in the dim lighting of the hall, her black eyes laughing a challenge.

'I'll... *hell*!' He let out a groan that was close to a howl of pain as Olivia slipped her hand between his legs.

There was no holding back after that. He attempted, briefly, to pull away, but she only laughed, a low, taunting, magical laugh that ripped to shreds what remained of his self-control. He was a man. She was a woman – a wicked, destructive, dangerous woman, but all the more desirable for that. It had been too many months since... God, he'd even forgotten her name.

He shut his eyes. *Yes*. All right then. He would give Ms Olivia Franklyn what she wanted – what he wanted too, if he were honest – and once it was over, they would go their separate ways.

As Olivia put a hand on his belt, he scooped her up in his arms and carried her up the stairs and into the blue-flowered bedroom. For a moment, as she gazed up at him, he thought he glimpsed a kind of shock in her eyes. Then he saw nothing but the pale perfection of her breasts as he lay over her, pushing back the red silk shirt and fumbling for the catch on her skimpy bra. He paused after a while to tease the pearly mounds with his fingertips, and when he heard her gasp, he lowered his lips and teased some more.

Her hips began to move, and she whispered, 'Luke?' in a voice that was both enticing and bewildered.

Luke, discovering he still had his jacket on, sat up and tossed it over a blue velvet chair. Next he removed his shoes and, with Olivia's eyes following his every movement, tugged off his sweatshirt and stood to unbuckle his belt. She stared up at him, still with that stunned look in her eyes, as he let his jeans drop on to the floor.

Seconds later, when he bent to unzip her tight black slacks, he felt her stiffen. Surprised, he paused to run his hands slowly, erotically down her hips. When that brought no reaction, he inserted a hand between her thighs.

Olivia's eyes dilated. 'Oh,' she moaned. 'Luke, please...'

'Anything you say.' He peeled off her pants.

God, she was gorgeous. But he couldn't wait now to admire her perfect body. Not when she was lying there all squirming and naked, her glorious eyes soft with desire...

She gasped when he entered her, but only once. After that she moved beneath him like the wanton she was, and when release came for both of them in the same moment, Olivia cried out, '*No*!' and then, '*Luke*!'

Time passed, and Luke rolled on to the bedspread as the aftershocks of pleasure died away. 'No?' he repeated groggily. 'Olivia, it's far too late for "no".'

'Yes. I didn't mean...'

'What did you mean?'

Sanity, at last, was returning. Slowly, though not slowly enough, Luke became aware of what he'd done.

While his sister lay recovering in hospital, he had been making love -no, lust – with the spoiled little miss who had put her there. How *could* he have done such a thing? Self-disgust curdled his stomach and threatened to rise up and choke him.

'I meant, no, I didn't know it would be as wonderful as this,' he heard Olivia say softly. 'But it was.'

Luke groaned. She was right there. It had, indeed, been memorable. Olivia Franklyn was damn good in bed, which was surprising considering... Oh. Oh, no! *What* had she just said? That she didn't know...

Hell and damnation! She couldn't be. Not this slinky, sophisticated little witch, with the body of a goddess and the wiles of an experienced alley cat. Yet she *had* tensed up when...

Luke closed his eyes, shutting out the white purity of the ceiling. 'Olivia,' he said. 'Was this your first time?'

She didn't answer, and he turned on the pillow to look at her.

She was smiling at him, a soft, sweet smile that made his blood turn cold. 'Mm,' she said. 'It was. I didn't mean for us to go this far really. But I'm glad we did.'

This time she wasn't lying. He'd stake his life on it.

'Shit!' he said.

Olivia giggled. 'Is it that bad?'

'Worse.' Shifting on to his side, he propped himself on one elbow and gazed down at her beautiful naked body on its bed of quilted flowers. 'I'm sorry. If I'd known...'

'What would you have done if you'd known?' She smiled angelically, and Luke was hard-pressed not to reach for her again.

'Nothing. Absolutely nothing,' he said with feeling.

'Then I'm glad you didn't know.'

'Why me?' He rolled on to his back and resumed his study of the ceiling.

'I don't understand...'

'Why did you pick on me to...' He brushed an arm across his sweating forehead. 'To be the first.'

'I didn't. I told you I only meant to make you stay.'

'Why?'

She was a long time answering that, and when she did, Luke was certain she wasn't telling the whole truth.

'You weren't as easy to catch as most men. I enjoy a challenge.'

'I am not a trout,' he snapped. 'And now that you've snagged me you'll have to throw me back.'

'Definitely not a trout,' she agreed. 'But what if I don't want to throw you back?'

She was laughing at him. He supposed he couldn't blame her. Turning on his side again, he lifted his head to examine her face. It was serene as a cloudless sky and devoid of guile, though he had reason to know that meant nothing.

'I mean it,' he said. 'This is it, Olivia. It's not going to happen again.'

'Didn't you like it?'

'You know damn well I did. That has nothing to do with it.'

'Because of Rosemary?'

'Yes. Among other reasons.'

The last thing he needed in his life at this time, was a beguiling little schemer like the woman lying seductively beside him. But there was no need to tell her that. He had just taken from her a gift no woman had given him before. In an odd way he was grateful, and the least he could do was spare her feelings. If she had any, which he seriously doubted.

Olivia raised a languid arm and trailed her nails across his chest. 'You have a nice chest,' she said. 'Not too much hair.'

Luke flinched as her hand moved down lower. 'Don't do that,' he said. 'It's over, Olivia.'

'But why?' She removed her hand with obvious reluctance. 'I don't want it to be over.'

'Then it's time you learned that you can't have everything you want.'

'Why not? I always have.'

Her honesty astonished him. 'Lucky you. But you see, I'm not your father. I don't have to cater to your whims.'

'Neither does he really. I haven't seen much of him since I started college.'

'Even though he pays for all this?' He waved at the expensively-furnished room.

Olivia raised a smooth, white shoulder. 'Oh, that's only because he feels guilty. He doesn't really care about me, you see. Though I do go to see him sometimes.'

'When you need money, I suppose.' Luke didn't believe her about the guilt.

'Mostly,' she admitted. 'But next year I'll have my own money. Mother left me an inheritance. I'll come into it on my twenty-third birthday.'

Was she only twenty-two, the same age as Rosemary? And already as cold and grasping as a sleek silver shark. He ran a brief, regretful eye over her lovely body, and swung his legs to the floor.

'Don't go,' Olivia said. 'We've got all night.'

'No. We haven't.' He stood up, turned his back on her and stepped into his jeans. 'Some of us have to work for a living, and I work better on a good night's sleep.' Not that he was likely to sleep tonight.

'Oh. What do you do?' she asked.

Luke recognised delaying tactics when he heard them, so he kept his answer brief.

'I'm a biologist. I work for Coastland Environment.'

'What does Coastland Environment do?'

He dragged his sweatshirt over his head. 'Our work has to do with surveying environmentally sensitive areas that developers want to build on, and convincing government bureaucracies that it can be done without destroying fish habitat or endangered flora or fauna. We also design compensation habitat and...' He paused, noting the mildly glazed look in her eyes. 'Want me to go on, or are you about to slip into a coma?'

Olivia ignored the gibe. 'Do you like doing all that?'

'Yes, I like it. That's why I do it.'

'But do you like working for somebody else?'

'Not particularly. I don't intend to work for somebody else forever.'

'Are you going to start your own company?'

'Yes.' He spun round, tired of questions he knew were only asked to detain him, and bent to collect his jacket from the floor. As he shrugged it on, he saw that Olivia was still lying naked on the bed.

She held out her hand. 'Please don't go.'

'I must,' he said, trying to look anywhere but at her perfect body. 'Look, Olivia, I'm sorry this happened...and since it can't happen again, it's best that I say goodbye and get it over with.'

She didn't answer, and when he finally made himself face her again, she had climbed beneath the blue-flowered bedspread and pulled it up around her neck. Above it, her face looked soft and sweet and very young.

Luke pushed a hand through his already dishevelled hair. 'If it helps at all, you were great,' he said.

Still she didn't speak, so he said, 'Thank you,' and then, 'Goodnight,' before striding to the door. If she went on looking at him like that, his resolution was likely to falter.

He couldn't afford to let that happen. Olivia Franklyn was long-term trouble he could do without.

Without meaning to, he slammed the door as he left, as if to emphasise the finality of his leaving.

He was halfway back to the apartment he shared with Rosemary, before it occurred to him that although he had made love to her with passion, he hadn't once kissed the woman he had left behind him in the bed.

Olivia watched the dawn rise over the birch trees at the back of the garden. If Luke had achieved his good night's sleep, then he had been luckier than he'd allowed her to be. She hadn't slept a wink.

It wasn't fair. All these years she had been attracting men she didn't much want, and now that she'd found one she did want, he'd walked out on her. For no good reason.

She wrapped her arms around her chest and wriggled voluptuously, remembering the feel of his body enfolding hers. To think that sex was like that. She had never really felt the urge until Luke. It was very strange. And if he thought he was going to get away with, 'Thank you and goodbye. You were great,' then he didn't know Olivia Franklyn.

How dare he reject her? She'd show him. And once she had him well and truly caught, she'd give him a taste of his own medicine. Next time *he* would be the one to be dismissed.

But not right away. She'd keep him for as long as she wanted him. Smiling dreamily, Olivia ran her hands over her flat stomach and thought about what they would do when she got him back. She hoped it wouldn't take long.

When Luke got home from work a few nights later, Rosemary was waiting for him.

'What's the matter?' he asked, picking up on the vibrations at once. 'Has something upset you?'

'Olivia Franklyn,' she snapped, flipping the pages of a magazine. 'She actually had the gall to phone and invite us to dinner.'

'Us?' Luke repeated. 'Did you say *us*?'

'Yes. I expect she planned to serve me as the main course. With caper sauce.'

Luke didn't laugh. 'Did she say *why* she wanted us for dinner?' he asked.

'No.' She threw the magazine viciously to one side. 'That is, she *said* she wanted to make amends. But she didn't sound a bit sorry.'

'Oh, she's sorry all right,' Luke muttered. 'But not for the reason she should be.'

Rosemary stared at him. 'What makes you say that?'

He shrugged. 'Just a feeling. What did you tell her?'

'That we were busy.'

'And she accepted that?'

'No. I hung up on her.'

Luke's mouth twisted in a grin that was more like a grimace. 'Good. Did she phone back?'

Rosemary frowned. If she hadn't known better, she would have sworn her brother was acquainted with Olivia. But he couldn't be. A week ago he hadn't known who she was.

'No,' she replied. 'Why do you ask?'

'No reason.' Luke prowled into the small living-room and flung himself full-length on the beige second-hand sofa, the one they'd bought together the day he finished college and removed her from their aunt and uncle's casual care.

Rosemary's grey eyes narrowed. Her brother was behaving very oddly. 'Is anything wrong?' she asked.

'Nope.' Luke settled a limp, green cushion behind his head. 'Busy day at work, that's all.'

Rosemary raised her eyebrows and left him to it.

Stupid cow! Olivia, too restless to stay home after her abortive phone call, paced up and down the grass strip separating the sands of Jericho Beach from the road. What right had that dull little mouse to turn down an invitation on Luke's behalf? If it hadn't been for Rosemary Harriman... If it hadn't been for Rosemary Harriman, the more logical side of Olivia's brain reminded her annoyingly, you would never have met her brother. And she isn't really dull. Only quiet.

She scowled at a passing sailboat, then stopped scowling as a large golden-retriever came bounding across the grass, put his paws on her chest and ran his tongue enthusiastically across her face.

'Down, Piggley! Bad boy. I *am* so sorry.' A small, worried-looking woman came twittering up as Olivia struggled to recover her balance. 'He's just a puppy, you see. Oh dear!' She put a hand to her mouth. 'He's got sand all over your pretty black sweater.'

Olivia bent down to pat the dog, who was now rolling on his back in the grass. 'It's all right. Dogs don't know about sweaters. I've got lots more.'

The woman blinked, smiled doubtfully and said, 'Oh, you are kind. Most people would make an awful fuss.'

'I like dogs.' Olivia was surprised by the look of shy approval in the woman's eyes. It was years since anyone had looked at her like that.

'I can see you do.' The woman nodded. 'Piggley knew you were a nice person at once. Didn't you, Piggley?'

Piggley wagged his tail and offered a friendly paw.

Olivia accepted it, lingered for a minute to fondle the dog's ears, then watched him amble away down the beach with his owner. A nice person, that woman had called her. No one ever called her nice. It must have been because she liked the dog.

One day, when she was home more, she would have a dog of her own. Dogs liked her, and when dogs showed affection they meant it. Not like her parents, who only pretended to love her.

Not like Luke either. But at least he didn't pretend.

Shoving her hands into the pockets of her designer jeans, Olivia glared at the shafts of sunlight falling on the mountains across the Inlet. Why couldn't Rosemary have been the pushover she had expected? It seemed Ms Goody-Two-Shoes wasn't as spineless as she'd thought. If she had been, she would have accepted that dinner invitation as the olive branch it wasn't.

Fine. Olivia made up her mind. There was no use whining over what she couldn't change. Plan One was a bust. Time to put Plan Two into action...

When she looked up, two tall young men were striding towards her, leering lustfully, so she spun on her heel and headed for the busy safety of the road.

Home at last. Luke parked his truck and jumped out on to the pavement. It had been a hot, difficult day – one problem after another – and that argument with the construction foreman hadn't helped. It would be good to put his feet up and have a long, cold beer before supper.

As he rounded the corner, a flash of red caught his attention. He paused. Nothing red belonged behind that bush beside the door. What the...?

No. It couldn't be. She wouldn't...

Even as he thought it, Luke knew that she would. And when Olivia Franklyn emerged from behind the bush, and collapsed at his feet in a cloud of some filmy red material that clung to every tantalising curve of her luscious body, he discovered that he wasn't even surprised.

In his heart he had known all along that he hadn't seen the last of the sexiest little she-devil it had ever been his pleasure, and misfortune, to take to bed.

It had merely been a matter of when, not if, she would make her move.

chapter three

Oh dear. Luke wasn't a bit pleased to see her. She could tell from the look in his eyes. Nice eyes usually, all black and velvety and intense – but the way they were raking her now was the opposite of nice. And if looks could kill, she'd be extinct.

'Get up,' he said.

Olivia reached for the step, bent her leg cautiously and winced. 'I think I've broken something.'

'Good. Now get up.'

'I c-can't.'

Luke placed his hands on his hips. She eyed him appreciatively. Mmm, he *did* look sensational. All hot and macho and glowering, with his backpack slung over one shoulder and his denim shirt unbuttoned to the waist.

'Really I can't,' she said, forcing a quiver into her voice.

When that had no visible effect, she pulled discreetly at the skirt of her red dress to expose an enticing glimpse of pale thigh while she squirmed a further few inches towards the step.

Luke, looking grim, extended a hand. 'Rosemary tells me that you're majoring in theatre,' he remarked.

Damn Rosemary. 'Yes, I am,' Olivia agreed, accepting the hand. 'And music. But mainly I'm interested in the production side of things.'

'You can say that again. I assume this little performance is an example of the kind of production you excel at.' He yanked her to her feet with no regard for possible broken bones. 'Now, pull yourself together and run along.'

Olivia clung to his hand, which was sweating profusely.

'I really did trip. I don't think I can walk without help.'

'Fine, I'll call an ambulance.'

'Oh, that's not necessary. If I could just rest in your apartment for a while...'

'Nice try. You can't. I told you it's over, Olivia. Why can't you just accept that, and find some other dupe to harass?'

OK, so he wasn't going to lower his defences. Not for a second. Time to up the ante.

'Luke,' she whispered, squeezing a handy supply of tears from beneath her eyelids. 'I do miss you...'

'You can't possibly miss me. You hardly know me.'

'I do know you. Intimately. Oh-h.' She stumbled, and grabbed for his shoulders, sliding forward and giving a little wriggle as her body connected with his torso. To her elation, his response was instantaneous. She could feel his arousal through the diaphanous folds of the dress she had bought specifically as a weapon of seduction.

It *wasn't* hopeless. He still wanted her, whether he was willing to admit it or not. She squirmed some more, and in the second before he seized her wrists to push her away, she felt his body thrust against hers.

'Why did you come?' he demanded, still holding her.

Olivia observed the moisture glistening on his neck. It was a hot May day, but not that hot. 'Because I want you,' she said, smiling the smile that had brought every other man she had turned it on to his knees.

Every man, but not Luke.

'I want you too,' he said. 'In my bed, but not in my life. Since that's not an option, I'll have to do without you.'

'But why? Do you hate me so much?' As soon as the words left her mouth Olivia realised she had let her guard down by allowing the depth of her hunger to show. But he *couldn't* just reject her out of hand. He couldn't. Not when he was the only man she had *really* wanted since...oh, since forever.

When his features softened marginally, she knew he'd picked up on her desperation. She didn't want that, didn't want him to be the one holding the upper hand. The whole idea had been to make him vulnerable to her, not the other way around.

'I don't hate you,' he said. 'I don't like you very much, but I don't hate you.'

'Nobody likes me much,' Olivia said matter-of-factly. 'What's that got to do with anything?' She tugged her wrists out of his grasp and backed against the dusty brick wall of the building.

Good grief, Luke thought. She really means it. She doesn't expect to be liked and has no idea why liking should have anything to do with sex.

What on earth had gone into the making of this extraordinary woman? He supposed he would never know, because the more he saw of her, the more convinced he became that she was trouble to be avoided at all costs. And it *was* at a considerable cost. There was no denying he wanted her, wanted her with the most pernicious, painful ache he had ever endured for the need of a woman. He hadn't been able to get her off his mind for more than a few scattered minutes all week. No wonder she'd found it so easy to snag Michael. The phrase *femme fatale* came to mind. It might have been coined especially for her.

'Look,' he said, as gently as he could. 'I know you don't understand, but most men – decent men, at any rate – want to feel something besides lust for the women they sleep with. One night stands happen all the time, but that's all they are. Those relationships don't last, because they're not meant to. That's the way it is with you and me. So please, be a good girl and leave me and Rosemary in peace. Do you think you can manage that?'

'Don't patronise me,' Olivia snapped.

Luke resisted an urge to catch her beautiful, angry face in

his hands and press a kiss on those soft and sultry lips. She was lovelier than ever when she had her dander up. Her eyes were flashing black diamonds, and her skin glowed with the brightness of fire.

'I didn't mean to patronise you,' he said.

She was right though. His words *had* been patronising... but only because, for a few seconds there, she had reminded him of a lost little girl. 'Listen,' he said, 'I'm sorry, but I've had a long day and Rosemary's expecting me for supper. Do you want me to call you a taxi?'

'No, thank you. I have my Mercedes.'

She made the announcement with a shrug and a dismissive toss of her head, and Luke guessed she was salvaging her pride. A Mercedes yet. That certainly put him in his place.

He smiled and touched a hand to her cheek. 'Goodbye, Olivia.'

Briefly, Luke thought she meant to protest, but the thin fellow who lived downstairs arrived on the step at that moment, and she turned her killer smile on him instead.

June passed with no word from Olivia, and Luke began to believe he'd heard the last of her. Sometimes, in the small hours of the night, his body made him regret sending her away, but in the clear light of early morning he always knew he'd had no other choice.

Rosemary, now recovered from her brief period of mourning over Michael, sat her exams and seemed confident of the results. In the ever-present heat of July, the rains of spring had become a cool and distant memory.

When the phone rang one particularly stifling evening, Luke answered it with no presentiment of disaster.

'Luke?' said the voice he had been trying so hard to forget. 'Is that you?'

He pushed his supper away and laid down a half-completed crossword. 'Who did you expect? Olivia, I told you...'

'Yes, yes I know you did, and I *have* been leaving you alone. But now I can't.'

What was she up to? 'Of course you can,' he snapped, resenting the ache in his groin that just the sound of her voice could induce.

'No, really, I can't. There's something I have to tell you. Something you have to know about.'

'Then tell me.' He stood up, leaving his plate of leftover Chinese food on the kitchen table, and began to pace back and forth in front of the window. Across the street, a large woman in an orange sun hat was walking two beribboned poodles.

'I'd rather tell you in person,' Olivia said.

'I don't doubt it. But it's not going to happen.' As the ache in his groin became a throbbing agony, he returned to the table to put down the phone.

Olivia must have sensed he was about to break the connection, because moments before he did, she cried out, 'Luke, please, don't hang up. I'm pregnant!'

Luke dropped the receiver on to the floor.

After what seemed like hours, but probably was only a few seconds, he bent to pick it up. As he straightened, one of the poodles began to bark.

'What did you say?' he asked. He must have heard wrong. Surely, even Olivia...

'I said that I was pregnant.'

So matter-of-fact, so unemotional. He swiped a damp hand across his face. This wasn't real. It couldn't be. And Olivia Franklyn couldn't be pregnant by him. As out of control as he knew he had been that night, he hadn't been *that* irresponsible...

'You can't be,' he said.

'But I am.'

'Then it's not mine.'

'*Luke*! How could you? You know you're the only man

I've ever...I mean, there's never been anyone but you.'

'I know I was the first. That's not the same thing.'

'The first and the last,' Olivia said.

'I don't believe you.' This couldn't be happening. It was only another of the Beauty-from-hell's little schemes.

'It's true. I can prove it to you. Please, will you at least talk to me about it?'

Luke groaned, and cast a despairing glance at the remains of his supper congealing on the plate. 'All right. Where?'

He couldn't refuse to see her. If he did, he would wonder for the rest of his life if a child of his loins had been born to a woman no more cut out to be a mother, than those spoiled poodles yapping at passing cars across the street. Not that it was likely to come to that. Olivia wasn't the type to be inconvenienced for nine months.

Yet – she *was* unpredictable. Anything was possible...

'You could come to my place,' Olivia said.

'No.' Luke's reaction was instinctive, born of a healthy sense of self-preservation.

'Alida's Coffee Bar, then. Do you know it?'

'Yes. Yes, I think so. Isn't it that new place on Fourth Avenue?'

'That's the one. Will you meet me there in half an hour?'

'An hour,' Luke replied, for no other reason than that he needed to assert a measure of control. It wasn't a matter of wanting to finish his supper, because he wouldn't be able to eat it without choking.

'Fine. I'll see you in an hour,' Olivia said.

In the end she was the one who hung up first.

She sat at a table near the window, waiting. The tacky pink clock behind the counter read eight o'clock. He was three minutes late, but he would come. She knew he would. Luke was a man who kept his promises.

A bearded man and a red-haired girl drifted through the door holding hands. They sat down at a pink-tiled table in front of her, practically eating each other with their eyes. Olivia felt a pang of something she didn't recognise. It couldn't be envy, because she had always despised such public moon-gazing in the past...

She jumped, as a chair scraped on the floor.

Luke, dressed in jeans and a short-sleeved blue shirt, took the seat across from her, rested his forearms on the table and said, 'Well?'

Olivia tried to meet his eyes, failed, swallowed a mouthful of tepid coffee and asked inanely, 'Would you like something to drink?'

'No. I'd like an explanation.'

She stared into her cup. Little globules of cream were floating on top of the coffee. 'It must have broken,' she said.

'What must?'

She smoothed the demure print skirt she had chosen because it looked vaguely maternal. 'The...the condom.'

'No. It didn't.'

All right, so she'd known he wouldn't fall for that – but it had been worth a try. 'I've been to see the doctor,' she said. 'I *am* going to have a baby.'

'Maybe you are. That doesn't mean I had anything to do with it.' His voice, hard and unaccommodating, told her what she already knew. Luke Harriman wasn't going to be any pushover.

'But there's never *been* anyone else,' she insisted, raising her eyes at last to blink at him beseechingly. 'You have to believe me.'

'I *don't* have to believe you. Why should I?' Thin, angry lines bracketed his jaw.

'Because it's true. Why would I lie to you?'

The coffee machine on the counter whirred and clattered.

When the noise died down, Luke said, 'Habit perhaps. But you could have any number of reasons.'

'Name one.'

'Money.'

She shook her head.

'No, I guess not...' His voice deepened, and he frowned down at the table as if he expected it to provide him with answers.

'Not money,' Olivia said. 'I have more than enough of my own.'

'Mm. I suppose...' He paused, then drew the words out one by one as if he were reluctant to voice them, 'You could, I suppose, imagine that you're in love...'

'But I'm not.' Olivia smiled sweetly. 'I just believe my baby should have a father.'

She waited for this well-rehearsed speech to take effect, watching a variety of emotions play across Luke's face. Doubt, disbelief, suspicion and, finally, a dawning acceptance of the possibility that she might be telling him the truth.

Yes! It *was* going to work. Olivia hugged her arms around her chest. If she played her cards right, Luke would eventually believe the child was his. And once she had him that far, the rest would follow.

'How do I know you're even pregnant?' he asked.

She had known he would ask that. 'I have a letter from my doctor. I told him you might not believe me.'

'I see. And I suppose you have it with you?' He turned his chair sideways and rested an ankle on his knee.

Olivia ran her tongue along her upper lip. Luke had wonderfully masculine legs. Long and strong and firm. She remembered how perfectly they had wound around her own...

Oh, she just *had* to make this work. And one day, when it suited her, she would send him off with a shrug like all the rest. No man was going to get away with treating Olivia Franklyn like a bad smell on the cook's day off from the kitchen. In the meantime, she would enjoy whatever pleasures she could take.

'Yes,' she said. 'I brought the letter with me.'

Luke extended a hand and watched her pretend to rummage through her purse. She knew exactly where she had put the damned letter. When she handed it to him, she produced what he supposed was her idea of a brave smile.

He ran his eye down the page.

'...to confirm that my patient, Olivia Franklyn, is approximately two and a half months into her pregnancy. Due date January... Signed, Anthony Crump, MD.'

Luke read it again, all the time unconsciously raking his fingers through his hair.

'How do I know who wrote this?' He tossed the letter on to the table. Olivia was entirely capable of manufacturing a letter and a doctor to suit her own ends.

'But...' She fluttered her impossible eyelashes. 'He's been my family doctor all my life. Why don't you ask him?'

'All right.' He picked up the letter again and made a mental note of the address. 'I will.'

He watched for some sign that Olivia was ready to back down, but she was nodding at him, pleased with his capitulation.

Christ! He *had* to be dreaming. Luke rubbed his eyes. This could only be a nightmare brought on by his own inexcusable lust. And what if Olivia *was* pregnant? What was he supposed to do about it? More importantly, how would he know the child was his?

He pushed back his chair and stood up. He had to get out of this trendy, tacky little coffee bar with its plastic panelled walls and too-bright lights; had to get outside where he could breathe air instead of coffee, well away from the temptation of enormous eyes filled with reproach – as if *he* were the one responsible for this mess. Which he couldn't be.

Nonetheless, he would see this Dr Crump. He had to if he was going to prevent the jaws of Olivia's mantrap from closing inescapably on his life.

Luke wasn't a drinker, but he was drinking now.

Two days had passed since his meeting with Olivia in Alida's Coffee Bar, and he had just come from Dr Crump's house. Apparently the old man had virtually retired, but he still kept in touch with a few of his long-time patients, one of whom, he assured Luke, was Olivia.

''Course she's pregnant,' the doctor had huffed through his moustache. 'Hope you're not trying to dodge your responsibility, young man. Pretty little thing, Olivia. Known her all her life. Fond of her. You see you do right by her, d'you hear me?'

Luke heard him, which was why he was currently holding up the bar of a seedy downtown hotel trying to forget he'd ever heard of Olivia Franklyn. Her child *couldn't* be his. Sure, accidents happened, but he would have known... wouldn't he?

Hell. Luke ordered another drink.

By the time he'd consumed three more whiskys, the mirror behind the bar was reflecting an assortment of heads, most of which seemed to be his.

He stood up, waited for the room to stop spinning, and lurched for the exit.

A jeering voice yelled, 'Wrong way, buster,' seconds before he ended up with his face plastered against the beer-spattered wall. In that moment, the drink-induced haze blurring his vision began to clear, and he knew he had to pull himself together. Peeling himself off the wall, he placed one foot carefully in front of the other and succeeded in making his way out into the night.

Air rushed against his skin, a door slammed, and he propped himself against a street lamp until he could gather sufficient breath to carry him home. It would help though if his body didn't feel as if it had been kicked to a pulp by steel-toed boots.

The throbbing in his head reminded him forcibly of what he'd known all along. No problem was ever solved by drink. And this particular problem, with her supple body and sexy siren smile, *must* be handled with a clear head.

By the following morning Luke knew what he had to do.

Around ten o'clock he phoned Olivia and arranged to meet her on Jericho Beach. The forecast threatened rain, but he didn't care. For this meeting he needed air and space, not the confining pink walls of Alida's.

He found Olivia sitting on a log with her knees drawn up to her chin. In her brief white shorts and a black tank top that provided no protection against the wind, she looked like a sea-sprite from one of the fairy tales his mother had read to him as a child. Or she did, until she twisted around to face him. Then she became the woman who had haunted his dreams for three months – the woman who held what remained of his life in her pretty white hands.

He sat astride the log, deliberately leaving a wide space between them.

'I want the truth,' he said, fixing his gaze on her delicate profile.

'Of course.' Her voice was soft as the wind stirring the trees. 'I've always told you the truth.'

'Have you? Look at me, Olivia.'

Obligingly, she swung a leg over the log and raised her eyes to his. Her heart-shaped face was guilelessly questioning. 'Yes?'

'This baby you're having. Can you look me in the eye and tell me, on everything you hold sacred, that you've never been with anyone but me? And don't think of lying to me, Lady. Not this time.'

Olivia's smile was soft and sad, and her big, pansy eyes, staring into his, made him feel like the worst kind of heel ever to walk the streets of Vancouver.

Out on the choppy water, a boat with red sails was scurrying for shelter. Closer to hand, a cacophony of seagulls protested the coming of the storm.

Luke laid damp palms on his thighs and waited for her answer.

chapter four

Olivia licked her lips and tasted salt. She could see the muscles, taut with tension, beneath the dark blue T-shirt stretched across Luke's chest. There was no question that the success of her latest plan, certainly her immediate future, depended on how she answered his question.

Funny, she didn't like lying to Luke. She hadn't thought it would matter because there was nothing she really considered sacred – but now, transfixed by the demanding darkness of his eyes, she felt a discomfort so acute it was almost pain.

The salt taste in her mouth intensified. 'No. I've never made love with anyone but you,' she told him. 'I haven't wanted to.' That much, at least, was the truth.

Luke's eyes were still clouded with doubt. What else could she say that might convince him? She could think of only one thing, and there was always the risk he might take her up on it...

Olivia made up her mind. Risk-taking was part of her heritage. Where would her father be if, early in his career, he hadn't been willing to take chances?

'If you don't believe me, we can always ask about DNA testing,' she said.

He didn't move, didn't react in any way she could put her finger on. Yet she knew at once that his attitude had changed. After a few seconds he nodded and, to her bewilderment, his body seemed to relax.

'No, that won't be necessary,' he said. 'I'm not entirely sure why, but I believe you. So what do you want me to do?'

'Do?' She hadn't expected that, hadn't expected him to accept responsibility without a fight. For some reason it made achieving her goal less satisfactory, less of a triumph than she'd imagined.

'Yes. *Do*.' His head snapped up, and she had to steel herself not to cringe from the contempt in his eyes. Whether it was directed at her or at himself she wasn't sure.

She took a deep breath and replied as composedly as she could. 'I want you to marry me, please.'

'Please?' Luke gave a kind of snort, swung a leg over the log and stood up. '*Please*? Olivia, you're not asking me to pass you the salt and pepper!'

'I was only being polite.' Olivia was annoyed. She had put considerable thought into the way she would phrase her proposal.

Luke lifted both hands to his temples as if he couldn't believe what he was hearing. 'You want to have this child then?' he said.

'Of course I do. Are you suggesting...'

'No.' He turned his back, took a few restless paces down the beach. 'But it's the easy way out. I'm surprised you don't want to take it.'

If he only knew! 'No,' she said. 'I want to have your baby.'

If that didn't hook him nothing would – though it was a good thing he wasn't actually looking at her.

'Marriage is for keeps, you know.' Luke crossed his arms, and she watched the rising wind lift his hair.

That's what you think. Olivia almost spoke out loud. As far as she was concerned, marriage was for as long as it took her to show Luke Harriman he couldn't reject her out of hand and get away with it. Men didn't reject her. She rejected them. It hadn't been easy waiting nearly two months for her revenge.

'Of course marriage is for keeps,' she said, in the gentle

tone she sometimes used to lull men into thinking *she* was gentle. 'Do you mind so very much?'

He turned to look at her then and, in spite of her resentment, the emptiness in his eyes made her flinch.

'Yes,' he said. 'I mind. But it's not the child's fault I couldn't keep my jeans zippered up. I know what it's like to be unwanted. I won't inflict that kind of neglect on any child of mine.'

'What about me?' Olivia thrust out her lower lip. '*I'm* the one who has to have it.'

Luke smiled, a resigned, cynical smile that made her want to scratch it off his face. 'You, my sweet, are a survivor. I've no doubt you'll get through it very comfortably.'

Olivia frowned. He had no business to make surviving sound like a character flaw – even though he was right. She *was* a survivor.

'I was unwanted too,' she told him, lifting her chin indignantly.

'Don't be ridiculous. You had two doting parents who adored you.'

'I didn't. Mother was hit by a car when I was seventeen. But in any case, neither of my parents really wanted me. They pretended to, but they didn't. Not after my brother was killed.'

'Nonsense. Why would they pretend?'

'It's *not* nonsense. They always loved Raymond best.'

'Why? I expect he was just as much of a spoiled brat as you are.'

Olivia resisted an immediate inclination to leap up and spit in his eye. Making him angry wouldn't achieve her goal. What was that saying about catching more flies with honey...? Luke was hardly a fly, but by the time she was finished with him he'd be well and truly stuck in her web.

'That's not very kind of you.' Sniffing softly, she lowered her eyelashes and scuffed the sand with the toe of her running shoe.

'It wasn't meant to be.'

Olivia waited, saying nothing, and after a while he said in a less aggressive tone, 'You're right in a way though. I can't pretend I'm happy about this mess. But if we're going to go through with it, we may as well try to get along.'

She looked up, hoping to see a softening of his features, some indication that he was finally succumbing to her charms. But all she saw was an expression of grim resignation and something that was probably a kind of dazed disbelief. Luke Harriman might be falling in with her plans but he had not, yet, fully accepted his fate.

'You *are* going to marry me then?' She asked just to be sure.

Luke took a step towards her, then stopped. 'Is that what you really want? Marriage to a man who doesn't love you? I'm willing to support the child, of course…'

'I don't want support. I want a husband.'

He nodded. 'Yes. I see. I suppose you have a right to expect that.'

'Yes. I have.'

The look he gave her was hard, and impossible to ignore. 'Olivia, marriage isn't a game. It's a commitment that's meant to last a lifetime. You can't decide you want a father for your child, then change your mind once you've got your own way.'

Luke was altogether too perceptive. But in this case he was wrong. She could change her mind whenever she chose to. And she would.

'I know.' She stood up and went to stand in front of him, languidly swinging her hips. 'I want commitment, Luke. For the sake of our child.' That phrase had a nice ring to it. She'd used it just last month in her theatre class.

Luke frowned, and she knew he wasn't entirely taken in.

'Fine,' he said. 'But don't try any of your tricks on me, Olivia. I'll marry you, and I'll do my damnedest to make the marriage work. Can you say the same?'

'Of course.' She tilted her face up and put everything she had into her smile.

Luke drew in his breath. When he released it, he took her face in both hands and kissed her.

She guessed he meant it to be a brief kiss given only to seal the bargain they had made. But almost at once it turned into something else. The moment she returned the pressure of his lips, he lowered his arms, gripped her by the hips and pulled her close. With only a thin layer of clothing between them, all the erotic memories came sweeping back, and the fires she had kept banked for two months burst into hot, hungry flames.

She pushed her fingers beneath the neck of Luke's T-shirt, feeling the muscles pull across his back. His tongue thrust against her mouth.

Then, for the first time in her life, Olivia tasted the tart sweetness of mint and man.

Oh yes! *Yes*. Was *this* what a kiss was meant to be? He hadn't kissed her that first time...

Luke's tongue thrust deeper, and the past no longer mattered. There was only the sound of the sea and the feel of Luke's arms around her body...and his mouth. His warm, drugging, wonderfully passionate mouth...

Her moment of ecstasy was shattered when a handful of sand hit the back of her legs. Somewhere close by a child's laugh was followed the scolding tones of an embarrassed mother.

'Let's go home,' Olivia whispered against Luke's mouth.

The moment she spoke, the first drops of rain splashed on to her head.

'No.' Luke broke away from her and sank on to the log, breathing heavily. 'Let's not ask for more trouble than we've already got.' The edge of his mouth turned down in cynical amusement. 'Though it looks as if at least one aspect of our marriage is destined for success.'

'Don't sound so gloomy. That's the best part.'

Luke attempted a hopelessly unsuccessful smile. 'I'm afraid you may be right,' he agreed.

Afraid? What did he mean by that? Not that it mattered, of course.

She was going to marry Luke Harriman – for better, for worse – and for a while. He would discover soon enough that he had made the biggest mistake of his life when he turned her down.

Several more raindrops landed on her head before the clouds above them opened in earnest. Luke took her hand, and together they ran up the beach to the shelter of his truck.

'You're *what*? Luke, you can't marry Olivia!'

Rosemary stood with her hands behind her back, glaring at the brother who lay sprawled across the sofa holding an empty bottle of beer in his hand.

'I can, you know,' Luke replied, with a chilling lack of romantic ardour.

'But why? I know you said she's pregnant, but...you're not trying to tell me you're in love with her?'

'No. She's not very loveable.'

'Then you *can't*. Even if the child *is* yours. She doesn't have to have it.'

'Yes, she does. I want her to have it.'

Rosemary ran a hand through her hair. 'You do?' she said blankly.

He nodded. 'It's mine too, you see.'

'Yes, but – you never said you wanted children. At least not yet.'

'I don't. But since this one happens to be on the way, I'll have to make the best of it.'

'But Olivia's not the best of it. She'll only make you miserable. And for what?'

'For my own self respect, among other things. I have to

be able to live with myself, Rosie. I can't turn my back on my own child.' Luke, unable to bear what looked like the shimmer of tears in his sister's eyes, rolled off the sofa and prowled restlessly across to the window.

The woman with the poodles was there again. One of them was relieving itself on a newly planted tree. Luke put his hands on the sill and thumped his forehead against the glass.

'You don't have to turn your back on him. Or her,' Rosemary persisted. 'You can always support him financially...'

'Olivia doesn't need financial support. She says she needs a husband.'

'Sure she does, until the day you cease to amuse her. She has a very short attention span, Luke. Once she's got you well and truly hooked, she'll dump you and leave the baby with a nanny.'

'Oh, no she won't.' Luke pinned his gaze on the nearest poodle. 'Because I have no intention of being dumped. I agreed to marry her so my child will have at least one parent he can count on – who'll love him, and make an effort to turn him into a decent human being. I can't count on Olivia for that. You, of all people, know what it's like to be raised as no more than an obligation.'

'Yes, I do see that.' Rosemary sounded forlorn as a lost child on a crowded street. 'But are you *sure* the baby's yours?'

'As sure as I can be. Olivia swears she's never been to bed with anyone but me – and for some reason I seem to believe her.'

Rosemary didn't answer, and when he heard a door shut, he knew she had left.

Damn. She was hurting, and furious with him, of course. Who could blame her? Hell, he was furious with himself. But it was too late to undo what had been done, and now he must pay the price for those brief moments of uncontrolled passion.

He *would* marry Olivia. And he would make their marriage work, whether or not he got any help from her beyond the obvious. Luke scowled as a familiar pressure against his jeans reminded him of what had got him into this mess in the first place.

He dropped his forehead back against the glass, and thought of the last conversation he'd had with his unblushing bride.

He had reminded her that it was time they broke the news of their engagement to her father.

Olivia had dismissed the idea with a shrug. 'It's not necessary,' she'd said. 'He probably won't come to the wedding anyway.'

Luke, with difficulty resisting an urge to shake her, had replied that it most certainly *was* necessary, and of course her father would come.

In the interests of harmony, he didn't add that he was curious to see what kind of man had sired the beautiful, unscrupulous seductress who was about to become his lawfully-wedded wife.

An iron-haired lady in an apron ushered Luke into the library at The Cedars.

'Come in, come in. Sit down.' A thin, balding man with a monk-like ring of white hair looked up irritably from a well-worn leather chair placed too close to a crackling, unseasonable fire.

Luke, thankful he'd decided to wear a sports shirt instead of a suit, took his seat in a second leather chair beside the fire and immediately edged it back from the heat.

'You didn't bring Olivia with you?' Joe rose briskly and went to a small, oriental cabinet bearing a silver tray of drinks and assorted glasses. Without asking Luke what he wanted, he measured out two substantial shots of single-malt whisky.

'No.' Luke weighed the options of telling Olivia's father the unvarnished truth. That he was tired of half-truths and deception, and had earlier taken it upon himself to phone the older man. 'As far as I know, Olivia doesn't know I'm here.'

'I see.' The unusually pale blue eyes, so unlike his daughter's, didn't blink, but a muscle twitched in Joe's left eyelid as he handed Luke his whisky and returned to the heat of the fire. 'I suppose by that you mean that Olivia hasn't chosen to involve me in her wedding plans. It doesn't surprise me.'

Luke smiled ruefully. 'I told her I planned to talk to you. But she wasn't home when I went to pick her up.'

'So you came without her. Very wise. My daughter has a habit of going her own way. As no doubt you've found out for yourself.'

'Mm.' Luke studied Joe's face for some sign that Olivia's indifference to him mattered, but all he saw was a thin nose protruding from the white, mask-like skin of a man who spent too much time indoors. What a strange, cold relationship this father and daughter must have.

A log cracked in the fireplace, and Joe blinked and said, 'I'll pay for the wedding, of course.'

He might have been offering to pay for a round of golf.

'There's no need. I can support my family without help,' Then, realising he had spoken with unnecessary belligerence, Luke added wryly, 'Just.'

The mask cracked, and Joe Franklyn laughed. 'I like your honesty,' he said. 'Do you love her?'

Ouch! Luke hesitated. He had an idea Joe found the thought of anyone loving his daughter surprising, but that didn't mean he'd appreciate the truth.

'She's carrying my child,' he said finally, and drained the remaining whisky in one gulp.

Joe sat totally still, a white-haired statue in a dapper cashmere suit. Someone upstairs switched on a radio.

After what seemed like minutes, but was probably only

seconds, Joe reached for a box of Cuban cigars, extracted one and snipped off the end with silver clippers.

The library filled with the pungent odour of expensive smoke.

'I suppose I ought to call you a blackguard and a scoundrel and order you out of my house,' Joe said at last.

'Are you going to?' Luke asked.

'No. What purpose would that serve? You've agreed to marry her, haven't you?'

Didn't he *mind*? Luke wondered how he would feel if Olivia were his daughter. Relieved, perhaps. At least she'd be some other man's responsibility. 'Yes,' he acknowledged. 'I'm going to marry her.'

'Good. You'll have your hands full.'

Definitely not your average over-protective father. Relief was the only explanation.

'You and Olivia,' Luke said, trying to find a way to put it diplomatically. 'Your relationship is – unusual.'

'That's one way of putting it.' Joe concentrated on the tip of his cigar, waiting until the silence was well past awkward before admitting with apparent indifference, 'Olivia changed after her brother died. I'm afraid I didn't notice it at first. Had too much else on my mind.'

'That's understandable.'

'Yes.' The muscle in Joe's eyelid began to twitch again. 'My wife took Raymond's death very hard. She was never the same afterwards. Lost interest in everything, including, to an extent, Olivia. I don't mean she didn't love her, but she couldn't seem to find the energy to do anything about it.'

'That must have been difficult for you – as well as for Olivia.'

'It was. But I should have seen what was happening. By the time I paid attention, it was too late. Olivia was no longer the loving, affectionate little girl she'd been before. She seemed to be playing a part all the time. Nothing I could call her on, mind you. On the surface she was still my little Moonbeam. But I could tell it was a charade – as if all the sweetness had gone out of her and she was only pretending it hadn't.'

Luke nodded. He had often had exactly that impression himself.

'I tried taking her to a psychiatrist,' Joe went on. 'Damned charlatan wasn't any help. Said she was having trouble adjusting to her brother's death. As if we didn't know that.'

'Mm.' Luke hadn't taken to Olivia's father at first, but now he felt the first stirrings of sympathy.

'So Olivia has been – the way she is – ever since?' he asked, feeling his way, not wanting to add to Joe's burdens.

'More or less. I thought things might change when her mother was killed, but they didn't. Olivia played the part of the grieving daughter to perfection, and then carried on as before. She left home as soon as she could. I saw no reason...' He broke off as voices sounded in the hall, followed by the sharp tap of heels on the polished parquet floor.

Moments later the library door was flung open, and Olivia stood on the threshold letting in a draft of welcome cold air.

Trouble, Luke decided, observing his bride's unusually high colour and sparking eyes with resignation. In her slim-fitting black dress and ridiculous high heels, she reminded him of a temperamental thoroughbred waiting to strike out at anyone who came near her.

He regarded her in silence.

'Talking about me?' she asked, with heavy sarcasm.

'We wouldn't have had the chance if you'd come with me. As I asked you to,' Luke pointed out mildly.

'I told you there was no need.'

'And I told you that there was.'

Joe cleared his throat. 'Good evening, Olivia. How are you?'

Olivia threw her father a dismissive glance, stalked across to the window and stood facing the room with her arms crossed aggressively on her chest. 'Apart from the fact that it's insanely hot in here, I'm fine,' she said. 'Why shouldn't I be?'

Joe gave her a look Luke couldn't interpret and exhaled a fresh cloud of smoke. 'As I remember it, a certain amount of nausea isn't uncommon in your condition.'

Olivia glowered at him. 'The only thing that makes me nauseous is your cigar. As for...' She broke off and turned accusingly on Luke. 'You told him.'

'Somebody had to. I agree it should have been you.'

'You'd no right...'

'I had every right since I'm the baby's father. And *your* father has a right to know he's going to be a grandfather.'

'Olivia isn't interested in my rights.' Joe spoke as if he were stating a dull but irrefutable fact. 'Mind you, she has a healthy respect for her own.'

'Damn you, Dad...'

Luke felt his irritation mount as he shifted his gaze from glowering daughter to impassive father, and back again. This was ridiculous. It was bad enough that he was about to marry a woman he lusted after, but couldn't respect and barely trusted. He was not about to put up with a pointless family feud into the bargain.

'That's no way to talk to your father,' he said, rising to his feet and striding over to the window to take Olivia firmly by the shoulders. 'Apologise.'

'I will not. I don't have to do what you say.'

He'd forgotten how lovely she was when she was angry. Heat crackled through his fingers as if he'd touched an exposed electric wire. Immediately he lowered his arms. He would *not* allow his libido to distract him now. If he let Olivia get the better of him at this stage, their marriage was destined for disaster.

'No,' he agreed. 'You don't have to do what I say. On the other hand, you do expect me to marry you.'

When Olivia's beautiful dark eyes narrowed, Luke braced himself, expecting her to take up the challenge. He was careful to keep his expression blank. If she detected even the faintest sign of weakness, he was lost.

They faced each other in silence, each waiting for the other one to blink. In the end, Luke's none-too-subtle threat must have got through to her.

'All right,' she said, tossing her head theatrically. 'I'll apologise if it makes you happy.'

'Accepted,' Joe said quickly. 'Luke, would you please pour us all another drink?'

Joe Franklyn had a very small smile on his thin lips as he raised his empty glass. A gesture that looked to Luke very much like a toast to the man who had wrung an apology from his daughter.

He refilled Joe's glass and asked Olivia what she wanted to drink.

'A Bloody Luke,' she snapped.

Luke raised his eyebrows.

'Oh, how silly of me,' she exclaimed, raising a hand to her mouth. 'I meant a Bloody Mary, of course.'

'Very amusing,' he said. 'Would you like me to add ice or acid? On the other hand, since alcohol is clearly not good for pregnant women, I think you'd be better off with a Club Soda – don't you?'

Joe gave a dry chuckle of amusement and, to Luke's astonishment, even Olivia permitted herself a smile of agreement. He returned it with an uncomplicated grin, relieved to discover she wasn't wholly incapable of laughing at herself.

'Sit down,' Joe said, waving his daughter to the library's leather love-seat. 'Time we started making arrangements for this wedding. It's not every year my daughter gets married.'

Luke threw Olivia a warning glance. He didn't trust her not to reply that her wedding plans were none of her father's business.

Instead, after giving Joe a frown that was more puzzled than indignant, she said, 'All right. I mean to get married in red.'

Ah. The first gauntlet had been tossed his way. Luke nodded agreeably. 'Whatever you wish. You look very seductive in red.'

Olivia, balked of opposition, said, 'I suppose you want a small wedding.'

Knowing she was testing him, Luke replied, 'It seems appropriate in the circumstances. But if you want a big crowd...'

'I don't,' Olivia interrupted hastily. 'I hate crowds.'

The corner of Luke's mouth tipped up. He had won a victory. A small one, but nonetheless a victory. No doubt his marriage to Olivia would consist of a series of these minor skirmishes.

He hoped they would all be won as easily.

'Did you drive, or take a taxi?' Luke asked, as they descended the steps of the Franklyn mansion two hours later.

The night was cool, fragrant, with a new moon in the sky and a hint of rain dampening the air – a night made for lovers and the warmth of bodies lovingly entwined.

Olivia sighed. Luke wouldn't even get close enough to hold her hand.

'I took a taxi,' she said. 'You'll have to drive me home.'

'I will if you ask nicely.'

'And if I don't?'

'You'll have to take another taxi, won't you?' He walked around to the driver's side of the Ranger.

Olivia stood with her hands on her hips on the damp grass bordering the driveway. 'You wouldn't dare leave me.'

'Try me.' He swung himself into the cab.

She went on glaring until it dawned on her that instead of watching her performance, Luke was warming up the engine. It growled softly as he shifted into gear.

He wouldn't...

The Ranger started to back towards the gates – and in that instant Olivia knew Luke most definitely *would* leave her behind. Without a qualm. He'd probably even enjoy it. The realisation galvanised her.

'Hey,' she shouted, running after him. 'Wait. I'm coming with you.'

Luke drew to a stop and leaned amiably out of the window. 'Well?'

Olivia gritted her teeth and said, 'Please.'

He nodded, and leaned over to open her door.

'Was that so difficult?' he asked, extending a hand to draw her up beside him.

'No,' Olivia admitted. She frowned. What was it about Luke that made him unlike any other man she'd ever met? And why did she always react to him in ways she knew were likely to get her exactly the opposite of what she wanted? If he had been any other man, she would have smiled and preened and given him all the 'Please' and 'Thanks' he could ask for.

She smoothed the black silk covering her knees. The fact of the matter was that if Luke had been any other man, she wouldn't have to marry him in order to get her revenge.

Not that it was only revenge she wanted. She and Luke were now officially engaged, yet he was adamantly refusing to return to her bed. He said they might as well have something to look forward to, and that the frustration was his penance for being a total fool.

Olivia definitely didn't appreciate being a penance, and she certainly didn't see why she should suffer along with him. Perhaps tonight she would make him change his mind?

Beguiled   67

She turned to smile at his unresponsive profile. 'I'm sorry I was out when you came to fetch me,' she said in her sweetest, most placating tone.

'Why were you?'

'I went shopping and got stuck in traffic.' Both statements were true. Luke wasn't to know she had deliberately left her shopping to the end of the day in order to avoid him. She hadn't expected him to carry out his threat to visit her father without her.

'Ah,' he said. 'Shopping. And to think I thought you didn't mean to come.'

Damn him. 'I did tell you there was no sense in talking to my father,' she snapped.

'Yes, you did.' Luke swerved to avoid a black cat darting across the road. 'But you were wrong, weren't you? I get the impression your dad is delighted you're getting married – and not only because of the child. Remarkably generous of him, considering.'

As usual, Olivia found herself wanting to argue. But she couldn't. Her father *had* seemed pleased. Once or twice this evening she had even come close to believing he actually cared...

'You should have agreed to let him pay for everything.' Olivia dragged her thoughts to safer ground.

'I did agree to let him pay for the reception. As he pointed out, the father-of-the-bride usually does.'

'Yes, but he would have paid for a honeymoon in Europe as well...'

'Olivia,' Luke interrupted. 'It's bad enough that I have to move into your townhouse until the baby's born...'

'What's bad about it? I like my townhouse.'

'I know you do. But *I* should be paying for the lease.'

'I told you it's already paid. Till the end of the year. And you're still paying Rosemary's rent. So if Dad wants to give us a honeymoon...'

'No.' Luke pulled the truck rather too fast around a corner and narrowly missed a second cat. 'What is it with Vancouver's feline population?' he growled. 'If they've all come down with a death wish, maybe I ought to help them out.'

'Don't even think it,' Olivia said. 'Cats don't know about traffic.'

'Or anything else if you ask me. Stupid creatures.'

'They are not stupid. They're just cats.'

Luke slanted her a glance she couldn't interpret. 'You *like* cats?' he asked.

'I like all animals.'

'Amazing.' He shook his head and returned his attention to the road.

'Don't you?' Olivia asked, placing a hand on his arm.

He shook it off. 'Don't I what? Like animals? Sure I do. I spent my teen years on a farm with several cats. But I prefer them to stay the hell out from under my wheels.'

'Oh.' Olivia sat back, relieved. That was all right then. He didn't actually hate animals.

It didn't occur to her to wonder why it mattered.

She decided to postpone any further discussion of the honeymoon. If Luke insisted on a week on Vancouver Island, when they could so easily have a whole two months in Europe, she supposed she could put up with it. By the end of that week she would have him so besotted, he would agree to go anywhere she wanted. And when that day came, her revenge would be complete.

That was the whole point of them getting married. Funny, quite often these days she forgot.

Luke pulled his truck up to the curb in front of Athington Woods. When they reached her doorstep he kissed her dutifully on the cheek.

'Please come in,' she said, favouring him with her most beguiling smile.

Luke shook his head. 'Nope.'

Olivia pouted and gave a little wriggle. 'I promise that I'll be good.'

'I know you will. Very, very good. Once we're married.'

Just to pay him back, and before he could guess what she was up to, Olivia pulled down the zipper of his fawn-coloured trousers, inserted her hand briefly and effectively, then shut the door in his face.

Luke gave a roar of outrage and raised his fist to hammer for admittance. Then he changed his mind and waited for the agony of frustration to pass.

'Little witch,' he muttered, walking stiffly down the driveway. 'Just you wait till we're married, Olivia Franklyn. Try a trick like that on me then, and you'll soon find out what happens.'

By the time he had climbed painfully into the cab of his truck, his lips were parted in a grin of pure anticipation.

chapter five

Luke signed the register with a steady hand, then moved back to stand next to his scarlet bride.

Olivia had stuck to her guns about getting married in red. He knew she'd expected him to object, but he'd seen no reason to. The colour suited her, made her look like a sexy little firefly in slinky silk. Was there a man in the congregation who didn't wish he could change places with Luke Harriman tonight?

Yet, if they only knew, what they saw was all they would get. Olivia was packaging. Pretty, glittery packaging, nothing more. He had tried, these last few weeks, to get past the gaudy outer layers to the core of the woman wrapped inside, but he'd come to the conclusion he couldn't find it because there was very little there.

Olivia pushed at a stray wisp of hair, drawing Luke's eyes to the red veil covering her head. As if sensing his gaze on her, she looked up at him and smiled. Immediately, and in spite of his deep reservations about this marriage, his heart began to beat faster, and he was hard pressed not to haul her into his arms and make love to her at once – amidst the clutter of register, pens and church papers that littered the minister's small desk.

He reminded himself that relief would come soon enough now. All day he had kept his mind focused on the night that lay ahead. It was the only thought that had so far got him through his wedding day, and prevented him from boarding the next plane to nowhere.

That, and the thought of his child.

The organ began to play again, and he tucked Olivia's

hand in his elbow and prepared to face the smiling congregation.

Olivia's scarlet train swirled gracefully over the slim silk skirt of her dress as she twirled in front of the long mirror, which had hung on the wall of her bedroom at The Cedars for as long she remembered.

She'd done it! Luke Harriman was hers. Tonight, at last, she would have him in her bed. Her skin prickled at the thought. He had looked so handsome and glamorous in the church; so unbearably desirable in his dark, formal clothes, that for a few seconds in the vestry she had dreamed of falling into his arms and making love to him – right there on the Rev Stephen Lyle's untidy desk.

Giggling, Olivia ran across to the window. Where *was* her new husband? She glanced round the garden, and discovered him draped against a cherry tree in animated conversation with her cousin, Margaret, who'd been her bridesmaid. Margaret was laughing delightedly at something he'd said. Olivia shrugged. It wasn't the first time she'd noticed that women were drawn to Luke like a bunch of pins chasing a magnet. Only now she had the right to chase them off.

Smiling complacently, she returned to the mirror, gave her train a quick flip and decided it was time to detach her cousin from her new husband.

By the time she reached the garden, Margaret had moved on to try her charms on Luke's best man, Charlie Caldicott. Good luck to both of them. Today she was feeling magnanimous.

Luke was with his sister and the minister. Rosemary, all starry-eyed, looked just as she had when Michael had been her boyfriend.

Olivia studied the Rev Stephen Lyle with more attention than she'd paid him up till now.

Mm. Not bad. Nice dark eyes and a way of using them that made him look sincere. Not a patch on Luke though. She switched her gaze to her tall husband who was still propping up the trunk of the cherry tree, apparently absorbed by the antics of a small yellow finch balanced on a branch above his head. He didn't notice her until she touched his arm.

'Luke, darling,' she purred, linking her fingers through his arm. 'Did you miss me?'

'Miss you? You've only been gone a few minutes.'

She had been gone half an hour.

Hiding her irritation, Olivia smiled and said, 'Come and cut the cake.' This wasn't the time to set him straight on his obligations as a husband.

'If you like,' Luke agreed. Taking her hand, he led her across the lawn to a long table on which a masterpiece of the confectioner's art sat waiting to be divided among the guests.

Olivia glanced at her husband's face, not sure what she expected to see, and immediately wished she'd kept her attention on the cake. Luke had always had a faintly piratical air about him, but at this moment he looked as if he were waiting to walk the plank. Not flattering, and not at all what she'd had in mind when she decided to marry him. He was *supposed* to look eager, and passionately devoted to his bride.

Stretching her lips into a smile for the benefit of her audience, Olivia picked up the silver-handled cake knife, moved close to Luke and rubbed her leg discreetly against his thigh.

'It's not that bad, is it?' she whispered. 'This is supposed to be the happiest day of your life.'

Out of the side of his mouth Luke growled, 'Stop it,' and closed his hand over her fist. Together they sliced cleanly though the cake.

Olivia had an uneasy feeling as she laid the knife down,

that her husband wished he could slice as effortlessly through the bonds that had so recently united them.

She would soon change that. Before long he'd be begging for her favours.

Mrs Crump led a burst of clapping from the assembled guests. Seconds later, a light breeze whispered through the garden and stole her hat.

By the time it had been recovered from the neighbour's compost heap by Charlie, Olivia had collapsed against Luke's shoulder in a fit of giggles.

Luke, looking much less forbidding, said she'd better get ready to leave before she disgraced them both.

Half an hour later, in the limousine on the way to the ferry, he laughed out loud for the first time that day when she told him Mrs Crump's hat reminded her of her father's satellite dish.

Olivia touched his hand, and he put an arm around her shoulders and pulled her to his side. She breathed in the fresh, clean scent of his body and thought of the night that lay ahead – quite forgetting that she had only married him for a while.

Luke held out his hand. 'Want me to carry you over the threshold?'

Olivia cast a dubious eye at the wood frame cabin with the faded curtains and peeling yellow paint. 'I don't know. This place is a dump. When you told me you'd rented a cottage on the beach between Parksville and Nanaimo, I pictured climbing roses, fresh paint and a picket fence.'

'Did you? I pictured bed.'

Olivia grinned, pleased, and accepted his outstretched hand. 'How do you know it won't have bugs in it?'

'I don't. But we'll give them a run for their money if it has.'

Her grin became a full-throated laugh. Luke was fun

when he wanted to be. Fun and sexy. What more could she want in a man?

When he unlocked the door and scooped her up in his arms, she linked her hands behind his neck and waited to see what would happen next.

To her disappointment, what happened was that he dumped her upright on the brown and white tiled floor of an alcove that she supposed was meant to pass for a kitchen, and went to fetch their suitcases from the car. Olivia didn't think much of the car. Luke had rented it in Nanaimo, and it was small and grey and inexpensive.

He returned to the cottage almost at once, and slung the suitcases on to a worn tweed sofa with canary yellow cushions. 'Well?' he said. 'Did you find any bugs?'

'I didn't look.'

'Scared?'

'Of course not. Why should I be scared of a bunch of bugs.'

'You're scared of mice.' He started towards the bedroom.

'I am not.'

Luke paused, then turned slowly around.

Oh, oh. Mistake. Big mistake. There was a glint in his eye that told her she'd been caught in a trap of her own making.

'Is that so?' he said softly. 'Not even a bit scared?'

It was too late to backtrack. 'Not a bit,' she admitted. 'I only said I was that day because I didn't want you to leave. But you knew that, didn't you?'

'I wasn't sure at first. Do you realise we wouldn't be here, wouldn't be in this predicament at all if you'd told the truth?'

'Yes.' Olivia lowered her eyelashes. 'But I *wanted* to be in this predicament.' She held out her arms and tipped her head engagingly to the side. 'Don't scold me, Luke. You've made me wait long enough for this day.'

'It's been precisely three weeks since our engagement. That's hardly a long wait.'

'Yes it is. I usually get what I want right away.'

'Then you're in for a change, aren't you?'

Damn. She had put his back up – just when she'd wanted to seduce him. Never mind, that was an error easily reversed.

She smiled and took a step towards him, still with her arms enticingly outstretched.

Luke turned on his heel and stalked into the bedroom. He reminded her of a large black bear that couldn't make up its mind whether she was a bedtime snack or something he wanted to squash.

Olivia followed. By the time she got there he was peeling back the yellow chenille bedspread, and then the blankets.

'OK,' he said, straightening, 'let's get on with it.' He shrugged off his jacket and slung it over a rickety wooden chair.

Olivia blinked at him. 'But…'

He paused halfway through pulling off his tie. 'I thought you wanted what you want right away. I'm here to oblige.'

Olivia glared at him. 'Not like *that*,' she said, backing towards the door.

'How then?' The tie joined the jacket.

'I…damn it, Luke, I'm not a machine.'

She could be though. Easily. His shirt was off now and he was starting on his belt, and the sensations she had never for one moment forgotten were cascading over her in aching great waves.

Luke removed his trousers, flung himself on to the bed and lay still, hands behind his head, watching her.

'I'm all yours,' he said. 'Isn't that why I'm here?'

She understood then. Luke knew exactly what she'd had in mind from the beginning. He obviously half-suspected that her pregnancy was deliberate – a ploy to get him into bed. And he was damned if he would give her the satisfaction of admitting that he wanted her, every bit as much as she wanted him.

All right, if that was the way he chose to play it...

Olivia raised both hands and flipped her long hair languidly over her shoulders. Then she unfastened the top button on the jacket of her red and white travelling suit.

Luke watched her impassively from the bed, the brief shorts he had on concealing nothing. She finished unbuttoning and tossed her jacket on top of his. The skirt followed. She noted with satisfaction that her efforts were having their intended effect. When she was down to nothing but the small, white triangle of her panties, she hesitated, trying to decide on her next move.

Luke didn't stir, so she turned her back on him as if she meant to leave the room.

'Where do you think you're going?' His voice sounded strangled, as if it were being squeezed through a tube.

'I thought I'd see if there was anything to eat.' It was the first thing that came into her mind.

'There isn't. Besides, *you* wouldn't know how to cook it, and I don't want to. Come to bed.'

'Later.' Olivia sauntered out into the kitchen.

She opened a cupboard at random and was glad when the hinges creaked loudly. Luke would know she wasn't only pretending to be occupied.

From the bedroom behind her she heard a growling noise, like thunder working up to an explosion. Then bare feet thudded on the tiles, a pair of sun-tanned arms closed around her waist and her back was yanked forcibly against a man's naked body.

Olivia released her breath and tried to swivel round. She couldn't move.

'Let me go,' she said.

'Why?'

'Because...because the bed's in the other room.' She squirmed, and was instantly and triumphantly aware of Luke's response.

Before she had time to think, he had dragged her away from the cupboards and backed her up against the door of the fridge.

'What did you say?' He placed his hands on either side of her head, trapping her against the yellowing enamel.

Her mouth was only inches from his neck. She could see the taut sinews moving beneath his skin, smell the warm, musky scent of his desire. Behind her, the fridge made a humming noise, and she felt the throbbing of its motor up and down her spine.

She gasped, and without quite knowing why, bent her head to nip sharply at the base of Luke's throat.

He sucked in his breath. His hands closed over her hips. Then her panties were sliding down her legs, and she was groping for the waistband of his shorts. Thick hair brushed across her chest as his mouth closed deliciously over first one erect nipple, circling and teasing with his tongue, and then the other.

Olivia had never known such exquisite torture. 'Luke,' she moaned. 'Luke, the bed...'

Luke was too busy to answer.

And they never made it to the bed. Not that time.

He parted her thighs and entered her right there against the fridge. It hummed and throbbed against the bareness of her back. Only the pressure of his body, and the warm palms gripping her bottom prevented her from collapsing in agony and ecstasy to the floor.

Afterwards, Olivia was certain that no matter how old she lived to be, she would never again be able to hear the hum of a fridge without being transported back to the passion of this hot August evening on the very first day of their marriage.

Luke pushed a swatch of damp hair out of his eyes, easing himself upright and allowing Olivia to slide free. 'What was that you said about bed?' he asked, his breath rasping out in short gasps.

Olivia bent down to pick up her panties. When she straightened, she discovered Luke had his hand on her backside and was propelling her purposefully in the direction of the bedroom.

She giggled and offered no resistance.

Luke enjoyed his honeymoon on the whole. He hadn't expected to, hadn't even been sure he deserved to – but his lovely, self-absorbed little bride turned out to be so incredibly good in bed that his mind refused to dwell on anything beyond the hungers of the moment.

And it wasn't only a matter of bed. He had no complaints about her on sand or in the sea – or up against the fridge. His lips curved pleasurably at the memory.

He was dimly aware that before long this idyll would be over, that the real world would intrude, and his life with Olivia would begin in earnest. He was also realistic enough to know that his marriage was unlikely to run smoothly.

In the meantime, he would take what he'd been given and be thankful.

The week wasn't without its challenges. Luke hadn't expected Olivia to know how to cook, and was pleasantly surprised to discover she had actually taken cooking classes. However, his pleasure evaporated the day she came home from the supermarket with a receipt that amounted to most of his month's salary.

'Caviar!' he exclaimed, slamming six jars on to the flimsy plastic table. 'Saffron! Olivia what do we need with caviar and saffron? And have you any idea how much imported truffles cost?'

Olivia shrugged. 'It doesn't matter. I have the money.'

'Not any more, you don't. Not since you married me.'

'Of course I have. Dad opened an account for me as soon as we got engaged. He said you were an honest young fellow with principles, but he didn't want to see me going short because of that.'

'He *what*?' Luke crashed a fist on the table, making all the expensive jars jump.

'Opened an account for me,' Olivia repeated patiently. 'So you needn't worry about all this.' She waved a careless hand at the overburdened table.

'Olivia.' With a great effort, Luke succeeded in keeping his voice level. 'You have to understand something. I told your father I could support you. And I can. I mean to. I will not be dependent on my wife's rich father, just because she won't give up luxuries that the average family has never even heard of.' He flicked a disparaging thumb at the jar of truffles. 'Do you understand what I'm saying?'

Olivia shrugged and stuck out her lip like the spoiled little girl he sometimes forgot she was. 'That's so old-fashioned. Why should I do without the things I want, just because you've got some silly idea that you have to be the provider. We're not living in cave-man times, Luke.' She gave him an irritable slap on the arm. Immediately he grabbed her wrist, said, 'Oh yes we are,' and bore her off to the bedroom.

Most of their disagreements ended that way – but Luke knew that sooner or later there would come a reckoning. This week was an oasis in time, one he might as well make the most of while he could. Because once they moved back to Vancouver, things would change. He would return to work, Olivia to university, and they would have to start making plans for the baby.

Olivia, for some reason, refused to talk about the baby any time he tried to bring the subject up.

On the last night of their honeymoon, the two of them sat

on a log on the beach gazing quietly at the path of moonlight on the water. Somewhere in the woods a frog croaked, and the gentle swish of the waves formed a timeless background to a week the like of which they both knew they would never know again.

Olivia reached for his hand. 'Why don't we stay on here?' she asked. 'We don't *have* to go back tomorrow.'

'I thought you weren't impressed with the cottage. You said it was a dump.'

'I know. It is. But I like the peace and the ocean – and being alone with you. I don't want you to go back to work.'

'I have to.'

'Why?'

'For one thing I was only given a week off.'

'But you don't *have* to work.'

He frowned and stood up, and she added quickly, 'Anyway you can always phone them up, and say you won't be back until after I start classes in September.'

'No. I can't.' Luke shoved his hands into the pockets of his denim shorts. 'They've already given me an extra week at a time when everybody else is working overtime.'

'What difference does it make when you take your holidays?'

'A big difference. Nobody gets time off during the fish window. It's our busiest time of year. My being away now, means everybody else's load gets doubled.'

'What's the fish window?'

He could tell she didn't care. 'It's a period of roughly two months when most of the fish are in the rivers or out to sea. That's when we work on habitat enhancement in the streams and creeks so that...' He broke off. Olivia wasn't listening. He supposed in her place he wouldn't have listened either.

'So why not just quit your job?' She seemed genuinely bewildered. 'Then they can hire someone else, and you and I can stay on here.'

'Olivia, they haven't *time* to hire or train anyone else. Not now. And in any case, I've no intention of quitting my job before I'm ready to do so.'

'But...'

Luke shifted his shoulders in an attempt to shrug off the load of irritation that was Olivia, and made his way to the edge of the ocean. His bare feet scrunched on dry seaweed, and he didn't stop until the waves were lapping at his feet.

Her rubber sandals slapped up beside him. 'Luke, why are you walking away from me? I only want to be with you.'

Luke sighed. 'I know you do.' He extended an arm and drew her against his side. Was there any point in explaining, yet again, to this lovely, hedonistic creature he had married, that she couldn't have everything she wanted?

He decided not to try. It was the last night they would spend here together, and he could think of more stimulating ways to pass the time.

Smiling, he took both her hands in his and pulled her after him until they were standing waist deep in the ocean.

Soon his denim shorts were floating on the water. A short time later they were joined by a pair of rubber sandals and the bottom half of a blue-and-white bikini.

chapter six

Luke was late again. Irritated, Olivia pulled a pan of grilled swordfish out of the oven, slid her own portion on to a delicate porcelain plate and left Luke's cooling on the counter. Damn him. She'd been at special pains to cook him a meal he would enjoy, and now it was all going to be spoiled.

For good measure, she slammed the oven door before dumping a helping of crisp fried potatoes over her fish and carrying her plate through to the den that doubled as a dining-room.

Why couldn't Luke come home on time for once?

Cooking nice meals for him was part of her campaign to beguile him into falling madly in love with her – on the principle of reaching his heart through his stomach. But how could it work if he never came home in time to eat?

She knew she'd succeeded in captivating him in bed – but it seemed that wasn't enough. Beyond bed, a kind of barrier existed. Luke was polite, patient most of the time, and he appeared determined to act the part of a textbook husband. But he never looked at her with the hungry, hopeful eyes of other men, or told her that he couldn't live without her.

Olivia couldn't understand it. In the past, every man she'd so much as glanced at had collapsed in worshipful adoration at her feet.

Luke didn't worship her. Sometimes, in spite of bed, she thought he looked on her as no more than a pretty nuisance, designed merely to complicate his life.

She swallowed a mouthful of swordfish and got up to fetch the salad that, in her exasperation, she had forgotten to take out of the fridge. It was an attractive salad, bright with contrasting greens. She had enjoyed making it, as she enjoyed most cooking when she was in the mood.

If only Luke wasn't so unreasonable about the cost of food. His objections took half the fun out of it. On the other hand, if she complained about his penny-pinching, he had a habit of taking over the cooking himself, and that meant either tuna casseroles or macaroni cheese.

It was all so stupid when she had a bank account just waiting to be spent – and a father who was willing to replenish it the moment it ran out. Obstinately, Luke refused to touch her father's money and told her she shouldn't touch it either.

'If you weren't prepared to live within my means, you shouldn't have married me,' he said when she protested.

Olivia slammed the salad bowl on to the table, but it didn't relieve her frustration.

She had just sat down again when she heard Luke's key in the lock. Seconds later her husband strode in, his hair dishevelled, the sheen of sweat on his skin and a black smear of dirt across his forehead.

Olivia's welcoming smile faded. 'Where have you been?' she demanded. 'Your supper's been ready for hours.' A little exaggeration never hurt.

'Working.' Luke slung his grubby backpack on to the floor that Mrs Giles, the cleaning lady Luke didn't know about, had polished only that morning. 'I told you this was the busy season. I've got contractors breathing down my neck; the bosses haven't stopped growling in six weeks – and just to help things out, a road shoulder collapsed into one of my spawning creeks this morning. What have *you* done to keep busy?'

OK, so this wasn't a good time to complain about his lateness. If only he would quit that stupid job.

'I cooked you a nice piece of fish,' she said mildly. If she told him swordfish, he'd say it was too expensive.

'*Fish*,' Luke muttered. 'I never want to hear that word again.'

Her disappointment must have been plain to see, because immediately his surly expression softened and he came over to pat her reassuringly on the shoulder.

'Sorry,' he said. 'You went to a lot of trouble, didn't you? Of course I'll eat your fish. Just give me time to clean up and I'll be with you.'

Olivia twisted her hands in her lap and nodded mutely. 'Of course,' she said, turning up the pathos.

As she listened to the shower sluicing away the evidence of Luke's workday, Olivia came to the conclusion she couldn't have done better if she'd tried. Her crestfallen look had been genuine, and he'd reacted with instant contrition and guilt. Maybe she could work on that guilt and persuade him to take tomorrow off.

She waited until he'd appreciatively consumed the swordfish, along with a large slice of blueberry shortcake, before broaching the touchy subject of his job.

'It's our anniversary tomorrow,' she announced over coffee.

'Anniversary? What anniversary?' His cup clattered back into its fine china saucer.

'Our one month anniversary. Tomorrow we'll have been married a whole month. What shall we do to celebrate?'

'I don't know.' Luke didn't look as though he saw much to celebrate. 'I don't have a lot of spare time at the moment.'

'You'd have time if you took the day off.'

Olivia didn't miss the instant stiffening of his jaw. 'How often do I have to tell you I don't *take* days off at this time of year?'

'But you could. If you were ill.'

'Yes, I suppose I could if I wanted to lie. I don't.'

Olivia sighed. She might have known he'd say that. And now he was mad at her for asking. 'I didn't mean that,' she said quickly. 'I just wanted to spend the day with you.' She blinked very fast but, annoyingly, this time the tears wouldn't come.

Luke pushed away his coffee and stood up. 'You'll be back in class soon,' he said curtly. 'Then maybe you won't be so bored. Do you think you'll manage to finish up the term?'

'Finish the term? Why ever not?'

'You're having a baby. Remember?'

'Oh. Yes, of course. But not till January.'

Luke, who had been heading for the sitting room and the newspaper, swung round and came back. 'Shouldn't you be putting on weight?' he asked, placing his fists on the table and gazing down at her with his eyebrows drawn together.

'Weight? You want me to get fatter?'

He shook his head. 'No, but it's only natural.'

'Oh. Yes, I suppose it is.' She gave him an extra bright smile. 'I'm bound to start gaining soon, aren't I?'

'Have you been to the doctor recently?'

'I'm going next week.'

'Good. You're feeling all right then?'

Olivia thought fast. Was this the opening she'd been looking for? Would Luke be all solicitous and sweet if he thought she wasn't well?

'I have been a little queasy,' she admitted, with what she hoped was a gallant smile. 'But I'm sure it'll pass.'

'Yes.' He paused. 'Is he...has the baby started kicking?'

'Oh no, it's much too soon.' She had no idea when babies were supposed to start kicking, but it was a safe bet he hadn't either.

'Is it?'

She nodded, and at that point he seemed to lose interest, because no more was said on the subject of their child.

That night, when Olivia reached for her husband in the

big bed with the blue-and-white cover, he pulled her head on to his shoulder and said they'd better take it easy for a while.

'You said you've been queasy. We don't want to hurt the baby,' he explained.

Olivia thought of arguing, but decided not to. If Luke hadn't been so busy, and so exhausted by the time he came home, he would probably have asked about the kicking a lot sooner.

As it was, now that he *had* asked, something would have to be done.

The following evening, when Luke came home from work, Olivia greeted him with the news that she had been to see the doctor.

'That's good,' he said. 'What did he say?'

'That it's perfectly all right to have sex.'

'Have sex? Dr Crump said that?'

'Well, no, actually he cleared his throat a lot and mumbled something about the act of love between a man and a woman.'

Luke laughed. 'That sounds more like it.'

'But he said it was just fine,' Olivia reiterated quickly.

'Good.' Luke shot her the funny, fishy look he often sent her way when she said something he didn't quite trust. 'Just give me time to take off my clothes.'

Olivia sat down on the arm of her favourite yellow chair. 'I didn't mean right this minute. Your supper...'

'Will wait.'

'But you're all dirty.'

'Soon remedied.'

She was still gazing at him with her mouth half-open when he put his hands on her upper arms, pulled her to her feet and pointed her in the direction of the bathroom.

'Hey, what are you doing?' she exclaimed. 'It's not me that needs the shower.'

'I was thinking of killing two birds with one stone.'

'I hate that expression. Who wants to kill birds? And anyway, you're not making sense.'

'Oh, yes I am. I want a shower. You, apparently, want sex. Why not satisfy both our needs at once?' He opened the bathroom door with one hand and urged her inside with the other.

'But...'

Luke ignored her and began to remove his shirt.

Olivia watched him, biting her lip as she tried to decide how to handle this odd, unfamiliar Luke. What was the matter with him? Usually he at least tried to be agreeable. But there was nothing agreeable about this bloodless, coldly practical man who seemed to expect her to jump into the shower with him and get a bothersome duty over with before he settled down to enjoy his meal.

He kicked off his shoes, and Olivia made up her mind.

Slowly she unzipped her striped summer dress, allowing it to drop to the floor. Then she reached past him to turn on the shower and stepped under the cool, cleansing stream without bothering to remove her bra and panties.

Behind her, Luke said something she didn't like the sound of. Then he was beside her, in front of her, his hands on her back – unhooking the bra, sliding the panties down over her hips...

Olivia gave a small sigh and kicked them into a corner.

When he grinned, a piratical grin that heated her blood, she linked her arms around his neck and jumped up to wind her legs around his waist.

Luke let out an expletive and backed her up against the tiles. She waited, watching the shower mist tumbling about his shoulders.

He was magnificent when all wet and silky like this, with his hair plastered to his head and his dark eyes hot and provocative. As the water splashed over them, cool yet arousing, Olivia basked in his strength, and in her power to make that strength her own.

She scraped her nails down his back, laughing at his gasp of surprise. Then it was her turn to gasp as his fingers probed between her thighs, touching and caressing, taking her to the point of no return.

'Luke,' she moaned. 'I...'

He didn't allow her to finish. Nor did she want him to as his lips trapped hers in a kiss so erotic she thought she would happily die of desire.

Water sluiced over them, slapping on to the tiles and sliding over their bodies until Olivia no longer knew whether the heat she felt was inside her or all around them.

When, together, they reached the nirvana she'd been seeking, Olivia let out a cry that was as much unholy triumph as satisfaction.

Afterwards Luke was unusually taciturn, and when she asked him what was the matter, he at first grunted and then said, 'Nothing. Why should there be?'

Since Olivia could think of no useful response, she decided to wait out his mood and hope it changed for the better, once it came time to go to bed.

It did change, but not for the better, and not in any way she understood.

When Luke made love to her that night, it was with a thoroughness, and a hard determination, that was nothing like the passionate abandon she had come to expect of his lovemaking. There was passion tonight, but no laughter and no gentleness. And although, as always, he made certain she wasn't left wanting, it was as if only his body was with her in the bed.

His heart, she was sure, was somewhere else entirely.

Again Olivia asked what was wrong, but his only response was to run a hand across her flat stomach and begin the whole soulless process again.

By the time she fell asleep she was stiff, exhausted and, in one sense at least, intensely unsatisfied.

In the morning, once her head cleared, she remembered that Luke had only married her for the baby. It had been too easy to forget that these past weeks. Yet if she solved the problem in the obvious way, would he then say goodbye and leave her?

No, surely not. Luke wasn't like that. Sooner or later she would be the one who left.

It would be better, perhaps, to wait a while before closing the chapter on his baby – better to give him time to find out that he was crazy about her. He was bound to come to that point sooner or later.

They all did.

'Time,' Luke growled a week later, as he banged down the phone on a laconic functionary from BC Environment. 'That's what everyone wants. Time. And we don't have it.'

He dialled a number, trying to explain to the indignant client who answered his call, that there was nothing he could do to expedite his application to build a retail shopping complex near a possible spawning ground.

The client, who wasn't prepared to be reasonable, treated Luke to his highly-coloured opinion of government ministries in general, and BC Environment in particular.

Luke made sympathetic noises and hung up. And this was only the *start* of his day.

It was after seven when he returned to the townhouse. Olivia, thank heaven, was back at university, and he hoped to God she'd had a busy day. A bored, restless wife wanting extra attention was a problem he could do without tonight.

It wasn't that he hadn't become used to having her around – the same way people learned to tolerate pretty, manipulative children – and physically he couldn't ask for a more exciting partner. But always there was an emptiness; a sense that beneath the lovely face and sexual gymnastics lay a lack of warmth, an absorption with self that would forever preclude a truly intimate relationship. There was also the suspicion, formless a week ago but now beginning to take shape, that things were not as they had seemed on the day he married her.

'Luke! You're back. Whatever happened this time?'

She was smiling. He allowed himself to relax. It looked as though tonight he was to be spared recriminations and sulks.

'Work happened,' he replied, returning her smile tiredly. 'But it won't be this bad for much longer. The fish window's almost over.'

'Oh. Good.' She beamed at him, and at once he felt more alive, less exhausted. 'I haven't made supper, I'm afraid. Do you think we could go out? We never did get to celebrate our anniversary.'

Luke suppressed a groan. The last thing he wanted was to go out. But Olivia *had* been less demanding this past week. It wouldn't kill him to take her for a meal.

'All right,' he said. 'Pietro's?'

'Oh. I thought...'

'I know what you thought. We can't afford it.'

Olivia sighed. 'All right then. Pietro's.'

She was disappointed. Damn. Luke went into the bathroom, turned on the shower, and planted a fist on the nearest blue tile.

Would she never understand that he couldn't touch a penny of her father's money if he wanted to keep his self-respect? Or that next year, when the lease ran out, he would insist on moving to an apartment he could afford?

Probably not. Luke muttered a few choice words, and got on with the business of washing off the day's accumulation of dust.

Luke felt Olivia squeeze his arm as they walked along the tree-shadowed pavement. It was a warm night for early September, the air unusually still and scented with the first hint of autumn. Close at hand, the silence was broken by the soft meowing of a cat.

'I *liked* Pietro's,' Olivia said. 'I didn't think I would, but it was nice – you know, intimate.'

'I liked it too,' Luke agreed. He patted her hand. 'And the company could have been worse.'

'Pig.' Olivia shoved him with her hip, but he knew she wasn't seriously offended.

It *had* been a pleasant interlude. Pietro's was small and unpretentious, but the staff were friendly and the food good. For the first time since he had met her, Olivia had seemed genuinely interested in the tribulations of his job. Only when he pressed her for details of her childhood had the conversation faltered. Briefly, before switching the subject back to him, she had mentioned a birthday forgotten by her parents.

Poor little girl, he'd thought, surprised to find himself sympathising with Olivia. Even his aunt and uncle had remembered birthdays. Perhaps, next year, *he* would surprise her with a party. It couldn't make up for the past, but it might help build a bridge to the future.

'I've been thinking,' Olivia said now, giving an endearing little hop along the pavement as she attempted to keep pace with his long strides.

Luke slowed down. 'Have you? Never mind, I doubt if it's fatal.' He didn't want her to get serious now. The evening had been a success, and he planned to keep it that way.

'No, really.' She refused to be put off. 'I was thinking it's time we had Rosemary to dinner.'

Luke stopped dead beneath a streetlight. 'I thought you didn't like Rosemary.'

'I didn't much, but she is your sister. Anyway, I was

wrong about her. She's not nearly as wimpish as I thought. I'm sure I could get to like her if I knew her better.'

Luke studied her face under the artificial light. What was she up to now, this beautiful, bewitching wife of his? Was this some scheme to manipulate him into accepting her father's largess?

'Rosemary is not in the least wimpish,' Luke said sharply. 'Olivia, isn't it about time ...?' He broke off. She wasn't listening.

'Look,' she said, pointing to a furry shape lurking beneath the thick foliage of a nearby laurel hedge. 'Do you think it's a racoon?' The shape moved, and she added delightedly, 'Oh no, it's not. It's a cat.'

'So it is,' Luke agreed, taking her arm. 'Come on, I think it's going to rain.'

'Of course it isn't. Oh, isn't he gorgeous.' Shaking off his restraining hand, Olivia ran down the pavement to crouch beside a monstrous Persian, which sat swishing its tail back and forth as it watched her with glittery silver eyes.

'He's just a cat,' Luke said, overcome by a sudden urgent need to get her home. He didn't think the Vancouver City Police would take kindly to what they would probably term 'lewd and indecent behaviour in a private hedge'.

'Olivia,' he said again, injecting a note of authority into his voice. 'I said come on.'

But Olivia, oblivious to the stains on her red and black dress, was kneeling on a patch of damp grass blissfully stroking the cat.

Afterwards, Luke could never remember the exact sequence of the events that followed, but he did remember, vividly, his emotions.

The cat, apparently resenting the invasion of its privacy, gave a meow of protest and shot to its feet in a flurry of fur and spread claws. Olivia jumped up, and in the same moment a silver station wagon with its radio blaring came spinning round the corner on two wheels.

'Cat!' shrieked Olivia, as the cat darted directly into the path of the oncoming car.

'Olivia!' Luke thundered, hurling himself after her as she dashed in pursuit of the cat.

He caught her just seconds before the station wagon hit her.

The ominous screech of wheels gave him the adrenaline he needed to jerk her out of its path and on to the pavement.

'Are you all right?' he demanded tersely, as he picked her up and inspected her for damage.

'I...I think so. The handle bumped my hip, and my arm's a bit sore...'

'Are you crazy, woman?' the driver of the car was shouting as he skidded to a stop. 'You could have been killed.'

Luke's arms tightened around a trembling Olivia. 'She's no more crazy than you are,' he snapped. 'Do you always drive like a drunken maniac on crack?'

The driver, a youngish man with an impressive scowl, looked ready to get out and start a fight. But something in Luke's stance must have stopped him, because after glowering for a few more seconds, he hurled a couple of unimaginative insults and took off.

'The cat,' Olivia murmured into Luke's shirt. 'Is he all right?'

Luke, who had been hanging on to his temper by sheer willpower, decided it wasn't worth the effort, and exploded.

'I don't give a damn about the stupid cat,' he roared. 'That fellow was right. What the devil did you think you were doing? Trying to get yourself killed over a *cat*? You're not a two-year-old, for heaven's sake.'

Olivia removed herself haughtily from his arms. 'Don't shout at me,' she said, in what he thought of as her imperious-little-rich-girl voice.

'Then don't behave like an idiot.'

'Why not? Why should you care?'

'Because you're my wife, that's why. And you happen to be carrying my child.'

'Oh. Yes, of course. The child.' Olivia's voice became even more disdainful.

Luke was past caring. 'Right,' he said. 'We're going straight home to fetch the truck, and then we're getting you to the hospital for a check-up.' He took her unbruised arm and pointed her firmly in the direction of home.

She tried to pull away. 'I don't need to go to the hospital. I'm fine.'

'That remains to be seen.'

'*Luke.*' Olivia stood still and turned squarely to face him. 'I am *not* going to any hospital, and that's that.'

'Oh yes you are. Preferably under your own steam, but if necessary I'll pick you up and carry you.'

She glared at him, her eyes snapping fire beneath the streetlight.

'I mean it,' he said.

Olivia went on glaring.

Luke waited.

'Oh, very well,' she said sulkily, 'I'll go to Dr Crump if you like.'

'No. Not Dr Crump. The hospital's closer – and he's an old man and probably asleep.'

'But…'

'Don't argue with me, Olivia. There's no point. I won't be responsible for something happening to you or the baby because *I* didn't take reasonable precautions.'

'They're not reasonable…'

Luke, still recovering from the shock of seeing his wife narrowly escape an early death, gave up all attempt at rational persuasion and said, 'Shut up.'

To his relief and amazement, Olivia took him at his word.

As they walked in stony silence down the street, a door

opened and a woman in a housecoat called shrilly, 'Kitty, kitty. Here, kitty.'

A large grey Persian streaked past them and ran up the path into the house.

Olivia said nothing, but Luke felt her body relax against his side. With considerable effort, he succeeded in repressing the pointed words that came to mind.

Luke lounged in a chair in the hospital's hygienic white waiting room inhaling the smell of disinfectant.

Olivia had disappeared behind a screen half-an-hour ago, and he'd been told a doctor would examine her shortly. He didn't really believe there was much wrong with her, beyond a few bruises that were no more than she deserved. But in the circumstances, he was taking no chances.

A brisk, red-haired woman walked up to him carrying a clipboard.

'I've examined your wife, Mr Harriman. She'll be with you in a minute. Some nasty bruises, and I've stitched the cut on her arm. Outside of that, she should be fine.'

Luke rose to his feet. 'Thank you,' he said. 'And…the baby?'

'Baby?' The doctor's eyebrows went up.

'Yes, my wife's expecting. Didn't she tell you?'

'No, Mr Harriman, she didn't. She must be in the very early stages though. I don't think you need to worry.'

'The baby's due at the end of January, Doctor.' Luke wondered why his head suddenly felt hot while the rest of his body had gone cold. In the background somewhere a child was crying, a monotonous howl of discontent.

'January, Mr Harriman?' The doctor shook her head. 'Oh no, very little chance of that. I can assure you that I examined her quite thoroughly.'

Luke took a deep breath. 'I see. Yes, of course. Thank you, Doctor.'

The doctor walked away looking puzzled, and Luke sat down again and picked up a copy of *People* that was lying on the floor beside his chair. The printed words and pictures danced crazily in front of his eyes. They made no sense, so he rolled the magazine into a cylinder, slapped it twice against his thigh and stood up.

A grey-haired woman behind the counter eyed him with wary curiosity and opened her mouth to speak. Luke didn't notice her, because at that moment Olivia emerged from behind her screen and came towards him wearing her most angelic smile.

'The doctor says I'm fine,' she said, and held up her cheek for his kiss.

chapter seven

Olivia's smile froze. Something was wrong. Very wrong. Luke was looking at her as if she were Medusa, about to turn him into stone. He didn't speak, and his eyes had a cold, mirrored look about them, which would have frightened her if he'd been anyone but Luke.

'Luke?' she said, lowering the cheek that obviously wasn't going to be kissed. 'What is it? What's the matter. I told you I'm fine.'

He did speak then, in a voice so quiet and hard, she barely recognised it.

'You lied to me, didn't you?'

'Lied to you? Of course not.' She forced her smile to stay in place. 'What are talking about?'

She knew, but she had to be certain...

The door to Emergency burst open and a man raced in carrying a child with blood gushing from his leg. A woman on a stretcher groaned. Luke glanced at her blankly, then turned to stare around the busy ward as if he had suddenly become aware of where he was.

He jerked his head at the exit. 'Out.'

'What?' Olivia wasn't used to being spoken to in that tone.

'Out,' he repeated. 'Now.'

She considered, briefly, telling him to speak to her nicely, but thought better of it after assessing the look on his face. What she saw in the line of his mouth, and in his eyes, was a raging hurt so savage he could scarcely contain it.

The man with the bleeding child was shouting. Olivia glanced at him, squared her shoulders and walked past Luke into the night.

They didn't speak as he drove the Ranger through the darkened streets. She wondered if his anger was so great he was incapable of speech, but there was nothing to be gained by finding out. In his present state, one wrong word and he was likely to drive straight into a lamp-post.

As soon as they reached Athington Woods, Luke jumped out of the truck and strode ahead of her up the path with his hands in his pockets; his back so stiff she could almost see the sinews pulling beneath his shirt.

Oh Lord, what should she do now? He'd been angry before, but never *this* angry.

Olivia lifted her chin and followed him. Given his mood, it might be smarter to run away, but she wasn't in the habit of running – or of conceding any battle.

Dimly, and without altogether understanding why, she was aware that the hardest battle of her life lay ahead. But she would win it. She had to.

Luke unlocked the front door and swept inside without troubling to see if she was following.

Olivia hesitated, but only for a second. Then she followed him, kicking the door shut with the high heel of the elegant black shoe, which Dr Crump had said was too risky for pregnant mothers.

When they reached the sitting room, Luke stopped in the centre of the floor, shrugged off his jacket and swung to face her.

'No more games, Olivia. You're not pregnant, are you?'

'I...I'm not now.'

Oh, if only she'd disposed of her mythical baby a week ago; told him she'd had a miscarriage. He might have believed her then. But a week ago she had needed more time to make him love her, before taking away the whole foundation of their marriage.

'No,' Luke threw his jacket on to the sofa. 'Not now. Nor were you ever.'

'I was...'

'Sit down,' he ordered.

Olivia, hearing the iron in his voice, decided to do as he said. She slumped wearily into her familiar yellow chair. Her shoes felt tight and she kicked them off, listening to first one and then the other thud on to the carpet.

'I want the truth from you, Olivia.' Luke spoke with a wholly unnatural restraint. 'Not another of your fabrications. Not this time. Now tell me, why? Why did you do it?'

Olivia raised her eyes from the brown-and-gold carpet, and saw that he had moved across the room to stand with his back to the open window. Was he so close to losing control that he couldn't allow himself to stand near her? And how *could* she tell him the truth? She wasn't even sure what the truth was – except that she didn't want to lose him.

It was all supposed to have been so easy. She would marry him; he would fall besottedly in love with her, and when the time was right she would leave him.

Only the time wasn't right, she didn't want to leave him – and he wasn't remotely in love with her. He never had been.

She pressed her hands together in her lap. It *might* not be too late, even now, if he still wanted her as much as she wanted him...?

Something of her thoughts must have shown on her face, because Luke said harshly, 'No. Don't even think it. I won't accept any more lies.'

Olivia believed him. Lies wouldn't help. But maybe, just maybe, she could beguile him into accepting an explanation.

'If you'll wait a minute I'll tell you everything,' she said. 'I have to go to the bathroom.'

His mouth turned down, and he gave her a long, level look that didn't auger well. 'Go on then,' he said. 'We're going to settle this however long it takes.'

Olivia padded into the bathroom, turned on the tap and gave her face a thorough wash in cold water. Then she worked on her make-up until she had achieved a look of translucent fragility with emphasis on her eyes. She hoped they looked sufficiently sad and soulful to make Luke believe in her penitence. As a finishing touch, she dabbed on her newest scent – the one with the fragrance of lilies.

'You wasted your time,' Luke snapped, the moment she returned to the sitting room. 'I've been married to you long enough to know you're as tough as old leather – and no damned lily.'

Olivia started to say she didn't know what he meant, but the way he was standing dissuaded her. If he'd had a tail, it would have been twitching like that of a tiger waiting to spring. His hands, curled tightly on his thighs, made her think of a tiger's threatening paws.

She sat down hastily, clinging to the arms of her chair and lowering her eyelashes in a fetching demonstration of remorse. 'I'm sorry,' she said softly, 'but I couldn't think of any other way to make you pay attention. You wouldn't have anything to do with me, you see.' She held out her hands, palms upward in supplication.

'For a damned good reason. I didn't *want* anything to do with you.'

'I know.' She hated admitting it. It was almost like admitting defeat. 'But I *had* to make you listen to me. How else was I going to get you back?'

Luke moved away from the window and came towards her. The scent of new-mown grass drifted behind him to mingle with the tense air in the room. Olivia stiffened and lifted her chin, but suddenly he veered to the right and went to stand with his back to the empty fireplace.

'Why?' he said again, folding his arms and scowling in a way she found particularly intimidating.

'Why?' Olivia tried to look mystified. 'Why did I have to get you back?'

'Yes.' His voice was as clipped as sharp scissors.

'Because...' She hesitated. What could she tell him? That she had needed to get him back because she loved him? He wouldn't believe her. She wouldn't believe herself. The truth? But what was the truth?

'I think that I wanted you back,' she said finally, when her silence had stretched beyond reason, 'because you'd given me something I no longer wanted to do without. Not once I knew what it was like.' That, at least, he might believe.

'Sex?' he scoffed. 'If that's what you're talking about, you certainly didn't need *me*. At least half the student population of the university would have been only *too* delighted to oblige you.'

Olivia winced, surprised at how much his contempt hurt. 'Yes, that may be true,' she agreed. 'But I didn't *want* half the student population. I wanted you.'

Someone in the building began to play the piano. The notes of Chopin's *Fantasy Impromptu* drifted plaintively through the window as she finished speaking.

'Maybe,' she heard herself saying, 'I wanted you because I knew I couldn't have you.'

'I see. Thank you for that bit of honesty.' Only the whiteness of Luke's knuckles betrayed how tenuous was his hold on his temper. 'So it was mainly on a whim you decided to wreck my life? And all because the beautiful Olivia Franklyn couldn't accept that not *every* man in the country was dying to grovel at her feet?'

'No,' Olivia cried, cringing from the sting of words that hurt as much as any physical attack. She hadn't felt this destroyed, this abandoned, since the day her parents forgot her birthday. 'I admired you because you *didn't* grovel.'

It was true. She had wanted to reduce Luke to the weak-kneed adoration of all the others. Yet she had been attracted to him precisely because he *wouldn't* bend to her whims. Was that also why she wanted so desperately to keep him? Until tonight, she hadn't known how much.

'Have I...have I *really* wrecked your life?' she asked, horrified to hear a quiver in her voice.

'Cut out the play acting,' Luke said tiredly. 'No. You haven't. Now that I know the truth, I won't let you.'

What? What truth was he talking about? And did he really think she was putting on an act? 'I don't understand,' she said, blinking hard, and raising her hand to brush away a tear that had nothing to do with poor Phantom. Oh, if only she had his warm, furry body to hug now ...

'Stop it, Olivia.' Luke's harsh voice sliced through her misery. 'You know exactly what I mean. You invented a child who didn't exist, for no other reason than to get your own way.'

Well, yes. She had. And looking at Luke now, the man she had so carelessly deceived, it occurred to her for the first time in her life that revenge was not necessarily sweet. Luke was hurting. He had wanted that baby. Funny, she had fully intended to hurt him, yet now that she had succeeded beyond her wildest dreams, she would have given anything to undo what she had done. Because if she couldn't undo it, she would lose him.

Except that she never lost. There *had* to be a way she could win him back.

Olivia stopped clutching the arms of her chair and sat up very straight. 'It wasn't just to get my own way,' she said. 'I admired you, Luke, even if I didn't know it then. And I *am* sorry. Truly I am.'

'Sorry? You think sorry fixes anything? I'm *married* to you, Olivia, supposedly until death do us part. Married for no damn reason to a woman who has never loved anyone but herself. Have you *any* idea what you've done?'

He turned away from her as if he couldn't bear to look at her any more, then propped an elbow on the mantel and bowed his head.

Olivia *hadn't* any clear idea, but she knew she had to say

something to appease him. He didn't even seem angry any longer. Just appalled.

'Yes,' she said. 'I know that I've hurt you. I guess you wanted that baby. But it's not true that I've never loved anyone but myself. I did once love two people very much.' She tossed her head, pushing the memory away. 'All I can tell you now is that I really *am* sorry.'

'You said that already. It doesn't help.'

Speechless, Olivia fixed her eyes on the strong column of his neck, and when he swung to face her without warning, she had no time to look away.

Dear God. She flinched, once again reaching for the arms of her chair. Could she really be the cause of such blazing emptiness? Such devastation?

'Did it matter so much to you?' she asked. 'The baby, I mean?'

'Of course it mattered. Why in hell do you think I married you?'

OK. So he was over that brief period of stunned mourning for the child who never was – and now he was ready to strike back. Olivia braced herself. What could she do to deflect him? There was nothing more she could say. Except... She took a deep breath.

'I'm not pregnant now. I took care not to be. But – but I could be.' For a few seconds she didn't believe the voice she was hearing was her own.

Then she saw Luke's eyes and knew it was.

Silence, broken only by the rhythmic ticking of the antique clock above the fireplace. The piano had long since gone quiet. Luke picked up a Dresden shepherdess, stared at it and put it down without comment.

After an eternity, he said, 'You expect me to believe you'd be willing to have a real child? You, who lied to me for no other reason than to get your own way?'

'That *wasn't* the only reason.'

'All right, your own way plus sex, which amounts to the same thing.'

Sex. Olivia clutched at the word now as if it were a lifeline. 'But you like sex. We're good together. We could have a baby if you want one.'

'Sure, then you could arrange a convenient miscarriage the moment it became inconvenient. Do you really believe I could bring myself to touch you now?'

Help! Olivia prayed desperately to the God she had ignored for twelve years. *Please help me*!

This was far worse than she had ever imagined. Forcing herself out of the comforting embrace of her chair, she stood up and walked steadily towards the man – whose presence in her life, she had just discovered, meant more to her than anything in the world.

He didn't move, but when she touched a hand to his unexpectedly damp cheek, he started back as if her fingers were snakes of fire.

'Don't try it, Olivia,' he warned. 'I've had about all I can take.'

She nodded, and moved away at once so he wouldn't see the tears that, once again, she hadn't needed Phantom's aid to manufacture.

Crossing to the window, she rested her hands on the sill and gazed mindlessly out into the night. The moon was a pale wedge of lemon suspended in the sky. As she watched it, seeking inspiration, a breeze came up and gently stroked her hair.

Olivia had no idea how long she stood there, feeling but not speaking. It seemed like forever before Luke broke the silence.

'How did you do it?' he asked, no longer as if he cared, but as if it were something he ought to know. 'Dr Crump wasn't lying. He was ready to drag out his shotgun if I didn't marry you.'

'No, he wasn't lying.' Olivia pinned her attention on the moon. 'I told him I'd done a home pregnancy test, twice just to be sure, and that I needed his confirmation because I wasn't sure you'd believe me.'

She heard Luke draw in his breath. 'Olivia, he's a doctor. He wouldn't confirm it on your word alone.'

'He did. He's retired, you see. Has been for years. I see him sometimes because he's an old family friend, but he's not my regular doctor any more. He's getting a bit dithery, and I knew he *would* take my word for it. He likes me, I think.' She didn't add that Dr Crump was about the only person she knew who did. It would sound too self-pitying.

Behind her Luke groaned. 'My God. Olivia, are you telling me I was trapped on the word of a well-meaning old fool, and a woman who makes lying a way of life?'

Did she? Did she make lying a way of life? She hadn't needed to lie before she met Luke – whose voice was so filled with loathing she couldn't bear it.

Slowly, holding her breath, she turned to face him.

He was still draped against the mantel, but the moment their eyes met, he straightened. Without a word, he picked up his jacket, slung it over his shoulder and strode into the hall.

'Where are you going?' Olivia cried, tripping over her feet as she scurried after him.

'Away.'

'But you can't. It's late. We...we have to talk.'

'We have talked.'

Was he leaving her? Just like that? She held out a beseeching hand which he ignored.

'Luke,' she pleaded. 'Please. Don't leave me.'

When he reached the door he paused to say over his shoulder, 'Tell me, when did you plan to break the news of your *miscarriage*? It did occur to me, about a week ago, that you seemed to have forgotten you were pregnant.'

'You didn't say anything.'

'How could I? The idea was absurd. I tried to put it out of my mind.'

He hadn't entirely succeeded though. Olivia remembered the night he had made love to her as if she were merely a handy receptacle for lust.

'You haven't answered me,' Luke said.

Olivia raised her eyes, which had been riveted on the scuff marks on his shoes. 'What?' she whispered.

'When did you plan to break the news of your miscarriage?'

Did he have to sound so hateful? So filled with disgust? 'I don't know,' she said. 'Soon. I hadn't decided.'

He nodded and put his hand on the doorknob. 'It makes no difference, I suppose. Goodbye, Olivia. I'll be back to collect my things – later, while you're in class.'

'Wait!' she shrieked, grabbing on to his elbow. 'Luke, you *can't* leave me. Not now. We're married. Please, I didn't mean...'

He shook her off. 'I don't care what you meant, Olivia. This time it *is* over.'

'Oh please, don't go. I promise I won't lie to you again. We can have a baby if that's what you want...'

'It isn't. Not with you.'

'But we *are* married. You can't...'

'I can do anything I like. Just as you've always done. As for being married – that was always a farce, wasn't it?'

'But...' She watched, frozen, as he opened the door. It creaked slightly, as if in protest, then his footsteps sounded on the gravel.

By the time the movement came back into her limbs, he was already switching on the engine of his truck.

'Luke!' she screamed, running down the driveway with her skirt flapping madly around her knees. 'Luke, come back.'

But Luke had already pulled on to the road, and by the time she reached the pavement, gasping and clutching a painful stitch in her side, her husband was already out of sight.

Olivia stood staring down the empty street for a long time. She didn't notice that the breeze had become a chilling autumn wind, and when her fingers turned numb, she merely flexed them and went on staring. It wasn't until she began to lose the feeling in her feet, that she at last dragged herself back to the house.

The pianist chose that moment to pick out a rollicking little dance tune on the keys.

'Stop,' she groaned, covering her ears with frozen hands. 'Please, please just STOP.'

The light streaming from the open doorway mocked her with its beaming good cheer.

Only once before had she felt this desolate, as if the world as she knew it were at an end. But she had been a child then, and it hadn't been like this.

Back in his rented apartment, Luke unbuttoned his shirt and decided he couldn't stay there brooding all night. He had never loved Olivia, never completely trusted her. Why should he *care* that his marriage was over? It wasn't as if there was a baby to think about...

The bitterness that had earlier threatened to engulf him intensified until he could taste it in his mouth. How *dare* Olivia play games with him like that? How dare she trade on his basic sense of fairness, for no other reason than that she wanted him in bed? Luke swiped an arm across his face. Maybe some men would be flattered.

He wasn't.

Olivia. He had surely paid the price for his lack of restraint there – for those fleeting moments of uncontrolled lust – and something told him he hadn't finished paying.

With a stifled curse, Luke pulled his shirt out of his belt

and threw it at a chair. What, in the long run, did it all matter? Life and fish windows would go on.

The only difference was that now there would be no baby.

Luke sat on the edge of the sofa with his elbows on his knees and his face buried in his hands.

The following morning, when Olivia opened her eyes after a tormented and nearly sleepless night, Luke wasn't back. She waited for him all day, but he didn't come.

The next day she returned to her classes and, in the evening, when she came home, all his clothes and possessions were gone.

All that remained to remind her of her marriage, was a small cake of mud on the doormat that carried the imprint of Luke's boot.

The week that followed was the worst one of her life.

She spent it alternately mourning her loss, and trying to come to terms with the reality of being alone once again.

At first she convinced herself Luke would soon return. Then she was forced to accept the possibility that he wouldn't. It took her a little longer to realise he had taken a part of herself with him when he left. She missed him. Quite desperately.

The knowledge appalled her. For a long time she had thought losing Phantom was the worst thing that could ever happen to her. She knew better now.

Losing Luke was a hundred times worse.

She wouldn't, *couldn't* give him up without a fight. It wasn't her way, and if that was what he expected of her, then he didn't know the woman he had married.

He had been gone five days when Olivia woke in the middle of the night, saw a bright shaft of moonlight on the wall and knew for certain he was back. She reached for him, murmuring his name – and touched the crisp coldness of unoccupied sheets.

It was only a dream.

chapter eight

On a pale October morning, one week after his marriage to Olivia had ended, Luke steered the Ranger up her driveway, slammed on his brakes and jumped to the ground with the motor still growling.

He held a sturdy cardboard box in his hands as if it were a bomb.

Yesterday afternoon a parcel had been delivered to his apartment. When Luke had come home and unwrapped it, he discovered it contained a beautifully preserved original edition of Darwin's *Origin of the Species*.

'I don't believe it,' he'd exclaimed, placing a hand reverently over the book's leather spine. 'Who...? What...?'

With his free hand, he searched the box for a card, and almost at once his initial awe at receiving such a treasure was replaced by a furious resentment because he couldn't keep it.

The book, as he might have guessed, was a gift from Olivia.

By the time he had carried the box to her front porch, his mood, already volatile, had worsened.

He glowered at the inanimate cause of his ill-humour, not wanting to enter the house, yet knowing he couldn't leave Olivia's gift on the step – any more than he could risk consigning it to the mail. He still had his key, and the Darwin was much too valuable to leave to the tender mercies of some crackhead, looking for something to steal in order to buy drugs. If *only* he'd never laid eyes on that remarkable book...

Luke removed the key from his wallet, shoved open the door and laid the box on the floor. Right. That was done. He cast a last, regretful glance at the gift Olivia must have known he had coveted for years, and started to back out of the door.

Just before it closed he heard a sound.

Ignore it, he told himself. Ignore it and get out. Fast!

He took three steps down the path, and stopped. Silence. Maybe he'd been dreaming, caught up in memories of a marriage that was over. He took another couple of steps. A blackbird perched high in the branches of a birch tree began to sing.

Luke stopped again. It was no good, he couldn't just walk away. He had to *know*. Scowling, he returned to the door, opened it a crack, and listened.

He hadn't been mistaken. There was nothing wrong with his hearing.

What he had heard, as he had suspected all along, was the sound of Olivia sobbing.

A familiar ache swelled in his chest. He clenched his teeth and slouched against the doorframe that was still damp from yesterday's rain.

What in hell was he going to do now? And why wasn't Olivia in class as she was supposed to be?

As he hesitated, the sobbing rose in intensity until it became one long, keening wail.

Ahh! OK. Luke ground his fist against the door post. Now he got it. This had all the earmarks of one of Olivia's schemes. She had guessed he would return the books in person, and had waited for him like a clever little spider waiting for a fly. Her web, naturally, was baited with the one lure experience had taught her was likely to entrap him.

Tears.

And he was tempted. Lord, was he tempted. He knew what she was up to, but it made no difference. The thought of walking into their bedroom to find her tumbled and sobbing on the bed, then stretching himself out beside her, taking her trembling body in his arms...

'*Hold it right there, Harriman.*'

At first Luke thought the voice came from somewhere above his head. When he realised it was his own, he knew he had to get out before he lost his mind.

Closing his ears to the escalating wails from the bedroom, he snapped the door shut and strode towards his truck.

He had one foot in the cab, and was about to slide on to the seat when he heard the sharp crunch of gravel behind him. He braced himself as a pair of oh-so-familiar arms closed around his waist.

No! Absolutely not. He was *not* going to fall for that again — even though the enthusiastic reaction of his body was telling him to give in like a ram in rut.

Without attempting to look at her, Luke detached Olivia's clinging arms and made to slide out of reach.

He wasn't fast enough. Before he could move, she had her fingers hooked into the back of his belt. He suppressed a groan as her busy hands worked their way inside his waistband and began an agonising exploration.

Luke let out a string of graphic expletives. 'No,' he snapped, reaching behind him for her wrists. 'No, Olivia. It's over. Can't you get that into your bright, beautiful head?'

For answer, she raised a leg and wrapped it around his knees.

'What the...?' He tried to shake her off, but she clung on like a mollusc gripping rock. If she'd been a man he would have kicked her off. But this was Olivia, his wife. Much as he might like to, he couldn't hurt her.

'Olivia...' he began.

Olivia laughed, leaning backwards and as Luke made a grab for the Ranger, he lost his balance. A second later, the two of them thudded to the ground in a tangle of flailing arms and legs. They struggled briefly and then, somehow, Olivia was beneath him, spread out on the lush green grass that came to the edge of the driveway.

'Hi,' she whispered, running a finger along his lower lip. 'I've missed you.'

While Luke fought to regain his breath and his temper, she coiled her arms around his neck.

He groaned. She was wearing that impossible red dress again, and even through his jeans and sweatshirt he could feel every supple, enticing curve of her woman's body. As she meant him to.

A plane droned overhead, and he smelt the damp, sweet scent of cut grass. He hadn't known wet grass could be an aphrodisiac...

As Luke struggled to subdue the treachorous reaction of his body, all at once Olivia began to move. Right there on the edge of the driveway, in full view of all the tenants of Athington Woods and passing cars, she rocked her hips in a slow, erotic rhythm as old as time.

Luke put a hand under her skirt and ran it down the length of her thigh. She wasn't wearing panties or stockings. Oh God, he had missed this, missed it like hell. She was so damn sexy...

Beneath him, Olivia gave a small, triumphant giggle. That giggle – so familiar and yet so maddening – succeeded in piercing the haze of lust and frustration that had him in its thrall.

What was he doing? Was he crazy? Dear heaven, if this was all it took to make him forget not only the constraints of civilisation, but everything this woman was and had been, she must be even more lethal than he'd thought.

Closing his eyes against the danger squirming beneath him, Luke rolled on to the grass and sat up, his hands hanging loosely between his knees.

Olivia held out her arms. 'Don't go,' she said. 'I can see you want me.'

'You, and anyone within a radius of thirty metres can see

that.' Luke cast a bleak eye at the evidence of arousal his tight jeans couldn't conceal. 'Yes, I want you. I also want to do things to you which are probably illegal. Unfortunately that isn't going to happen.'

'Oh.' Olivia gave him a sultry smile and raised her knees to show him what he already knew – that she had nothing on underneath the dress. 'Why not? I've never tried kinky.' She jumped to her feet in a rustle of sexy red silk. 'Come on, let's go inside.'

For two seconds, even now, Luke was tempted to take her up on her invitation – until he caught the glitter of victory in her eyes.

Reality hit him in the gut.

'No,' he said, though he doubted if she knew the meaning of the word.

Olivia produced another reproachful and unbearably seductive smile.

Luke shook his head. 'I said no. It won't work.'

She opened her mouth to protest, but Luke had had enough. Rising swiftly to his feet, he took her by the shoulders, pointed her in the direction of the house and gave her a quick swat on the behind.

By the time she swung around, he was safely out of reach in the Ranger.

'Wait,' she yelled, running after him.

Luke didn't wait. With a farewell wave, he gunned the engine and roared off down the driveway in a cloud of dust and flying gravel.

Olivia put her hands on her hips and glared after him. 'All right, Luke Harriman,' she shouted. 'All right. You may have won this round, but you needn't think I've given up on you yet.'

Two weeks passed with no word from Olivia, and Luke began to hope she had finally learned the meaning of 'No.'

Most of the time he was relieved. Yet sometimes, at night, the hungers of his body betrayed him, and memory wouldn't let her go. She might be a woman without a heart, but there had been times when that hadn't mattered – times he couldn't forget...

It wasn't that he wanted Olivia back, he assured himself. She was a selfish, frivolous society miss who, as far as he could see, would never be of any use to him or anyone else. Except in bed, of course, and that he was determined to renounce.

The fact that Olivia was a walking invitation to bed, was exactly what had landed him in this fix in the first place.

On the second Friday, after a slow week at work that had Luke thinking seriously of speeding up his plans to go into business for himself, Joe Franklyn called.

He wanted Luke to come for drinks at six o'clock on the following day. Luke thought about refusing, but when his father-in-law assured him that Olivia was unlikely to be present, he agreed. If Olivia did show up, he could always leave. In the meantime, it wouldn't hurt him to keep her father happy.

Any man who had produced a daughter like Olivia, deserved whatever small satisfactions he could get.

To Luke's relief, there was no sign of a red Mercedes when he arrived at The Cedars just before six. The iron-haired housekeeper, whose name he had learned was Mrs Cavendish, ushered him straight into the library.

Joe's fire, stoked to combat the drafts of autumn, blasted Luke as he stepped across the threshold.

Pale eyes regarded him without blinking. 'Sit down.' Joe waved his cigar vaguely at the hearth.

Taking his time about it, Luke pulled his usual chair well away from the heat and sat down. He crossed his legs and waited for the older man to speak.

'All right, young man.' Joe placed his cigar carefully in an antique glass ashtray and steepled his fingers beneath his chin. 'Now tell me what you propose to do about my daughter.'

'Do? Nothing, sir. Although naturally I'll co-operate if she wants a quick divorce.'

'She doesn't.' Joe reached for his cigar and exhaled a cloud of smoke, that snaked across the room before rising slowly to hang in a dusty grey balloon near the ceiling.

'In that case,' Luke said equably, 'I'm willing to wait until she accepts the inevitable. There's no particular need to rush things.'

'Hmm.' Joe jerked his head at the silver tray of bottles and mixes. 'Help yourself to a drink. I'll have rye and water.'

Luke got up and poured the drinks, glad of a respite from the fire. When he sat down again, Joe said gruffly, 'She says she loves you.'

Luke pinned his gaze on a row of maroon-coloured classics that looked as though they'd never been opened. 'No offence, but I don't think Olivia loves anyone.'

He sensed, rather than saw, the other man retreat into his chair like an aged crab. Damn. Perhaps he could have found a more tactful way to put that. But he wasn't going to lie to Olivia's father. There had been enough lies told already.

'I've wondered about that myself over the years,' Joe admitted, in a tone that gave no hint of his true feelings. He pressed a knuckle to the corner of his eye. 'But you mustn't judge her too harshly. Her mother's depression can't have been easy for a child to understand. I didn't understand it myself.'

'I'm sure that's true.' Luke kept his gaze focused on the books. 'Unfortunately it doesn't alter the present.' He hesitated, choosing his next words with care. 'You say she told you the reason why I left her?'

'Yes. Yes, she did.' An unusual thickness deepened Joe's voice. 'She seems to think that what she did came under the heading of "All's fair in love and war." She can't accept that you don't see it that way.'

'Can you accept it, sir?' Not for the first time, Luke wondered what it must be like to have fathered Olivia.

Joe's eyelid twitched. 'Sure. I felt like throwing her out myself, when I learned the grandchild she'd promised me was a lie. But she's all I've got. And you, I think, may be the only man who can deal with her.'

Luke pulled his gaze from a shelf featuring the collected works of Joseph Conrad, and swivelled to face Olivia's father. It couldn't be easy for a man of Joe's temperament to admit he couldn't handle his own daughter. 'I don't want to deal with her,' he said. 'I never did. And I no longer feel any obligation.'

Joe rubbed his other eye then pinched the top of his nose. 'Nonetheless, she is your wife. And she wants you back.'

'I know that. I'm sorry I can't oblige.'

'You dislike her that much?'

Luke reminded himself again that he was talking to Olivia's father. 'I don't dislike her,' he said. 'What's the point? She's her own worst enemy. But I do refuse to have her in my life. I apologise if that offends you...'

'It doesn't offend me.' Joe drew on his cigar then put it down. 'I'd be surprised if you felt any other way. But the fact remains, she's my daughter. I'll always want what's best for her and, as far as I'm concerned, that means you.'

Did all the Franklyns imagine they could have whatever they wanted?

'That's out of the question,' Luke said, smiling to soften the blow.

'Hmm.' Joe leaned forward and held out his hands to the fire. 'In my experience nothing's out of the question, given the right incentive. Olivia tells me you plan to go into business for yourself.'

'Yes. Soon, I hope.' What had his career plans to do with

anything?

'You'll need backing for that. She also tells me you haven't any money.'

'My sister and I had a small legacy from our parents which was invested for us. A few years ago I re-invested it. That and a bank loan should be enough. I plan to start small and expand slowly.'

'Hmm.' Joe studied the tip of his cigar. 'What if I agreed to back you free of charge? Then you wouldn't need a loan, and you'd get your business up and running that much sooner.'

Luke suppressed his initial response, which was to swear at Olivia's father and walk out. After a pause, he said tersely, 'I couldn't accept your offer.'

'Olivia said you'd say that. All right, what *would* it take to persuade you to give my daughter another chance?'

Did Joe really imagine he could be bought? 'Nothing,' he said. 'If I was prepared to have her back, which I'm not, it would take nothing.' He paused as the implications of Joe's offer sank in. 'Did Olivia *ask* you to bribe me?'

'I wouldn't put it that way. She asked me to do anything I could to get you back for her. And whatever you may think, young man, I honestly believe she cares more for you than she's ever cared for anyone. Unless you count her dog.'

'Phantom? Yes, she told me about him. She seems to have an affinity with animals.'

'Mmm. Animals and you. Do you suppose there's a connection?' Joe smiled thinly.

Luke returned his smile with a small shrug.

'Right,' Joe said. 'What do I tell her then? That you'll think about it?'

Nice try. Luke shook his head. He'd heard that Joe's business success was based largely on bull-headed tenacity, and an ability to wear down the opposition.

A log snapped in the fireplace, sending a shower of

bright sparks on to the hearth. Luke loosened his tie. The room was insufferably hot. 'No, don't tell her that,' he said. 'It wouldn't be true.'

'You set great store on truth, don't you?' Joe frowned into the flames as another shower of sparks hit the hearth.

'Yes. I do.' Seeing no reason to prolong the interview, Luke stood up. 'I'm sorry things didn't work out.'

'So am I.' Joe went on staring into the fire. 'So am I.'

Luke opened the door and waited in case he meant to say more. But his father-in-law seemed to have forgotten he was there.

'Goodbye, sir,' he said, and stepped into the comparatively cool air of the hall.

Joe didn't answer, and when Luke looked back into the room he saw that he had picked up a poker and was coaxing even further heat from the fireplace.

The moment Luke was free of the house he removed his tie and drew in a long draught of crisp evening air. Thank God that was over. He wouldn't have lasted much longer in Joe's furnace.

Stuffing his tie into his pocket, he headed for the Ranger.

Someone had closed the heavy iron gates since his arrival. He was on his way to open them, when he became aware of an unusual shadow beneath one of the two tall cedar trees guarding the entrance. He waited, and the shadow moved, gradually transforming itself into the outline of a woman.

'Hello, Luke,' Olivia said. 'I've been waiting for you. Did you have a nice talk with Dad?'

Luke shut his eyes. Oh lord, not *now* when he had thought himself safe. He swiped a hand across his forehead and looked again.

He wasn't hallucinating. This was definitely Olivia, beautiful and appealing as ever – and working on another of her schemes. The woman just didn't give up. He groaned silently, even though he admired her tenacity in a way. She wasn't her father's daughter for nothing...

Olivia, her body softly shadowed in the moonlight, held out her hands and said, 'Surprised?'

Luke caught his breath. Yes, he was surprised. But he shouldn't have been. And in spite of everything he'd said to her father, he wanted to take her outstretched hands; wanted to take a whole lot more.

The knowledge hit him like a blow below the belt. Would he never be free of Olivia Franklyn?

'Yes,' he said. 'I am surprised. I thought you were bright enough to know when to quit.'

'But that wouldn't be bright.' Her low voice wound around his senses like warm honey. 'Why would I give up on the only man I've ever really wanted?'

'You don't know that's true. I'm the only one you've ever actually sampled. You're wasting your time, Olivia.'

He hoped to hell she was.

They were standing only a few inches apart, and the faint scent of lemon teased his nose. As he waited for her to speak, he saw her tense and go still.

'You mean it, don't you,' she said.

At last. Did he dare to believe he had finally got through to her?

'Yes,' he said. 'I told you I meant it from the first. There's no going back, Olivia. Not for us.'

For a long time he half-wondered if she was breathing. Then her head moved up and down, twice, in what he took for acquiescence. Her long hair fell around her shoulders like a witch's cape.

'Yes,' she said. 'I see that now. Will you do one last thing for me, Luke.'

Luke switched to instant alert. 'That depends on what it is.'

'Of course. Please...please will you kiss me goodbye?'

chapter nine

It was her one hope. If Luke kissed her knowing that it would be for the last time, and then walked away from her without turning back, she would have to accept that it was over. But if he couldn't – then she would know that before long he would succumb as he had before.

'Luke?' Olivia lifted her face, hoping he could see the inviting curve of her lips in the soft light cast by the moon. 'Please.'

A car screeched past the gates, its radio blaring to wake the dead. Luke didn't seem to hear it.

'Please,' she repeated, blinking her eyelashes more out of habit than because she thought he could see them.

Luke squared his shoulders as if bracing for a punch on the jaw. 'Why? What good will it do?'

'For remembrance.' She flipped back her hair in an age-old gesture of seduction.

Luke took a half-step towards her, hesitated, then cupped his hands very gently around her face.

She held her breath as from the copse at the back of the house came the high-pitched gibbering of racoons. Another car passed, its lights briefly sweeping the lawns. Then Luke bent down and touched his lips to hers.

His kiss was light as the wings of a moth brushing her mouth – barely a kiss at all. Yet her stomach lurched instantly and turned a somersault, as it always did when Luke touched her.

She tried to draw him closer, but at once he dropped his arms and stepped back.

No! He *mustn't* leave her. Not like this. It wasn't enough.

It would never be enough.

'That was no kiss,' she whispered. 'I meant a proper one.'

For a moment, as he loomed over her like some black-coated highwayman in the moonlight, she was certain he meant to refuse. Then she felt his fingers on her cheek and knew he wouldn't.

'All right then.' His voice was slurred velvet stroking her nerve ends. 'On your head be it.' This time, when he took her face between his hands, his lips crushed hers with a savage passion that would have made her gasp if she'd been able.

She moaned and opened her mouth, inviting his tongue to probe deeper. When it did, with a ruthlessness more exhilarating than any more tender caress, she knew, even as she responded, that she had lost him.

This wasn't the kiss of a man who meant to make his peace with her. This was the kiss of a man who could take without being taken, seduce without being seduced and who, having fallen victim to her once, did not mean to fall that way again.

For a little while she allowed the kiss to go on. It felt so good to be close to him again, to taste him and feel the strength of his shoulders flexing beneath her fingers. So…right. He smelled clean and masculine, yet smoky from the aftermath of fire. When he slid his mouth down to her neck, she gasped and put her hands on his wrists.

This was unbearable. He was going to leave her. If she wanted to face herself in the mirror in the morning, it must stop. Bad enough that he was lost to her. If she lost her pride as well she'd have nothing left.

Luke didn't try to hold her. The moment he felt her strain against him, he released her.

'Goodnight,' he said, as if he were dropping her off after a casual first date. 'Sleep well.'

'What?' she said blankly.

'I said goodnight.'

'Oh.' Olivia nodded as the darkness fell around her. 'Yes. Of course. Goodnight.'

She watched him walk down the driveway to open the gates, then stride back to the Ranger. Her body felt frozen, unable to move as he backed on to the street and drove away.

By the time she had thawed sufficiently to run after him, there wasn't any point.

Olivia stumbled back through the gates, and into her father's house. She couldn't seem to remember where she was. Never mind. It didn't matter.

'What is it, Moonbeam?' her father asked. 'Why are you here?'

Moonbeam. He hadn't called her that since she was twelve. 'I don't really know,' she said, a comforting mug of cocoa in her hand as she moved over to sit down beside him by the fire. 'There didn't seem anywhere to go.'

'How did you get here?'

'In my car. No, no that's wrong. I came in a taxi. You said Luke was coming tonight, but I didn't want him to know I was waiting.'

'I see. I spoke to him, you know, but he wouldn't listen.'

'Yes, I know. He despises me.'

Her father didn't answer. The two of them sat in silence, by the Library fire, then after a while Joe said quietly, 'If you want him back you'll have your work cut out. You know that, don't you?'

'Yes, I know.' She took a small sip of cocoa and put the mug down. 'Oh, Dad. I don't know what to do.'

Joe, recognising a cry from the heart from his only living child, reached across the table to take her hand. Could this really be his cold-hearted daughter? This vulnerable young woman struggling to hold back her tears? A tearing sensation knifed through his chest. It had been so long, so damned long since he'd seen his Moonbeam cry.

'Don't,' he said. 'Don't cry, sweetheart. If you put your mind to it, you'll think of something. He says he doesn't hate you.'

Olivia drew her hand from his. 'I wish he did hate me. Hate's closer to love than contempt.'

'Are you *sure* you love him?'

She lowered her eyelashes. 'I think so. But I'm not sure I know what love is. Or even if it exists. All I know is that I do want Luke back, and I can't bear the thought of never...never being with him any more.'

'Hmm.' Joe massaged the back of his neck. 'Are you sure that's not just because you don't want him to be the one to end it?'

Olivia pressed her fingertips to her forehead. 'It was at first. How did you know?'

She sounded so weary, so drained, so unlike the cold, reserved little miss he'd grown used to, that Joe felt a brief but powerful urge to wring Luke Harriman's neck.

'I know you,' he said. 'You're my daughter.'

'Oh Dad.' She shook her head. 'You don't know me at all.'

'You may be right.' He sighed. 'Maybe I don't. But I've always loved you, Olivia.'

Olivia's head jerked up as if he'd shot her. 'That's not true. You know it isn't. You and Mother *didn't* love me. You wished *I'd* been the one killed instead of Raymond.'

'*What?*' Joe raised his hands to still a sudden roaring in his ears. 'How can you say such a thing? Of course we loved Raymond, but we could never, *ever* have wished you dead. You were both our children.' His voice broke on the last word, and he bowed his head.

Olivia gaped at him. What was he saying? Could she... could she believe him? Why, his shoulders were actually shaking. And yet...surely after all these years she would have *known*?

'I can't believe that,' she told him, fastening her gaze on the bright flames. 'After Raymond died, Mother always looked through me as if I wasn't there – even when she was talking to me. And you fussed over her when you were home, but you never fussed over me.'

'That is *not* true.' Joe slammed his palm on the table. 'So help me, I tried to get close to you. But you wouldn't let me. As for your mother...' The fire in his eyes clouded to smoke. 'She couldn't help it. She loved you, Olivia, but she was never the same after Raymond died. You were too young to understand about depression then. I wasn't much good at it myself.'

'You're saying Mother was depressed, and that made it all right for her to ignore me? For both of you to forget about my birthday...'

'Forget your...? What are you talking about? We gave you presents, held parties for you every year when you were younger...'

'Not every year. I didn't have a party the year I turned twelve. Even though you promised.' Olivia jumped up not because she had anywhere to go, but because she couldn't bear to keep still while all the hurtful memories came flooding back...memories of an excited, hopeful, anxious little girl waiting for the party that didn't happen. Then waiting for her father to come and make it right.

'You didn't come,' she cried, leaning over the sink, as nausea roiled in her stomach. 'There wasn't any party, and you didn't come. I waited until midnight.'

Behind her a chair scraped back. 'Olivia, I didn't know. I remember the birthday you're talking about. I was in New York, and I sent you a huge box full of presents. There was a big stuffed dog and a book about bears...'

Olivia gripped the edge of the sink. It felt like steel ice beneath her fingers. 'A box? I never got it.'

'But I sent it. By courier. You *must* have got it.'

'I didn't. And there wasn't any party either.' Just as now there wasn't any Luke.

'But I talked it over with your mother weeks before your birthday.' Her father's voice suddenly sounded old. 'She said of course she could organise a party for a few children... But she must have forgotten. Moonbeam, I'm sorry. I had no idea...' His voice trailed off as if something had caught in his throat.

In the end, when Olivia could stand the sound no longer, she turned around.

Her father was slumped over the table with his head on his arms.

Biting her lip, Olivia hurried over to touch him on the shoulder. She had never seen her controlled father like this. His sparse hair, silver against the reddish-bronze of the maple, reminded her of the ashes in his fireplace.

'Dad,' she said, 'You didn't even ask about my party when you came home. That's why I thought...'

Joe lifted his head, then abruptly pushed back his chair and stood up. 'I suppose I didn't,' he admitted. 'But if I'd guessed for one moment... Listen, Olivia, when I got home from New York I found your mother in bed with pneumonia. I suppose, in my worry over her, I did forget to ask you about your party.'

Olivia backed up against the table, needing its support. 'I was so sure you would come,' she whispered.

Her father ran a hand over the top of his head. When he lowered it, his eyelid was twitching. 'I got held up. Serious business problems plus bad weather. Then I came home to find your mother ill.'

Olivia was experiencing the oddest sensation in her stomach, as if a bag of something frozen had begun to thaw. She raised her hand, tentatively touched his cold cheek. It was damp as well as cold, so she wiped it with her thumb.

'I didn't know,' she said. 'I thought you didn't care.'

'Of course I cared.' Joe spoke as if a rubber band were wrapped around his throat. 'There was a letter inside that parcel...'

Olivia started to say something, but he cut her short. The next thing she knew, she was wrapped in his arms and he was pulling her head on to his shoulder, rocking her just as he had done in the old days when, as a little girl, she had fallen and bruised her knee or scraped her hand.

'Can we start over?' he asked, in a voice so cracked with regret it made her want to cry.

Could they? Wasn't it too late? She was so used to ignoring her father, to giving him only as much of herself as was necessary in order to keep him seeing to her needs...

Luke said she was selfish, and she was. It made life so much easier. Yet her father's arms felt good, comforting, had helped in a way to restore her confidence in herself. Maybe she *could* make things right with Luke somehow...

'We can *try* to start over,' she whispered.

Joe patted her shoulder. 'We'll have a long talk tomorrow,' he said. 'What you need now is a good night's sleep. And what I need is a damned good cigar.'

Olivia laughed, and laughing made her feel better. She was still smiling when she trailed obediently up the stairs to her old room.

Church bells? Olivia rubbed her eyes and turned over on her side. Was she dreaming still? She sat up, took in her blue flannel night-dress, blue velvet curtains and the cedar tree spreading its branches outside the window.

Of course. She had come home.

Twenty minutes later, dressed in the black skirt and red sweater she had worn the day before, Olivia made her way downstairs to find her father.

He was drinking coffee and smoking a cigar in the small

breakfast room overlooking the garden. Only the top of his head was visible above the Sunday paper, sporting a headline about a couple caught having sex in full view of passengers on Vancouver's Skytrain.

'Good reading, Dad?' she asked.

'Hmm?' Joe peered over the top of the paper. 'Doubt if you'd think so. I'm reading a report on mining in the Yukon.'

Olivia grimaced. 'Dull. Sex on the Skytrain sounds much more fun.'

Joe laid the paper on the table and cleared his throat.

Oh. He was embarrassed. 'It's all right, Dad,' she said. 'I was only teasing.'

Joe relaxed and produced a self-conscious smile. 'It's been a long time, hasn't it? Too long.'

She knew what he meant. He had teased her all the time when she was small, and she had teased him back with childish enjoyment.

'Yes,' she agreed, taking her seat at the glass-topped table. 'Much too long. Dad, what am I going to do?'

'You haven't given up then?'

'On Luke? Yes, I have for the moment. I don't know what else to do.'

Joe drew thoughtfully on his cigar. 'I'd say the best thing to do is let him alone for a while. Finish your degree, then go and do something useful. Luke's not the kind of man to admire a woman simply for being decorative.'

'I know that.' Olivia took a half-hearted mouthful of muffin and discovered she was hungry after all. Her father watched her eat with an indulgent smile, that at one time would have annoyed her. Odd that it didn't any more.

'What kind of useful did you have in mind?' she asked, licking the last moist crumb off her lips. 'I couldn't stand being a nurse, or one of those people who go around being cheerful in hospitals.'

Joe brushed a hand across his mouth. 'No, I can't see you as Florence Nightingale, myself. But I've no doubt something will come to you.'

Olivia wasn't as sanguine, although her father was right about one thing. The only way she could possibly hope to change Luke's mind about her, was by changing herself.

She could do it if she wanted to. She had always believed she could do anything she wanted.

Swallowing the last of her orange juice, Olivia let its tart sweetness slide slowly down her throat. 'Not Florence Nightingale,' she agreed. 'But I will definitely think of something.'

chapter ten

Luke glanced at his watch, stretched, and rose unhurriedly from his desk, in no real rush to leave just because it was Friday night and the rest of his staff had gone home hours ago.

There was nothing elegant about these offices overlooking the north arm of the Fraser, but the wall-to-wall drawing boards – evidence of a thriving and growing business that in just over eight months had bid on and won some substantial contracts – gave him as much pleasure as anything had since his marriage ended.

Now where in hell had that thought come from? There had been precious little pleasure about his marriage – except for bed – and that night at The Cedars, when he had kissed Olivia for the last time, he'd proved that he could let her go with little regret.

So why were there still times when he woke at night with the scent of lemon in his nose and the taste of mint tea on his tongue...?

In eight months, any rational man would have laid the memory of Olivia Franklyn to rest. Luke prided himself on being rational.

Memories! Better forget them. Only the present counted now.

He shrugged on his jacket before stuffing half a dozen files into his briefcase, switching on the alarm and heading for home.

Tomorrow his sister would graduate from the University of British Columbia. Hard to believe that not so long ago Rosie had been crying for Michael. Now she was planning to marry Stephen Lyle, whom Luke privately -well, mostly privately – regarded as a well-intentioned bore.

And if Rosemary was graduating...then so was Olivia.

He slammed the door behind him with considerably more force than was necessary. Yes, all right. His almost ex-wife would be there too – but only as a distant figure on the stage. For all he knew, she wouldn't even attend. Some people didn't.

He ran down the steps to the parking lot, jumped into his truck and drove off whistling *The Marseillaise* through his teeth.

He might have known Olivia wouldn't miss a chance to walk across a stage. 'F' came before 'H,' and, although he had been prepared for her to be there, when they called her name he found himself rising from his seat.

'Hold on there, Luke. Take it easy.' Stephen, who was seated beside him, put a sympathetic hand on his arm. Luke shook him off and restrained an impulse to tell his future brother-in-law to mind his own business. Stephen was only doing what he perceived to be his job.

The Chan Centre for the Performing Arts wasn't huge, but even from his vantage point at the front of one of the boxes, Olivia was too far away for him to make out the details of her features. Her figure hadn't changed though. No academic gown could conceal that. And her shoulder-length hair swung thick and shining as ever.

When she reached the edge of the platform, she raised her head and looked straight at him.

Luke caught his breath. Could she see him? No, that was impossible. Olivia couldn't know where he was sitting. He swallowed the bitter taste in his mouth and watched her as she walked off the stage looking small and vulnerable in that concealing black gown – and as innocent as he had reason to know she wasn't.

He followed her with his eyes, then lost her among the throng below the stage.

When Rosemary's turn came he clapped loudly, but could barely see her for the haze dimming his vision.

The remainder of the ceremony passed in a fog of confused memories of the woman who had once been his wife. He came back to earth only when the band, incongruously, began to play, *'It's a Small, Small World.'*

Afterwards, he stood with Stephen among the crowd of friends and parents gathered in the hot May sunshine on the tree-shaded terrace in front of the unusual circular building. Then Stephen spotted Rosemary and moved away.

Luke, following more slowly, thought he heard Rosemary laugh. He didn't turn to look. He couldn't. Because directly beside him stood Olivia.

'You haven't changed,' she said.

'No. Apparently not. Neither have you.'

'I hoped you'd be here.'

Luke shrugged. 'I hoped you wouldn't.'

Olivia's shoulders slumped and she lowered her head as if in shame.

He had to remind himself that she was only acting, wasn't truly capable of being hurt. Because in spite of all the grief she had put him through, what he wanted to do more than anything at this moment was take her in his arms and tell her he didn't mean it.

'So you still despise me.' Olivia kept her head down as if she were fascinated by the parade of shoes hurrying past them on the pavement.

Did he? Yes, he supposed he did. He also wanted to remove that ridiculous gown and the dark blue silk showing beneath it, and carry her to the nearest patch of grass.

'What I feel doesn't matter,' he said. 'It's been over eight months, Olivia. Soon you can apply for a divorce.'

'Always the gentleman.' She sighed. 'Why don't *you* apply?'

'Do you want me to?'

He remembered how, when they had first separated, his physical frustration had been so great he had thought a speedy divorce was his only hope of maintaining his reason. But, over time, he had come to realise that since there was no other woman in his life he couldn't live without, the matter of divorce was not urgent. Later, he had been so caught up in the business of incorporating Harriman's that it had been easier than he expected to keep his bodily needs under control.

Now, with Olivia standing only a few inches away from him, swaying her hips in what was undoubtedly a deliberate attempt to drive him mad, he was forced to acknowledge that the situation as it was could not continue.

'No, I don't want you to divorce me.' Her low voice broke into his thoughts. 'You know what I want.'

'Olivia we've been over that.'

'Yes, I suppose we have.' The sadness in her voice was a pain knifing through his groin. But when he heard her use a word Rosemary wouldn't have dreamed of allowing past her lips, all his sympathy evaporated.

'Don't talk like that,' he snapped. 'It doesn't suit you.'

'Doesn't it? Are you going to wash my mouth out with soap? Besides, I've heard you use that word more than once.'

'That's different,' Luke replied, knowing it wasn't.

'No, it's not. Anyway it's true. I do want you to...'

'That's enough!' Luke felt his temper rise along with other, more susceptible, body parts.

She shrugged, reminding him of a mutinous little girl. And right then and there, he lost it.

'All right,' he said. 'Lift your skirt and we'll get on with it right now.'

The moment he spoke he knew he should have known better. Olivia might be selfish and inconsiderate, but she had guts. And she relished a challenge. As he opened his mouth to say he hadn't meant it, she reached for the hem of her blue silk skirt and started to lift it.

'Olivia! What do you think you're doing?'

Joe Franklyn's voice jerked Luke abruptly from the heated trance in which he had been gazing at a tantalising view of Olivia's shapely legs.

He looked round to see that Joe had come up beside them, blue eyes flat and furious as they glared at his daughter.

'Luke told me to,' Olivia said, not visibly intimidated, but immediately allowing the blue skirt to drop around her calves.

'I...' Luke's angry denial died in his throat. He had been going to say he'd done nothing of the sort, but that wasn't strictly true. 'I wasn't serious,' he snapped. 'As you very well know.'

'You shouldn't say what you don't mean then, should you?' Olivia tossed her head. 'Not everyone understands your jokes.'

'Olivia.' Joe's voice held a warning. 'Behave yourself.'

'Good advice,' Luke agreed. He smiled stiffly at Joe. 'I'm here for my sister's graduation. I apologise if my misguided remark caused embarrassment.'

'Hmm.' Joe grunted, and slanted him a look that hinted at understanding. He turned to his daughter. 'Olivia, we have guests waiting for us at home.'

Olivia nodded. 'Will you come to my party?' she asked Luke. With her hands folded demurely in front of her, she might have been a shy Victorian miss inviting an acquaintance to take tea.

'No, thank you, I'll be attending my sister's celebration.' Luke knew he sounded as Victorian as she did, and didn't care.

She smiled sweetly and held out her hand. 'Of course. Goodbye then, Luke.'

He accepted her fingers reluctantly. They were cool and soft against his palm – and he had to force himself to let them go.

'Goodbye,' he said. And then, with an effort, 'Let me know when you're ready to discuss that divorce.' He turned his back on her without waiting for an answer.

As he searched for Rosemary and Stephen among the crowd, he thought he heard her low voice murmur, 'Never.'

Olivia kicked off her shoes, threw herself into her yellow chair and picked up the paper she had tossed on to the coffee table that morning.

Thank heaven the party, attended mainly by her father's friends, had ended before ten o'clock.

She was glad she hadn't agreed to spend the night at The Cedars. Joe had wanted her to, had even hinted that now she had her degree there was no reason for her to maintain a separate dwelling. She pretended not to hear him. Although she was glad to be reconciled with her father, and genuinely regretted the wasted years, that didn't mean she was prepared to give up her independence just when she had at last come into the inheritance left her by her mother.

She glanced at the paper. After reading a few paragraphs, she flipped to the entertainment page in the hope that it would take her mind off what had happened this afternoon. She hadn't meant to behave like a hormone-crazed schoolgirl, and had planned to greet Luke with ladylike poise. But seeing him again had made her forget all her vows about becoming the kind of woman he admired. All she had been able to think of was how much she wanted him. Accepting his challenge had been an instinctive reaction to the knowledge that she was as far from winning him back as she had ever been.

Common sense had flown out the window on wings of disappointment and hurt.

Yet she couldn't regret it. The look on Luke's face, scandalised, and at the same time glazed with desire, had proved that her cause was not *entirely* hopeless.

Olivia hugged her arms around her chest. At least she had living proof that even after eight long months Luke wanted her as much as she wanted him.

It wasn't a lot to hold on to, but it was something...

A section of the paper rustled off her knees on to the floor. She bent to pick it up, and her gaze fell on a picture of a sour-faced old man with his arm around a small spotted dog with floppy ears. Above the accompanying article was the headline, *'Veteran to be Parted from Dog Who Saved His Life.'*

Quickly, Olivia scanned the story. When she'd finished, she read it again.

The old man, a veteran living on his pension, had been ordered by local bureaucrats to get rid of his furry companion, a dog appropriately, if unoriginally, named Spot. Spot's frantic barking had apparently once woken his master just in time to save him when the sofa he was sleeping on caught fire. The article went on to say that if the old man insisted on keeping his dog he would have to leave his low-cost apartment.

Olivia scowled and read the story a third time. The dog was nine years old and had been with the man all her life. He said he would live on the streets before he gave her up.

'Poor dog,' Olivia muttered. 'She's too old to live on the street.' So, from the looks of him, was the old man. How *could* those heartless bureaucrats be so cruel?

She glanced at the clock, then reached for the phone. It might be late, but if she had anything to do with it, a small spotted dog and an old man would shortly be moving to a new home.

'Sign right here, Ms Franklyn, and it's yours.' The estate agent watched hungrily as Olivia took his narrow gold pen and signed her name with precision.

Irrationally, she wished she could sign Olivia Harriman. But she had declined to take Luke's name when they were married, at that time having had no intention of remaining his wife. Or so she'd deluded herself. Luke had been unflatteringly indifferent, and said she could call herself Olivia Borgia for all he cared.

'Done,' Olivia said, handing the pen back to its owner. 'I've arranged for work on the village to start next week.'

'Excellent.' The agent rubbed his hands in eager approval. 'It's been a pleasure doing business with you, Ms Franklyn.'

No doubt it had. The man was now many thousands of dollars richer. She, on the other hand, had a plot of land in a rural section of Richmond which was going to deplete her inheritance by several million.

She stood up, shook his hand, and left the plush offices with a strong sense that she had royally burned her boats.

It was two months since she had moved old Len Stivic and his dog to a two-bedroom cottage in Burnaby. She had looked at land from Chilliwack all the way to Horseshoe Bay, finally settling on a property in suburban Richmond.

Her father insisted she'd gone mad.

'You're going to do *what* with your mother's money?' he had exclaimed, blowing a storm of smoke signals at the library's beleaguered ceiling. 'My dear girl, have you any idea what such a project would involve?'

'Not much,' Olivia admitted. 'But I mean to learn. And I'm sure with your help...'

'Help? I have no intention of helping you build a – what did you call it? A *retirement village* for a load of shiftless old pensioners and their decrepit dogs...'

'And cats,' Olivia interrupted. 'Birds and hamsters too, if that's what they want.'

'What for? To feed the cats?' Joe snorted. 'The whole idea is ridiculous. What you need to do with that money is invest it.'

'I have invested it. That's why I have enough to begin the first phase of my village.'

'Village? Zoo, you mean. What's the point of all this, Olivia? Surely you don't expect that sort of nonsense to impress Luke?'

'I hope it will,' Olivia said. 'If I build this village with my own money he won't be able to say I've never done anything for anyone but myself. Besides, Luke's not the only reason I'm doing it. You're the one who said I ought to do something useful.'

'I see nothing *useful* about making it easy for a bunch of old fools to be irresponsible.'

'I'm doing it for their pets,' Olivia said. 'You can't expect *them* to be responsible.'

To some extent, she agreed with her father about the owners of the pets. Len Stivic was a sour old soul, and since moving him into a rented cottage she had met enough senior citizens in similar circumstances to know they weren't all rosy-cheeked grandmothers, or sweet old men who stood up when ladies entered the room. But she wasn't admitting that to her father. Not when she particularly wanted his co-operation and advice.

'Pets,' Joe muttered, clipping the end off a new cigar with a vicious snip. 'You always were besotted with dogs.'

Olivia didn't reply, but when her father said, 'Oh, all right, I'll take a look at your plans,' Olivia knew he would soon come around. She also knew, as the ecstatically happy estate agent closed the door behind her, that after today there could be no turning back.

Feeling as if she had deliberately walked over a precipice, Olivia walked out into the sticky heat of downtown Vancouver in July.

Whatever her father said, she *would* make her village work. She would. And not just for Luke. She might be selfish, but she *wasn't* useless. This was her chance to prove it to the world.

When a small voice in her head whispered, 'And to yourself,' she ignored it.

'I don't want to move. Spot and I are just fine where we are.' Len Stivic glared at Olivia from cataract-clouded eyes.

'I know,' Olivia explained for the fourth time. 'But the lease on this cottage is up. The family who own it want it back.'

'Over my dead body,' Len growled.

Olivia refrained, with difficulty, from assuring him that that too could be arranged. She had to think of ten-year-old Spot, who had become her good friend over the past year — a year during which the first phase of the village had been built and its tenants installed, along with their assortment of pets.

Although she hadn't banked on iguanas, toads, rats and the occasional ferret, she had swallowed her reservations and agreed to give them space after a diminutive old lady, called Mrs Woo, had looked her in the eye as she hesitated over a particularly ugly crow with a broken wing, and said, 'They are all God's creatures, you know.'

Olivia, who wasn't sure about God, and had a sneaking suspicion it wasn't legal to keep crows, said she supposed they were.

Len Stivic, taking advantage of her inattention, lit a cigarette and blew a steam of smelly smoke in her face. Olivia, who had learned more patience than she'd ever known she possessed over the past year, finally snapped. 'Mr Stivic,' she said, 'You'll either move from here willingly or be thrown out. What do you think will happen to Spot then?'

'Huh. He'll probably croak along of me. No place for us oldsters any more.'

'There *is* a place. At Hopeville.' Olivia, who hadn't spent almost a year dealing with obstinate old codgers like Len without learning when to stop arguing, marched into the kitchen to start his packing. It wasn't that she didn't understand Len's resistance to change, it was just that in this case he had little choice.

Not for the first time, Olivia wondered what she was doing in this business.

To her own surprise, she had become fond of most of her senior citizens, though she didn't think many of them liked her. 'Young bossyboots', she'd heard one woman call her.

The animals loved her though. Olivia smiled, thinking of all the four-footed friends she had made.

Len, shuffling up beside her, was moved to remark that she didn't look such a crab when she smiled.

'I'll try to remember that,' she replied dryly.

In truth, she didn't often feel like smiling. She was kept busy overseeing the construction and organisation of the village she had decided to name Hopeville, but being busy wasn't the same as happiness.

People thought she had called the village Hopeville for the hope it gave its elderly inhabitants. They were wrong. It was for the hope she still had of winning back the man who had opened her eyes to the true joy of living. And she wasn't thinking about sex.

Luke had called her twice, both times to ask if she was ready to proceed with a divorce. The first time she had asked him if he wanted to marry somebody else.

He had been silent for so long before he replied, 'No,' in an unnaturally clipped voice, that she hadn't asked him the second time he called.

Both times she had told him she was in no hurry if he wasn't, and he had seemed to be satisfied with that.

140   *Kay Gregory*

She wondered if he had he any idea that *she* was the moving force behind Hopeville. The village had been written up in the papers several times, but it was hardly the sort of news to rivet Luke's attention. She remembered he had read the front page, the sports page and sometimes the business section and editorials. Senior citizens and pets were not his bag, although he had a natural respect for all living creatures.

It didn't matter. She would see he had an invitation to the Hopeville benefit concert she was organising for the beginning of September. He wasn't a music lover, but with any luck he would come.

If not, she'd find some other way to meet him accidentally.

'What's the matter with *you*?' Rosemary paused in the doorway of the two-storey penthouse overlooking English Bay which Luke had recently bought. He was rooting gloomily through a litter of papers on the dining-room table. 'Have you lost your wallet under all that junk?'

'No, only an invitation I was planning to ignore.' He glanced at a flyer advertising camping equipment, and tossed it down in disgust. 'Why does everyone think that just because I'm a biologist, I need an inexhaustible supply of thermal underwear?'

'I've no idea.' Rosemary added her handbag to the clutter on the table and propped herself against the oak-panelled wall. 'What invitation? And if you're going to ignore it, why do you need it?'

'I *was* going to ignore it. Now I'm not. Charlie phoned and asked me if I'd escort his little sister, Celia. Apparently her boyfriend has the measles, and I'm sufficiently ancient not to pose a threat to his claim on her affections.'

'Oh. Escort her where?'

'To some charity concert. Something about old people and pets.'

'Hopeville,' Rosemary said.

Luke stopped shuffling through the papers and looked up. His sister's voice had gone unusually flat.

'Yes, that's it. What's wrong?'

Rosemary went into the kitchen, a designer's dream of black-and-white efficiency, and he watched through the connecting door as she poured herself a tall glass of water.

'Don't you know about Hopeville?' she asked.

'No. Should I?'

'It's been in the papers.'

She still sounded odd. What *was* Hopeville? A home for retired witches and their familiars? 'I must have missed it,' he said. 'Ah. Here's what I'm looking for.' He pounced on a square of glossy cardboard embossed with silver, and gave it a quick, disapproving appraisal. 'Great. Just the way I like to spend my evenings – listening to a bunch of screeching violins.'

Rosemary came back into the dining room. 'Just because *you* have a tin ear...'

'I know, I know. I've said I'll take her. Charlie's a good friend and I won't disappoint young Celia. She was a cute little thing the last time I saw her.'

Rosemary shook her head. 'You amaze me sometimes. Not many men would take their friend's teenage sister to a concert they don't want to go to. Why doesn't Charlie take her?'

'He'll be in Winnipeg.' Luke tried not to snap, but his temper was already fraying at the edges. He put the invitation in his pocket and began to sort the accumulation of clutter into something resembling order.

Rosemary left him to it and made her way out of the penthouse.

He was here. No longer a dream but glorious flesh and blood. For the first time in over a year, she was looking on the face of the man she loved.

Olivia put out a hand for support and found herself grasping empty air. She had purposely positioned herself at the top of the steps leading up to the Orpheum Theatre's coffee shop and bar, but she hadn't counted on her knees turning to sponge the moment she caught her first glimpse of Luke.

Taking a long, calming breath, she smiled glassily and extended her hand to a passing patron. The man's look of dazed admiration told her what she already knew – that she had chosen well when she picked her dress of slim-fitting emerald green silk with a slit up one side that extended from her ankle to a point of borderline indecency.

Luke *couldn't* be indifferent to her tonight. Her heart slammed against her ribcage as she touched the jewelled combs in her hair and waited for him to climb the steps towards her.

He wasn't looking her way. Olivia's smile stiffened as she followed the direction of his eyes.

No. He couldn't be... *Who* was that blonde bimbo hanging on to his arm like cheap baggage? She was laughing up at him as if they knew each other well. And he was grinning back, his attention solely on her.

Oh, how well she remembered that grin, too seldom seen after the first blissful week of their marriage.

Olivia dug her nails into her palms and was only able to maintain her welcoming smile by calling on every ounce of pride she possessed.

No wonder the bimbo was laughing. What woman wouldn't, when she had the magnificence that was Luke on her arm. Olivia had never seen him in evening clothes before, and the effect was breathtaking. She could tell at a glance that no rental agency was responsible for the superb cut of the dark cloth moulding his frame. And if she wasn't mistaken, those were Italian leather shoes.

Luke had come up in the world since last she saw him.

As he drew level with her, still absorbed by the girl on his arm, Olivia held out her hand and said, 'Good evening, Luke. I'm so glad you could come.'

He didn't look up at once. When he did, she added, 'Aren't you going to introduce me to your bim...um, friend?'

Luke had always been a master of self-control – when it suited him. She watched him force his fists to unclench. After a pause, he nodded curtly and replied with a coolness that belied the fire blazing from his eyes, 'Of course. This is Celia Caldicott. Celia, this is Olivia, my ex-wife.'

'Oh. What a surprise.' Celia giggled, a becoming blush tinting her youthful skin to dusty rose.

'Yes, it's a surprise for me too,' Olivia agreed. 'Especially as I'm not actually Luke's *ex*-wife. As far as I know, we're still married.'

'Not for long,' Luke snapped. 'Come on, Celia, we'd better find our seats.' He took the younger woman's arm and propelled her across the red carpet so rapidly she had to skip to keep up.

'See you at the reception,' Olivia called after them. She fastened her smile back in place and watched them until they disappeared behind one of the ornately gilded columns scattered around the foyer of the massive old building that at one time had been a thriving cinema.

Could he be serious about that giggly blonde child? She was attractive, but far too young for him...

'You're looking very pretty, my dear.'

Olivia started, and turned blindly towards the kindly voice she recognised as belonging to Dr Crump. 'Thank you, doctor,' she murmured. 'You're looking very smart yourself.'

The old man beamed and made warbling noises in his throat. 'Sorry to hear your father couldn't come.' He patted her hand. 'Hope he's on the mend.'

'Oh yes, it was just a bad cold. He didn't think it would be fair to cough all through the concert.'

'Good, good. Glad to hear it.' Dr Crump nodded approvingly.

His wife grabbed him briskly by the arm.

As Olivia turned to greet another guest, she heard Mrs Crump bellow, 'Don't let her compliments go to your head, you old fool. Didn't you notice? Young Olivia could hardly see you for the tears in her eyes.'

Tears? She wasn't crying. Olivia dashed a hand across her face, and was astonished when it came away damp.

Ignoring the curious stares of the crowd around the bar, she bit her lip and fastened a bleary gaze on the nearest shimmering chandelier. Briefly, she allowed herself to indulge in a pleasing fantasy in which the chandelier separated from the ceiling and landed squarely on Mrs Crump's permed head. Then she turned with a smile to tell the conductor how grateful she was that so many young, local musicians had agreed to donate their time and talent for this concert.

Behind the conductor came a group of tenants from Hopeville.

'Good evening, Mrs Woo,' Olivia said to the leader of the procession. 'And Mrs Bayliff. How lovely to see you. How is Attila today?' She bent down to shout into the ear of a plump little lady with the face of a bad-tempered cherub. 'Is his paw better?'

'It's a bloody mess,' Mrs Bayliff shouted back. She brightened. 'You ought to see the other cat though.'

Olivia didn't want to see the other cat. Convincing her tenants to keep their more pugnacious pets on their own property, was a never-ending battle she had yet to win.

The chimes heralding the start of the performance began to toll their monotonous warning and, as the countdown continued, Olivia was kept busy settling her tenants in their seats.

Just before the attendants closed the doors to the

auditorium, she hurried to her own seat at the front of the lower balcony. The orchestra began to play the Overture to Rossini's *La Scala di Seta*, and Olivia leaned back with a satisfied sigh.

All her hard work had been worth it. There would be no more Len Stivics and Spots left homeless on the streets of Vancouver. And now, at last, she could relax. At least she could if she could get her mind off Luke, who had brought his blonde bombshell to *her* concert.

Celia Caldicott. She'd heard that name somewhere... Oh. Yes, of course! *Charlie*. That was it. Charlie Caldicott, who had been Luke's best man at their wedding. Celia must be his sister. Maybe she wasn't a bimbo after all...?

Olivia closed her eyes and, as the pure notes of the oboe swept over her, she stopped wanting to cry and gave herself up to the joyful benediction of the music.

Luke rotated his shoulder blades as the endless wash of noise reverberated off the lavishly gilded walls. Another couple of hours and he'd be out of here, away from the cacophony of sound and, most particularly, away from Olivia.

He should have known, ought to have known, that she was behind his invitation. Instead he had assumed that the success of his business had landed him on some fund-raiser's list. Ironic that the fund raiser was Olivia, whom he had spent the past year relentlessly expunging from his mind – except at night. He hadn't yet learned to control his dreams.

Celia smiled up at him and mouthed, 'Thank you.' She was a sweet kid who genuinely loved music, and he hoped he wouldn't let her down because somewhere in this theatre, perhaps only a few feet away, Olivia was sitting half-naked in that incredibly indecent green dress. No woman had a right to look like that.

If anything, she had grown even more desirable in the months since their brief marriage had ended. There was a maturity about her now that hadn't been there before, an air of cool sophistication that made him long to peel away the façade and light a match to the fire he had no doubt still smouldered below the surface.

Olivia might have changed on the outside. Inside he knew she never would.

Christ, how long was this racket going on?

Beside him, Celia stirred happily, lost in the music, and he reminded himself he wasn't here to please himself.

When the intermission finally came, he managed to smile and assure her he was enjoying the concert.

'Good. I'm looking forward to the reception too,' she said.

'Reception?' He swallowed.

'Yes, afterwards. Didn't you hear your wife invite us?'

'She's not my wife,' Luke growled.

'Oh. But we *are* going to the reception, aren't we? All my friends from music school will be there.'

So would Olivia.

Luke gazed down at Celia's sweet, youthful face, filled with anticipation, and muttered a strangled, 'Of course. If you want to.'

Charlie owed him big-time for this.

Ten minutes later he settled back to endure the second half of the performance.

'You stayed awake,' Celia said approvingly at the end, as waves of enthusiastic applause thundered round the auditorium.

'Don't be cheeky.' Luke grinned and took her arm to escort her up the wide, carpeted stairway to the hall where the reception was to be held. As he neared the top, and the murmur of conversation grew louder, he began to feel as if he were climbing to his doom. Logically he knew that was ridiculous. Olivia was merely his ex-wife. A beautiful but mortal woman. She could spin no magic unless he let her.

Yet later, when he saw her draped fetchingly against a decorative pillar holding court to an admiring crowd of guests and musicians, it wasn't magic that kicked him in the ribs. It was undiluted lust.

A thin, distinguished-looking man with a small beard stepped forward to put his hand familiarly on Olivia's bare back. Luke, who was fighting to control something Rosemary had once gigglingly referred to as 'leaping loins', felt his jaw go rigid. After that it wasn't lust that moved him, but as he recognised later, pure instinct – the instinct of the male animal to drive off a potential rival for its mate.

It seemed to make no difference that Olivia was no longer his mate.

With a murmured, 'Excuse me,' to Celia, he stalked up beside Olivia and removed the offending hand from her back.

'Who the devil do you think you are?' the man with the beard demanded in a faintly European accent.

'Ms Franklyn's husband,' Luke said.

Olivia smiled sweetly. 'He's so possessive,' she gushed to the beard.

Luke wasn't sure if he groaned out loud or only inside his head. What was the matter with him? Had the witch put a hex on him, after all?

'My mistake,' he growled, and went off to look for Celia, whom he found leaning on the gallery balustrade surrounded by a crowd of chattering teenagers.

That was all right then. He left Celia gazing soulfully into the eyes of a budding Casanova with acne, and went to find himself a drink.

At the bar he tossed back a scotch and water which did

nothing to improve his state of mind. He was contemplating heading back to collect his charge when a low voice behind him murmured, 'Luke?'

He swung round. Olivia was standing so close to him he could feel her breath teasing his neck.

'Come and talk to me,' she said. 'There's a corner over there where we ought to be reasonably private.'

'I came with Celia,' he said.

'Yes. But you're my husband – as you just pointed out to one of Hopeville's most generous supporters. He's not amused. Don't you think you owe me the courtesy of a few minutes of your time?'

'I don't think I owe you anything. But I apologise for detaching you from the octopus. I didn't realise putting up with tentacles went with the job.'

'It doesn't,' she said. 'But I'm quite capable of handling men like that without your help.'

'Mm. You've had a lot of practice, I expect.'

Olivia put her hands behind her back and didn't deign to answer.

He'd forgotten how beautiful she was when she wanted to scratch his eyes out. 'What do you want to talk about,' he asked, relenting. Perhaps she had finally come round to thinking about divorce.

The fire in her eyes died down. He remembered that it always did when she thought she'd won.

'Lots of things,' she said. 'Come with me.'

Celia was still gazing into her Casanova's eyes. When Olivia jerked her head and began to walk away, Luke didn't hesitate. It was no hardship following Olivia. The view she presented from behind had always been an inspiration.

She came to a stop by an especially baroque pillar. Luke watched with narrowed eyes as she turned around, slung out her hip and treated him to an alluring glimpse of thigh and green silk.

Nice. Very nice. He clapped three times, slowly, then stepped forward to close his hands around her waist.

Olivia said, 'Mm,' and gave a satisfied little wriggle.

Luke smiled cynically and released her.

chapter eleven

'Right. Now what's this about?' Luke gave Olivia a look she recognised. It meant the game-playing was over.

She crossed her arms protectively. 'Us. It's about us. Half-an-hour ago you said you were my husband.'

'I also said that was a mistake. What do you want, Olivia?'

'You,' she said. What did he think she wanted? Had she ever pretended anything else?

'No.' Luke's reply was quiet but devastating.

'But I'm not the same person I was a year ago. I've changed.' Olivia tried to project an air of cool confidence. She wanted to come across as a capable, assured woman in her own right, not some pathetic, pleading cast-off of a wife.

'You *haven't* changed. Not in any way that counts. I wish you had.'

'You don't know that.' She slumped against the pillar, not yet defeated but glad of its support.

'I do know that.' He made an attempt at a smile that she supposed was meant to soften the blow. 'You still want what you want, when you want it. At the moment that happens to be me.'

Olivia laid her palms against the stylised flowers carved into the surface of the pillar. 'Not only at the moment,' she said. 'I've always wanted you.'

'Yes, because you couldn't bear to be denied anything you decided you ought to have. I'm sorry, Olivia. This conversation is a waste of time.'

He made to turn away, and at once Olivia cried out, 'No. No, Luke, that's not true. I've wondered myself...I mean it *is* true I don't like to lose. But it's more than that. Truly it is.'

Luke raised a sceptical eyebrow.

'Listen to me,' she insisted, his scepticism firing her indignation. 'Dammit, you're not the only good-looking man in Vancouver. I've had opportunities...'

Luke rested a hand on the pillar beside her head, moving his face so close to hers she could see the map of fine lines beside his eyes along with the dark sweep of lashes on his cheek.

'Yes. I'm sure you have,' he said.

So cold, almost bored, as if he didn't care. Yet something in his voice made her think that maybe, just maybe, he did.

'I didn't take those opportunities,' she told him, barely aware that she had raised her hand and was clasping the lapel of his jacket. 'I didn't want to. Because I was already married to you.'

'You needn't be, you know.' Luke removed her clutching fingers quite gently. There was a faint smell of whisky on his breath. It wasn't altogether unpleasant.

Olivia knew she had to remain calm. If she lost her temper now, as she was sorely tempted to do, Luke would undoubtedly turn his back on her and walk away – perhaps forever. As long as she could keep him talking, there was hope.

'Yes, I know.' She smiled composedly. 'But divorce is such a messy, unnecessary business. Why bother?'

Luke's mouth turned down. 'So you'll feel free to take up those opportunities, of course.'

'I'm already as free as I want to be.'

They were going round in circles. And if she pressed Luke any further he was likely to start divorce proceedings himself. In fact it was odd that he hadn't done so already, given the way he felt. Or rather, didn't feel. Olivia turned her face to the pillar, not willing for him to catch even the slightest reflection of her thoughts.

When she looked around again, he had moved away and was no longer close enough to touch.

'I'd like to talk to you about Hopeville,' Olivia said. It was all she could think of to make him stay.

'What about it?'

A burst of laughter erupted from one of the halls down below. Olivia winced. 'Did you know I'm the one who founded Hopeville? That without me it wouldn't exist?'

Was it her imagination, or did she see a flicker of surprise cross his face?

'I may have heard something,' he admitted. 'To be honest, I didn't pay a lot of attention. Why? Are you looking for a donation? I thought that was what this concert was all about.'

'It is. I thought maybe you didn't know.'

Luke shook his head. 'It makes no difference. Hopeville is a good cause, so Celia tells me. But, knowing you, it was founded for some reason that had nothing whatsoever to do with making life easier for the elderly, and everything to do with suiting Olivia Franklyn.'

'No!' She held out her hand, beseeching him to stop. 'That isn't true...'

Luke continued as if she hadn't spoken. 'And if that reason had anything to do with impressing me – then fine. I'm impressed. But that's as far as it goes. And now, if you don't mind, I'd better find Celia and take her home. I promised her parents we wouldn't be late.'

Olivia shrugged, allowing the narrow strap of her dress to slip down one arm. 'Why didn't *they* bring her?' She didn't ask because she cared, but because she wanted to keep Luke talking. There had to be some way of convincing him she wasn't as self-centred as he thought.

'Celia's only eighteen. I understand it's not cool to be seen out with your parents before you're twenty-one.' His smile was indulgent, as if he found Celia's childishness appealing.

'I wouldn't know,' Olivia snapped. 'It wasn't an option for me.'

Luke's smile vanished. 'Nor for me.'

Oh. She'd forgotten, briefly, that his childhood had been infinitely harsher than hers.

'Goodnight Olivia,' he said. 'And by the way, if you want to get through the lobby with your virtue intact, I suggest you pull up that strap. Give some thought to a divorce, won't you?'

He had reached the top of the stairs before Olivia rallied sufficiently to form a reply, but by then there wasn't any point.

A young couple sauntered past her on their way to inspect a wall of posters featuring the stars of long-ago movies. Oblivious to their startled stares, Olivia wrapped her arms around the pillar and pressed her forehead to the cold comfort of plaster and gilt.

She didn't see Luke pause on the top step to look back. If she had, she might have seen him wipe a hand around the back of his neck then close his fist over the balustrade as if it were her neck.

'So help me, Olivia,' he muttered as he ran down the stairs. 'So help me, one more second and I'd have had that dress off you – right then and there! And we'd have ended up back where we started.'

'Talking to yourself, Luke?' Celia came up to him, smiling pertly. 'I wondered where you'd got to.'

'Sorry. I met someone I used to know.'

'Yes,' Celia said dryly. 'Your wife. I saw you follow her up the stairs.'

Were *all* females put on earth to drive men crazy?

He took her arm, hustled her down to the cloakroom and told her it was time for them to leave.

Olivia steered the Mercedes between Hopeville's wrought

iron gates and parked in the tree-shaded lot reserved for visitors. She climbed out and surveyed the nearest row of cottages with pride. Today, with the sun shining on fresh paint and green lawns, the village looked trim and well-kept. A happy place for both people and animals.

The closest cottage, belonging to Mr and Mrs Starsky and their delightfully dim-witted afghan, Delilah, was painted a delicate shade of mint green. Their garden was a glorious tangle of fall flowers. In contrast, Len Stivic's cottage was painted grey, and sported stones in place of a lawn.

Typical of Len. Yet, if it hadn't been for him and Spot, Hopeville might never have existed. Still thinking of her most intractable tenant, she made her way to the cottage next door.

Mrs Bayliff appeared at her door with a spitting, yellow-eyed tabby cat in her arms.

'I came to see how Attila's paw is doing,' Olivia said.

'Coming up to scratch.' Mrs Bayliff cackled evilly at her own wit. 'Gave that Madame Dupont's sausage dog a sore nose when it got into my compost this morning, Attila did. Served Dupont right for saying Attila ought to be de-clawed.'

'De-clawing is cruel,' Olivia agreed. 'Painful, as well as dangerous for the cat. But I'm sure Mrs Dupont didn't mean it.'

'Oh, yes she did.' Mrs Bayliff poked her head forward like an elderly turtle emerging from its shell and squinted suspiciously at Olivia. 'What's the matter with you? You look sour as one of them crab apples Dupont's always making into jelly.'

Talk about the pot calling the kettle! 'I'm not sour,' Olivia said with a certain tartness. 'Just tired. I didn't sleep well last night.'

She hadn't slept well for the past week. Not since the concert that had sounded the death knell on her dreams of a second chance with Luke.

'Hmm!' Mrs Bayliff was unsympathetic. 'When you're as old as I am you won't expect to sleep. Something to look forward to, eh girlie?' She stabbed a finger at Olivia's chest, a wicked old cherub in aspic. Attila gave an accompanying wheeze.

What a pair, Olivia thought as she backed down the path.

Luckily, most of the residents were grateful to have a roof over their heads and a place where their pets were welcome, but there were always a few embittered old souls who liked nothing better than stirring up trouble. Those were usually the ones with no families and very few friends.

No wonder. They reminded Olivia of rusty nails always on the lookout for someone's tyre to puncture.

She drove home feeling depressed.

That evening, as she watched a romantic comedy on TV, Olivia thought again about Mrs Bayliff. The bitter old woman had done her best to make her feel bad. Would she be a sour old misery too when she was her age? It was a frightening thought. What had Mrs Bayliff said? Something about her having a sleepless old age to look forward to...

The couple on the screen ended the argument they'd been having with a flying double leap into bed. Olivia watched the man's blond hair settle on the pillow. Luke's hair was strong like that, only dark...

But she had lost Luke. He was never going to change his mind.

She gripped the arms of her chair and discovered a small tear where her manicured nail had pierced the fabric. Oh hell. Was she really going to spend the rest of her life growing old and bitter and resentful, until she reached a point where she had nothing better to do than quarrel with her neighbours and antagonise everyone around her? Did it even matter much if she did? She had never actually cared who she antagonised ...

Until she met Luke.

The thought brought her up short. Before Luke she hadn't known, or had forgotten, that there was more to life than taking care of her own needs. And in the end, taking care of herself and no one else had lost her the one man she had ever thought of loving.

The couple on the screen looked as though they were about to swallow each other whole, so Olivia switched off the set and stood up.

She was *not* going to turn into one of those cantankerous old crones no one cared about. If Luke wouldn't have her – then she would make a life without him. And maybe one day she would find someone else to relieve the restless emptiness of her nights. If that didn't happen – well there was certainly life beyond men. She had Hopeville and the father she was just getting to know again – and her health. So why allow herself to be tormented by what she couldn't have?

Olivia lifted her chin. The child she had once been had coped with loss by refusing to admit she needed love. The woman she had become would cope by any means that came to hand. It wouldn't be easy, but she would do it.

Although the air wasn't cold, she shivered suddenly. There was one last gift she had to give to Luke before she got on with her new life. And when she had given it she would cry. After that she would start to build her future – a future that would be the very best that she could make it.

Head held high, Olivia marched into her neat and sparkling kitchen and poured herself a small glass of wine.

'To the future,' she said, raising her glass to the watery sun streaming through the window. After a while, she added in a much quieter voice, 'Goodbye, my love. Goodbye.'

Dry leaves crackled under Luke's feet, as he strode morosely beside Lost Lagoon. With his hands thrust into the pockets of black jeans and the black collar of his jacket turned up around his ears, he guessed he looked more like the leader of a biker gang than a successful businessman with a growing reputation. His scowling visage did little to allay the impression.

He had been taciturn and glowering all day, since he had received a letter from Olivia that morning telling him she was filing for divorce.

'*I want you to be happy,*' she had written. '*So I'm giving you the only thing you seem to want. I know you won't believe me, but I'm sorry.*' This had been followed by an all but indecipherable signature that looked as though it had been blotted with something wet. He had thrown the letter on the table, furious for no reason he could identify and had set off for a walk.

His outrage would have been laughable, if it hadn't been so obvious it was sparked by a pain he was too obstinate to acknowledge.

'I never gave a damn about Olivia,' he muttered through gritted teeth.

'You married her,' the little voice in his head argued.

'Yes, I married her. What else could I do?'

'I don't know. What I do know is that you can't go on brooding over her forever. Either leave her to get on with the divorce, or go back to her and make your marriage work.'

The mist was lifting, the air was sweet, and not far away he could hear the insistent call of geese greeting the morning. 'Olivia's improved.' His conscience reminded him. 'Why? Because she spent money she didn't earn on her toy village. She only did that to impress me.'

'Have you any idea how arrogant that sounds? Olivia always loved animals. Maybe she did it for them.'

'Sure. Maybe she did.' He didn't believe it though. 'I swear, I'd rather be married to a python, than to Olivia Franklyn!'

An apt comparison. Luke made a face, but as a small brown duck waddled past him quacking about nothing, his grimace turned to a reluctant smile.

Olivia was about to start her car, after a particularly frustrating visit to the foreman of site number two of the village's development, when a peculiar noise coming from the Starsky cottage made her pause.

What was that? A cry of pain? She slid out of the car, and immediately a rotund little man bounded on to the step of the cottage. Tears streamed down his face as his mouth worked frantically to form words. A long-legged dog, obviously closely related to a shag carpet, ambled out and sat at his feet.

'What is it, Mr Starsky?' Olivia hurried up to the old man, instinctively catching his flailing hands.

That seemed to calm him. 'Vera,' he croaked. 'It's Vera.'

'Is Mrs Starsky ill?'

He nodded. 'She fell. In the kitchen. I don't think she's breathing.'

Oh God. The end to a perfect afternoon. 'Have you phoned the Emergency Services?' Olivia called, as she stepped around the dog and hurled herself through the open front door.

'No. Not yet. I didn't think...'

'Call them now. I'll see what I can do for Mrs Starsky.' She ran into the kitchen and knelt down beside a plump figure in a flowered apron who lay sprawled on her side on the black-and-white tiles. Beside her, a white puddle and the scattered remains of a broken blue milk jug gave evidence of the suddenness of her fall.

What had she read about not moving people after accidents? Olivia felt for Mrs Starsky's pulse. There didn't seem to be one. She held a hand close to the pinched nose. No breath either as far as she could tell.

Making up her mind, Olivia turned Mrs Starsky on to her back and tried to remember what she'd read about mouth-to-mouth resuscitation.

Pull out the tongue, tip the head back, hold the nose and

take a good breath. Cover the mouth and breathe in at intervals of...oh God, she couldn't remember. Never mind, do it anyway.

Behind her, she was vaguely aware of a man's voice stumbling over words, then of a receiver dropping back into place. After that she was conscious only of what she was doing and of the same voice saying, over and over, 'Vera, Vera, don't leave me.'

Loud panting sounded in Olivia's ear, and something that was probably a tongue swiped her neck.

She raised her head, cried, 'Mr Starsky, please get Delilah away,' and took another breath.

The panting stopped.

After a while, when she lifted her head again, Olivia thought she heard the shriek of sirens. She breathed into the flaccid mouth for the tenth – or was it the twentieth time – and felt... Oh, thank God, thank God.

Mrs Starsky's chest was rising. And falling. Rising again. Then she was, unbelievably, breathing on her own.

Olivia sat back on her heels, exhausted, her heart beating so fast it sounded like a drum roll in her ears. Seconds later she felt a hand on her shoulder. 'Good work, miss,' a gruff voice said. 'We'll take over now. You go and see to the old man.'

Olivia stood up stiffly as three large and competent-looking men in uniform swarmed into the cottage and surrounded Mrs Starsky. She backed away, and discovered Mr Starsky shaking on the window sill between two pots of golden yellow mums. His hand rested on Delilah's shaggy head. He was still crying, but now he was smiling through his tears.

'She's going to be all right, isn't she?' he said.

Olivia nodded. 'Yes. Yes, I think so.'

'You saved her life. You saved my Vera's life. Forty-five years we've been married.'

For the first time in her life, Olivia felt tears in her eyes that were wholly for the happiness of another human being. She had cried for animals many times and, less often, for herself. But never for an old man who loved his wife.

She brushed her knuckles over her eyes. It must be wonderful to be loved as much as that.

'I know you'll be married for many more,' she said, taking Mr Starsky's mottled hand.

He smiled and said, 'Yes. Thanks to you.'

Delilah offered her a paw.

Twenty minutes later, having refused all offers of a lift home, Olivia stumbled down the steps of the cottage and into the gathering dusk. She shivered at the unexpected sharpness of the wind and began to make her way quickly towards the parking lot. Delilah, long tail swinging, walked trustingly by her side.

She had only taken a dozen or so steps when a woman's voice said, 'Olivia? Olivia, is that you?'

Olivia groaned. Who the hell else would she be? And who wanted something from her now?

She turned resignedly. 'Yes? Who...? Oh.'

'Mm,' said Rosemary Harriman. 'I'm afraid it's me.'

chapter twelve

Rosemary's astonished gaze wandered from the retreating lights of the ambulance back to Olivia who, even in the pink-shaded dusk, looked as rumpled and bedraggled as a homeless cat. Her long hair hung in a mass of tangles and was dotted with what looked like milk. Her shoes were muddy, and her red sweater frayed at the sleeves. The dog she had with her, a moth-eaten but possibly pure-bred afghan, appeared positively elegant by comparison.

'Olivia?' Rosemary said. 'Are you all right?'

Olivia brushed a tangle out of her eyes. 'All right? I don't know. My workmen didn't show up, I slipped in the mud, and Mrs Starsky just tried to die on me. Apart from that, I suppose you could say I was all right.'

'Oh. This isn't a good time, is it?'

Olivia threw back her head and laughed with a touch of hysteria. 'A good time for what? If you feel like looking after Delilah for the night, then yes, I guess it's a good time. Mr Starsky has gone to the hospital with his wife, and there was no one else willing to look after her. But Custard will go straight for Delilah's eyes when I bring her home.'

Rosemary said, 'Oh,' again. Custard? Delilah? Had the events of the day gone to her sister-in-law's head?

'Right,' Olivia said. 'That's what I thought. Good night then. Give my love to Luke.' She turned her back and continued on her way.

'No, wait,' Rosemary called after her. 'I didn't mean... that is...who are Delilah and Custard?'

Olivia paused but didn't bother to turn around. 'This is

Delilah.' She bent down to touch the dog's shaggy head. 'Custard is my cat. I've only had him a couple of weeks but he rules the roost.'

Rosemary doubted if anyone, animal or human, could rule a roost owned by Olivia Franklyn. But she *could* imagine that the big, gangly dog was likely to get the worst of any territorial battle with a cat.

'I suppose I could take her,' she said doubtfully. The germ of an idea began to take shape in her mind.

'You could?' Olivia swivelled round, and became hopelessly entangled in Delilah's leash.

'I think so. There's a rule about no pets in our building but Luke's never paid much attention to rules. And she'll only be with us overnight. Won't she?'

'Oh yes. Mr Starsky says I can bring her back tomorrow.' Olivia turned in a circle to extricate herself from the leash, took a small step forward and peered mistrustfully at Rosemary, as if she couldn't believe she was offering to help.

'Then I'm sure it'll be OK.'

A light flashed on over the porch of the cottage next door. Olivia blinked and moved into the shadows. 'Why?' she asked. 'Why are you being nice to me? For that matter, why are you here?'

Rosemary turned up the collar of her jacket. 'Your next-door neighbour told me I'd probably find you at Hopeville. I wanted to talk to you about Luke.'

Olivia pulled Delilah close, as if seeking protection. 'What about him? You know I've filed for divorce.'

'Yes, I know. I wondered why.'

'Because that's what he wants. Now if you don't mind, I'd like to get home before I turn into an icicle.' She hesitated. 'Were you serious about taking Delilah?'

Rosemary smiled wryly. Olivia hadn't grown much sweeter in the months since they'd last met. Yet there *had* been something in her voice when she'd spoken of Luke and divorce... Perhaps, obliquely, she had been given the answer she was looking for.

There was only one way she could think of to find out.

Luke wouldn't be pleased, but she would risk that. She held out her hand for Delilah's leash. 'Yes, I'll take her,' she said. 'Can you fetch her in the morning before I leave?'

'Sure. Is nine o'clock OK?'

'Yes, fine.'

'Good. Thank you. I...' Olivia smiled suddenly, a wary, almost embarrassed smile. 'I do appreciate your help.'

Rosemary understood that, in that one sentence, an apology had been made and a tentative offer of friendship extended.

'It's no trouble,' she lied, accepting the offer at face value. Whatever Luke might think, Olivia *had* changed.

The two of them walked in silence to their cars.

'Luke?'

'Mm?' Luke sprinkled salt on eggs he'd already salted and went on reading the paper.

'Do you have to go to work today?'

'What?' He folded the paper and laid it beside his plate as his sister prepared to leave for class. 'Of course I do. I own the company, remember.'

'That's what I mean. It's up to you when you go in, isn't it?'

'Not entirely. I have appointments, meetings...'

'Today?'

He frowned. 'Not specifically today, no...'

'Then, please, could you possibly stay home until the afternoon? I have an early class, and Olivia won't be coming for Delilah until late.'

'Why on earth should I stay home?' Luke forked up a mouthful of scrambled egg. 'Are you sure you're feeling all right?'

'Of course I am. It's just that I don't like to leave Delilah alone. You never know what she might do.'

Delilah, hearing her name, thumped her tail.

'You might have thought of that, before you took her home last night.' Luke picked up the paper again so Rosemary wouldn't see how close he was to throwing it on the floor and stalking out. There was no point in resuming a battle he'd already fought and lost.

Half-an-hour ago, when Rosemary had strolled into the apartment with a nervous Delilah prancing at her heels, he had, at first, been speechless. When he finally found his voice, all he could think of to say was, 'What's that?'

'This is Delilah,' Rosemary had said blithely. 'Um...actually I'm looking after her for Olivia, who's looking after her for...'

'Hold it right there.' Luke made an unsuccessful attempt to keep his voice down. 'You're looking after her for *who*?'

'Whom,' Rosemary corrected him. 'Who isn't grammatically correct.'

'Neither am I.' Luke, who had been sprawled on the new, cream-coloured sofa reading an article on local drainage systems, stood up and advanced threateningly on his sister. 'Now say that again. You're looking after this four-legged shaggy carpet for *who*?'

Rosemary's smile was ingenuous. 'For Olivia. One of her residents had an attack of some sort and had to be taken to hospital. So there was no one to look after the dog. She would have taken Delilah home herself if she didn't already have a cat.'

'Rosemary.' Luke was only partially conscious that he never called his sister anything but Rosie. 'Rosemary, why have you been in touch with my wife? Has it slipped your mind that we're about to be divorced?'

'No, of course not. I...um...happened to run into her. And she asked me if I'd mind looking after Delilah.'

'Olivia asked *you*?'

'Yes. I think she thought I'd say no. But I didn't.'

'And why didn't you?' Luke went to stand with his back to the window to prevent himself from acting on his inclinations and boxing his sister's pointed ears. 'You don't like Olivia, and this ridiculous creature isn't your dog. Besides, in case you've forgotten, this is supposed to be a pet-free building.'

That, Luke realised as he studied Rosemary now across the table, had been a tactical error. Because Rosemary had immediately replied, 'I know, but you've always said rules are made to be broken. Especially stupid ones. After all, you do *own* this apartment.'

'I may own this apartment, but it's not a stupid rule. It keeps people like you from bringing home mutts like that.'

Delilah chose that moment to trot across the room and offer him a paw. That was when he made his second mistake, because instead of ignoring it, he bent down and shook it politely. Delilah, quivering with delight, offered the other paw.

Luke knew when he was defeated. Growling, 'Damned carpet,' he had accepted the paw and told Rosemary that Delilah could stay.

'Why don't *you* stay and look after her?' he asked his sister now. 'You can always get notes from someone else.'

Rosemary swallowed the dregs of her coffee. 'There's a test,' she explained. 'I'd rather not miss it.'

'And I'd rather not miss a morning's work.'

'Can't you do it here? You always bring your work home.'

'Yes, so I'm free to deal with problems at the office. Not so I can baby-sit a damned dog.'

Delilah stretched, rose slowly and shook herself. Then she padded over to Luke, put her head in his lap, and fixed his now tepid eggs with her best hypnotic stare.

Luke raised his hands in a gesture of surrender. 'OK, OK,' he groaned. 'You win, the pair of you. But Rosie, I swear, if you ever do anything remotely like this to me again, I'm leaving here – and without giving you a forwarding address. Do you understand me?'

Rosemary nodded, scooped up her books, and skedaddled out the door before he could change his mind.

Luke scraped the remains of his eggs into a bowl, set it on the floor and told Delilah to get on with it. Wriggling with gratitude, she did.

With the rest of the morning unexpectedly at his disposal, Luke pulled off his tie, poured himself a fresh cup of coffee and went back to reading the paper.

When he turned to the second section, a particularly bold headline caught his eye.

'HOPEVILLE BENEFACTRESS SAVES LIFE OF STRICKEN RESIDENT.'

Underneath, in smaller print, were the words, '"*She gave me back my wife*," claims grateful husband.'

Luke tightened his grip on the paper, crumpling its edges and lifting the page from the table. The printed words blurred momentarily, then came back into focus when he wiped his hand across his eyes. Behind him, Delilah heaved a sigh.

He began to read, at first with scepticism, then with a growing sense of – what? Pride? In his wife?

No. Pride wasn't an emotion he associated with Olivia.

He read on, convinced a different truth would soon emerge from the clean lines of print, a truth more in keeping with Olivia's nature. She was adept at destroying lives, not saving them.

He read the whole article through once, then started again at the beginning.

When he came to the line that read, 'A grateful Walter Starsky told this reporter that Olivia Franklyn also took it upon herself to care for the family dog,' Luke muttered, 'Hmm. They sure got that wrong, didn't they, Delilah?'

Delilah pricked up her ears. Luke patted her head and reached for the phone to call his office.

As soon as he hung up, the buzzer connecting the apartment to the front door gave a sharp beep.

What the hell...? He picked up the receiver and snapped, 'Yes?'

There was silence on the other end, and he was about to disconnect when a doubtful voice said, 'Luke?'

Oh no. Not *again*. He shoved both hands through his neatly brushed hair. Not when she was serving him with divorce papers ...

'What do you want?' He had never had the stomach for polite platitudes when it came to Olivia.

'I'm here to fetch Delilah. Rosemary told me she'd be here this morning.'

Damn her. Her voice was still as soft and sexy as silk...

'Rosemary told me most specifically that you wouldn't be coming until later.'

'Oh. Is she still here?'

'No. As I've no doubt you're quite well aware.'

'No. No, I wasn't. Is Delilah there?'

'Of course she's... Hell! Delilah, hold it. You can't...'

He was too late. Delilah already had – all over the kitchen floor, which now flaunted a saffron-coloured puddle.

'What's the matter?' Olivia's voice squeaked in alarm. 'Is she all right?'

'Of course she's all right. She just finished christening my kitchen.'

'Oh. I am sorry. Luke, can I please come up?'

Luke glared at the wet pool in the centre of his clean kitchen floor. What was he supposed to do now? He didn't want to see Olivia, didn't want her anywhere near him. On the other hand he did want to get rid of

Delilah, who was sniffing hopefully at a cupboard containing canned vegetables.

'I suppose you'll have to,' he said, and pushed the button to let her in. A minute later he answered her quiet knock on his door.

He jerked his head, indicating she could come in. 'There's your mutt. I have to congratulate you.'

Olivia looked puzzled – and as unbearably beautiful as ever in a black cashmere cloak with red trim that only served to remind him of the supple woman's figure it concealed.

'Congratulate me? On what?' Her eye fell on the paper, still open amidst the remains of breakfast. 'Oh, I see. It was nothing.'

'That's what I thought. Although it just so happens I wasn't talking about your heroics of last evening.'

Her eyes sparked dangerously. 'Instinct, Luke. Not heroics.'

'Whatever. I'll concede it was a job well done. That's not why I offered congratulations.'

'Why then?'

Luke opened his mouth to reply, but Delilah chose that moment to give up on the cupboard. When she took in that the visitor was Olivia, she gave an ecstatic bark and bounded across the floor to welcome her old friend.

Olivia said, 'Hi, Delilah, aren't you a beautiful girl then?' and crouched down to throw her arms around the squirming dog's neck.

Luke glowered. 'She is not a beautiful girl,' he said to the top of Olivia's head. 'She's a pain in the ass who has just piddled all over the floor.'

'Didn't you or Rosemary take her out?' Olivia stood up, and Delilah gave a protesting grumble and trotted back to the kitchen to see what she could do about the carrots.

'Take her out? No, Rosemary didn't. I doubt if it occurred to her.'

'Dogs need to be taken out,' Olivia said mildly. 'If you'll give me some rags I'll clean up the mess.'

Luke noticed she wouldn't look him in the eye. He was glad, because he knew all too well the effect those incredible eyes had on his libido. At the same time, her evasiveness only increased his suspicion that her arrival was a set-up. Clearing up her hairy decoy's mess was the least she could do. As far as he was concerned, she was getting off lightly.

'Here,' he said, going to the dispenser and pulling out a handful of paper towels. 'These should do it.'

Olivia unfastened her cloak and threw it over the back of a chair before she took the towels.

To Luke's amazement, she made a remarkably efficient job of wiping up the puddle. Delilah watched the operation, panting happily. Luke lounged in a corner with his arms crossed and clamped down firmly on the urge to pant himself.

It wasn't easy. Olivia's neat behind in trim, scarlet wool slacks was extraordinarily tempting.

By the time she had finished scrubbing the floor, the air was pungent with the smell of disinfectant. Luke handed her a plastic bag and took the towels to the garbage bin without comment.

When he returned, Olivia was in the bathroom. He could hear water splashing into the sink.

'You haven't yet told me what you meant,' she said, as soon as she returned to the living room. There was an edge to her voice he remembered well.

'About what?'

'Your congratulations.' She went to stand behind the pale green armchair as if she felt the need to put a barrier between them.

Luke threw his considerable length on to the sofa and crossed his arms behind his head.

'You'll get wrinkles in your shirt,' Olivia said.

He remembered she had always liked him in crisp white shirts and dark trousers, and vaguely regretted that he wasn't dressed in jeans.

'It doesn't matter,' he said. 'As for the congratulations – you're here aren't you? And so am I.'

'What's that supposed to mean?'

'That you cooked up a most imaginative little scheme to worm your way into my apartment. You even got Rosemary on your side.'

'What are you talking about?' Olivia closed her hands over the back of the chair and swallowed to relieve the tightness in her throat.

Had her soon-to-be-ex husband any idea what he was doing to her? Sprawled on the sofa with his legs invitingly apart and the top buttons of his shirt unfastened, he looked like a blatant invitation to sex in the morning.

She shut her eyes.

'I'm talking about yet another of your plots to get me into bed.' Luke's low voice penetrated her frustrated imaginings. 'That's what this is about, isn't it? You've never used a dog before. Very clever.'

'*What?*' Olivia's eyelids snapped up. How *dare* he...? No. She cut the thought off before it choked her.

'I said I'm talking about another of your plots...'

'I know what you said.' She bowed her head, and after a while it came to her that she couldn't expect Luke to see her presence in any other light. It wasn't his fault. Her track record spoke for itself.

'I didn't use Delilah,' she said wearily. 'Nor did I use Rosemary. I don't know how this happened. All I do know is that I told Rosemary I'd be here around nine. She said she'd be here. I thought you wouldn't be, because when we were...together...you always left around eight.'

'Are you saying *Rosemary* arranged this?'

'Of course not. It was just a mistake, I suppose.'

'Sure. A mistake. Very convenient.' He pulled a cushion from behind his shoulders, threw it at his feet and sat up.

Thank God. Olivia released breath she hadn't realised she was holding. If that gorgeous body had remained so temptingly displayed for much longer she would very likely have been reduced to going down on her knees and pleading with him to take her. For all the good it would have done her.

'It *must* have been a mistake,' she insisted. If he wouldn't love her, at least she had to make him see the truth.

'OK, it was a mistake. Now – are you going to take the dog and get out of here? Or do you have some other trick tucked up your sleeve?'

'It wasn't a trick.' Olivia released her grip on the chair, and her eye fell on a handsome, red Swedish glass bowl in the centre of the circular oak coffee table. She wished she had the nerve to pick it up and throw it at his disbelieving head. *That* might get through to him.

'Wasn't it?' Luke rolled up his sleeves as if he'd read her thoughts and was preparing to take action. 'All right, have it your way. Now – are you going to take the dog and get out?'

In that moment, all the months of pent-up tension stretched to their breaking point and snapped. Dammit, she was telling him the *truth*. She was also giving him the divorce he wanted – at a nearly unbearable cost to herself. Yet he still refused to believe she could perform a single act of kindness that wasn't motivated by egotism or self-interest.

Red flashed in front of her eyes. She didn't realise it was the Swedish glass bowl until she held it in her hands.

'What the...' Luke was on his feet, across the floor and wrestling it from her before she had a chance to make her move.

They stood inches apart, breathing hard, glaring at each other like two prize-fighters itching to pound the other one insensible.

Olivia was the first to break eye contact, and the moment she did Luke put the bowl back on the table and took her by the shoulders.

'What was that about?' he demanded. 'I won't put up with it, Olivia. Not any more.'

'Put up with what? I wouldn't have thrown it. At least, I don't think so.'

'Wouldn't you?' Luke gave a bark of a laugh and released her. When she started to speak, he spun away from her and went to stare out of the window.

Olivia gazed at his back as he leaned on the sill, supporting himself on his arms. How well she remembered that back...and the seductive curve of his taut buttocks.

She moistened her lips. Luke didn't move.

It was too much, the temptation too great. Olivia released her breath and padded across the pale green carpet to stand beside him. Deliberately, she brushed her hand against his thigh.

Luke moved away, leaving a space of several inches between them. Far below, the waters of the bay churned beneath the onslaught of the wind. No small sailboats had braved the sea this morning, and only a few grey freighters rolled stoically with the motion of the waves. On the small strip of beach, a lone woman was walking her dog.

For a moment Olivia wished she could be that woman out there braving the elements instead of up here with Luke, braving another kind of onslaught.

She doubted if Luke knew what he was doing to her, how much his withdrawal hurt. Though if he had known, perhaps he wouldn't have cared. He had never believed she was capable of honest suffering.

At one time, he might have been right.

Minutes passed, broken only by the muffled roar of traffic and the wailing of the wind. 'It wasn't a trick,' she said finally. 'Truly, I thought you were at work.'

Luke looked at her then, but she couldn't tell if he believed her or not.

'So why are you here?' he asked, in a funny, cracked voice.

'I told you. I came to fetch Delilah. If you'll give me her lead...'

'She's asleep.' He nodded at the kitchen, where Delilah was curled on her green blanket making little bubbling noises through her nose.

'Yes.' Olivia frowned. What had the fact that Delilah was asleep to do with anything? Puzzled, she put a hand on Luke's arm.

He stiffened at once, but this time he didn't pull away. Needles of fire sizzled through Olivia's fingertips, and she wasn't sure whether the heat came from him or from some place deep within herself.

'Luke...?' she murmured. 'Luke, I...'

She got no further. As she struggled to find words, he let out a sharp, explosive phrase and clamped his hands around her hips.

She recognised then what she should have seen from the beginning – that the fire blazing at her out of his eyes was not hostility, but a passion that burned as fiercely as her own.

Olivia gasped. Desire snaked hotly through her abdomen. What was he doing? He wanted her, yes. She knew that. But, with Luke, wanting meant nothing if he'd made up his mind not to have her.

She tried to pull away, but at once he moved a hand to the small of her back, pressing her against him as he rotated his thumb in small, delicious circles round and round the base of her spine.

Within seconds, she thought she would die of the sheer agony of wanting him.

'Luke, please,' she moaned. 'Oh, please...'

'Yes.' He answered her plea in a dark, husky voice that didn't sound as though it belonged to him. 'Yes. Why the hell not?'

Olivia moaned again, not daring to believe he meant it until he turned her around, put a hand on her bottom and hustled her ahead of him up the stairs. The wrought iron shuddered beneath the urgency of their feet.

Luke's bedroom was directly ahead of them, and at first all Olivia took in was the size of the enormous oak bed. Then he sat her down on its colourful patchwork quilt and, without pausing, pulled off her shoes, dropping them one after the other on to the burnt-orange carpet. After that he slid down the zipper on her slacks.

Still Olivia was afraid to believe.

She mustn't be taken in. He was torturing her, that was all...taking his revenge.

She cried out as he swung her legs on to the bed and tugged her slacks down over her ankles. Her panties briskly followed.

He stopped then, breathing hard, and sat on the edge of the bed inspecting his handiwork as if he were trying to decide whether or not to finish the job. And suddenly it was all too much to bear.

She couldn't take any more. Perhaps she owed him his revenge, but not now. Not like this.

With a low murmur of protest, she rolled over on to her stomach and buried her face in the thickness of the quilt.

Nothing happened. Luke didn't move, and neither did she. Then she heard him mutter something that sounded like, 'God help me,' and caught her breath as his palms slid purposefully across her bare buttocks and down the backs of her thighs.

'Take off your sweater,' he said, still in that rough, husky tone.

'What?' Warily, Olivia shifted on to her back and sat up.

'What are you...? Luke, why...?'

Luke was unbuttoning his shirt, but he paused to reply gruffly, 'Because it's been too damn long, that's why. Do you...want some help with that sweater?'

He meant it. He wasn't playing with her, he meant to go through with it. Not because he loved her, but because his need was as urgent and overwhelming as hers.

For a split second she heard a voice in her head saying, *'This is all wrong. This is nothing more than lust.'* But Luke's hands caught the bottom of her sweater, and it no longer mattered. She helped him tug it over her head.

He lay down beside her then, as virile and magnificent as she remembered. Turning on her side, she ran her hand slowly down his chest, over the flat, muscled planes of his stomach...

It wasn't until he lifted her up and rolled her over on top of him that she became aware of the tears streaming down her face.

He touched one damp cheek, and said quite gently, 'Tears, Olivia? We'll have to do something about that.'

He was as good as his word.

Soon, but not too soon, he carried her with him to the peak of remembered rapture, and in that place of light she had no need for tears.

chapter thirteen

Olivia lay in the warm circle of Luke's arms watching the grey clouds roll across the skylight above his bed. Two copper-coloured leaves, lifted by the wind, dropped on to the glass and remained there.

She thought of saying something to break the silence that had fallen between them since passion had drifted into satisfied lethargy – but no words came to her, and Luke seemed far away.

Was he angry? Filled with regret for a coming together that, for her, had been a thousand times sweeter than her memories? Or was he indifferent now that desire had been most gloriously sated?

With Luke it was impossible to tell.

In the end, when the rolling clouds above them turned from grey to an ominous shade of greenish black, she turned her head on the pillow to look at him – and discovered he was looking at her.

'Are you all right?' he asked, in a queer, stilted voice.

'Of course. I...are you?'

His face was so close she could see only his nose and the darkness in his eyes.

'Yes,' he said. 'I suppose I am.' He rolled away from her and pushed himself up against the headboard. 'Physically anyway, I'm as all right as I've been for...a long time.'

'Oh.' Olivia, feeling unaccountably abandoned, pulled back the quilt and slipped quickly beneath its comforting patchwork folds. 'Haven't you...I mean, hasn't there been anyone...?'

'No. Not yet.' He didn't give her a chance to complete the question.

Not yet? Did that mean that, as of now, she was still the only one. Olivia tried not to let her heart sing too loudly. Better not to tempt fate.

'There hasn't been anyone for me either,' she said. 'But, of course, you knew that.'

'Did I?'

'You should have. I told you...' She stopped. What was the use? She had told Luke a lot of things, and not all of them had proved to be true.

'So you did,' he agreed, and relapsed into silence as if it didn't matter. Which perhaps, to him, it didn't.

After that Olivia was afraid to speak in case he told her it was all over between them, just as he had done so many times before. Without meaning to, or even wanting to, she had begun to hope again.

Some time later Luke asked, 'How much of that story in the papers was true?'

Olivia blinked, and gradually brought her mind back from fantasies of a distant planet where all was forgiven and she and Luke lived together in harmony and love.

Papers? Story? What was he talking about...? Oh. Of course. *That* story. 'Most of it's true,' she said, not seriously expecting him to believe her. 'Except the part that said I was a heroine. The truth is that I acted without thinking.'

'Mmm.' He seemed to accept that. 'Lucky for Mrs Starsky your lack of thought turned out to be on target. You did very well.' He gave her shoulder a squeeze.

'Thank you. Are you surprised?'

Luke laughed. 'Are you?'

'I suppose I was.' Olivia wished he would look at her, but his gaze remained riveted on his antique oak tallboy. With his hair all damp and disordered, and his body still glistening with sweat, he looked so unbearably desirable that she was once again devastated by the depth of her hunger for this man. Throwing back the quilt, she turned on her side and flung her arm around his waist.

Automatically, Luke tensed. The wind blew another shower of leaves on to the skylight. He closed his eyes and listened to the roaring of the sea.

Why was it that even now, with desire satisfied, the touch of Olivia's hand was enough to send him spinning into orbit? What in hell was he going to do about her? Not having an answer, he lowered his head and let his forehead rest lightly on her hair.

'I should say I'm sorry,' he said. 'But I'm not going to.'

'I don't want you to be sorry.'

'I know.' He smoothed a hand down her naked back. 'That's exactly why I should be.'

He wasn't though. How could he be sorry that by giving his witch of a wife what she wanted, his body had achieved release from a frustration that had been growing more intolerable with every week that passed? He had been right to resist her, but the time had come for some kind of...what was that word Rosemary's Stephen was so tediously fond of using? Closure. That was it.

Making love with Olivia today had been a way of tying up loose ends and allowing the past to be laid to rest.

Had Rosemary guessed that? Was that why she had set him up? Because he had no doubt this meeting with Olivia was her doing. She'd had no right, of course. But, even so, he might, just maybe, find it in his heart to forgive his sister.

Olivia's cloak of glossy hair fell like expensive silk across his chest. He drew in his breath and inhaled the faint tartness of lemon shampoo.

Strange. He felt peaceful, contented, in a way he hadn't for a very long time. It was too bad that soon he would have to burst this small bubble of contentment...

It burst abruptly, and without any help from him, when

Olivia gave a little purr of satisfaction and slid her hand in between his thighs.

'What the...what are you trying to do to me?' he gasped.

'What do you think?'

Luke decided he wasn't capable of thought.

With a laugh that was part groan he flung himself back on to the pillows, curved his hands purposefully around her waist and lifted her up until she sat astride him.

'Beautiful,' he said, reaching up to touch the creamy smoothness of her breasts.

She gave a little gasp, giggled and bent over him, teasing his lips until they parted willingly to draw first one and then the other hardened peak into his mouth.

There was no holding back after that, and when the quilt slid to the floor they slid with it.

In the moment he entered her, Luke heard Olivia cry, 'Luke! Oh Luke, my love.'

Any response he might have made was lost in an explosion of passion. Their bodies were a single moving force. All memory of the world outside the bedroom vanished, and in that moment Luke was aware of nothing but the taste and feel and the bittersweet scent of the woman he held in his arms. He even forgot she was Olivia until, without warning, her moans of pleasure took on a different, startled note.

'What is it?' he asked, struggling to disentangle his legs from the folds of the quilt. 'Olivia...'

'Delilah,' she gasped. 'I think it's Delilah.'

Luke sat up. 'What...?'

He closed his eyes, then opened them again almost at once. Sure enough, standing behind Olivia was the big dog. She had her head down, and her pinkly extended tongue was enthusiastically washing her friend's back.

'Damned dog. Get out of here!' Luke roared.

Olivia laughed. 'It doesn't matter. She startled me, that's all. I expect she woke up and decided she wanted company.'

'Well, I don't.'

'Not even me?' Olivia asked.

Damn. He recognised the warning at once.

Somehow, some way, he was going to have to tell Olivia – again – that for the two of them there was no future written in the stars. Once, he would have gained a perverse kind of pleasure from telling her she wasn't going to get what she wanted. This time it would give him no pleasure at all.

Yet it had to be done.

'Not even you,' he replied, springing briskly to his feet and holding out his hand to help her up. 'Olivia, we've always worked well in bed – not to mention on the floor...' He gestured wryly at the rumpled quilt, now occupied by a panting Delilah. 'But that doesn't mean there's a hope in hell for us in any other way.'

In the greyish light, her dark eyes gazed at him, moist and huge, making him feel as if he'd slapped her in the face. Hell. He didn't want to hurt her. Not any more.

When he saw that she was trying not to shiver, he put his arm around her and said roughly. 'You're cold. Delilah, get off that quilt.'

Delilah didn't move, and Olivia looked reproachful. Luke swore and dragged the sheet off the bed, wrapping it securely about her shoulders. She looked small and lost in its voluminous white folds, reminding him of an underfed ghost.

Olivia didn't speak.

OK, so he was an award-winning jerk. Scowling, Luke shrugged on the clothes he had shed with such abandon an hour or so before. One black sock turned up on his bedside lamp.

When he had finished dressing, he found Olivia standing exactly where he had left her, still wrapped in the sheet and looking as though she'd forgotten how to move.

Damn. He suppressed a pang of something that couldn't

possibly be guilt. He had no reason to feel guilty. Not about Olivia.

'What's the matter?' he asked brusquely. 'Surely you understood…'

'What?' she interrupted,' her low voice unusually bleak. 'That I was just a one morning stand?'

He winced. 'If you want to put it that way.'

'I don't want to put it any way.' She folded her hands in the sheet, gripping it as if it were some kind of shield against hurt. 'I'll leave that up to you.'

'All right then.' Luke took a deep breath, wishing he could find some way to soften what needed to be said. 'Nothing's changed, Olivia. You're still the woman I married in good faith – and who I left when that faith was destroyed. I like sleeping…no, that's wrong. We don't do much sleeping, do we? I like making *love* to you. But I don't trust you.'

Olivia nodded, and again he felt a healthy stab of that feeling that couldn't be guilt. She looked so sad, so lost, so…defeated.

It was hard to think of Olivia defeated.

'I understand,' she said. 'I should. We've had this conversation before.'

Yes, he supposed they had. Luke picked up his tie and went to the mirror. The face that looked back at him was tight-lipped, hard – not the face of a man who had just been well and truly loved. He muttered a few choice phrases under his breath, knotted his tie, and discovered that Olivia was already standing by the door dressed in her red slacks and blouse.

As always, she looked like a beautiful firefly in red, a creature of the night who had glowed for him with transient passion. It was extinguished now. For good. It had to be.

They walked together down the stairs, not touching, with Delilah trotting behind them, bumping the backs of their legs with her nose. How different from their precipitate rush to bed. Luke's mouth turned down in cynical self-mockery.

To his surprise, Olivia made no attempt to change his mind. Once back on the lower level, she picked up her cloak, allowed him to slip it over her shoulders, and said quietly, 'You should have the divorce papers soon. My lawyer's been away, but he promised me they won't take much longer. He says everything ought to be reasonably straightforward — unless one of us plans to sue for alimony, of course.'

Reluctantly, Luke smiled. 'I don't. Do you?'

She shook her head. 'No. But I'll expect generous annual donations to Hopeville.'

His smile faded. Was she serious? He didn't mind giving to Hopeville, but he resented even the slightest hint of blackmail.

'Is that a threat?' he asked.

Olivia turned her back and went to collect Delilah's lead from the coffee table. 'What do you take me for, Luke?'

'I'm damned if I know.'

He watched her clip the lead on to Delilah's collar, admiring the graceful way she moved. When she straightened, her brows were drawn together in a ferocious frown.

'Peace,' Luke said, holding up his hands. 'Hopeville can count on my support.'

She gave him a formal little nod. 'Thank you.'

He thought she meant to add more but, in the end, all she did was pat Delilah on the head and walk towards the door.

'Aren't you going to say goodbye?' Absurdly, Luke felt rejected. Yet he was the one refusing to take things further.

'Goodbye,' Olivia said, and stepped into the hall.

He was still waiting for her to turn around when she put a hand behind her back and closed the door. Moments later, he heard the sound of the elevator descending.

Olivia was gone. With barely an argument, she had walked sedately out of his life.

Luke stalked into the kitchen, picked up the well-licked plate Delilah had pushed into a corner, and slammed it on to the counter with such force it cracked cleanly down the middle.

He was stopped for speeding on the way to work, and his temper wasn't improved when he arrived at the office to be informed by an anxious biologist, that the elevations on a recently-completed fish ladder were out by a good thirty centimetres.

'Do you realise that means it'll have to be rebuilt?' he roared. 'Have you any idea what that's going to cost?'

The unfortunate biologist nodded glumly, and Luke let out a stream of profanities that caused his shocked receptionist to give notice on the spot.

When he returned home from the office that evening, Rosemary rang him. 'Did you have a good afternoon?' she asked.

'No. I had a much better morning.'

'That's good,' she said vaguely.

'Thanks to you,' Luke added.

'Um...really?'

'Oh yes. Unlike your virtuous Reverend, my soon-to-be-ex wife has no scruples about bed.'

'That's not fair!' Rosemary spluttered. 'You ought to be pleased that Stephen respects me. It isn't easy for either of us.'

Luke's voice softened. 'I am pleased, Rosie. In fact I'd probably want to horsewhip the little...I mean, I'd hate to think Stephen was taking advantage of you. I shouldn't have said that. On the other hand, *you* shouldn't have set me up with Olivia.'

She didn't attempt to deny it. Luke always saw through her. 'I thought you said you had a *good* morning,' she said.

'I did.'

'Well, then...'

'Rosie, Olivia and I are finished. Over. *Kaput*. There's no sense prolonging the agony. I know you meant it for the best. But don't...ever...think of trying it again.' He spoke in the stern, brotherly tone she remembered from her childhood.

'I only wanted for you to be happy,' she protested.

'I know. I am happy. Now off you go and take a cold bath or something – whatever it is you do, in order to survive Stephen's estimable rectitude – and stop worrying about me. I'm fine. OK?'

'OK. Provided you stop sniping at Stephen. I do love him, you know.'

'I know.' He smiled crookedly. 'It's a deal. Goodnight, Rosie.'

Rosemary said coolly, 'Goodnight,' and Luke put down the phone. He lifted the Swedish glass bowl and examined it minutely for flaws.

Olivia tapped a nail against a brittle pink ball hanging from the big Christmas tree in the front hall of The Cedars.

Christmas Eve. She had stood in this same corner when she was a very small girl, touching the ornaments with reverence, charmed by their magical brilliance. In some ways nothing had changed, in spite of all the frozen years between.

When the basket on her arm let out a protesting meow, she set it down and lifted out a fluffy, yellow cat with golden eyes.

The cat settled into her arms with a smug purr.

'Olivia!' Joe exclaimed, from the top of the stairs. His slippered feet slapped each step as he hurried down. 'Where did that yellow puffball come from?'

'I brought him with me. This is Custard.'

'Ah, yes. Your cat.'

Her father kissed her perfunctorily on the cheek before bending down to give a watchful Custard a friendly scratch between the ears.

Olivia smiled, but her smile faded the moment Joe's attention shifted from the cat to her waistline, and then, after that, to her face. She hoped he wasn't about to ask questions. Questions she wasn't yet ready to answer. Time enough for that when she had accepted those answers herself.

'There's a fire in the library,' Joe said.

Olivia felt like saying, 'Of course there is,' but succeeded in biting her tongue. If she allowed the frayed edges of her nerves to show, her father would scent trouble immediately.

She followed him into the library, and waited while he went through the usual motions with his cigar before settling back comfortably in his chair.

Olivia perched tensely on the edge of her seat and hoped he would talk about the weather.

Instead he gave her a look that meant business and asked, 'What's happened to you, Olivia? You've changed.'

'I'm fine,' Olivia said quickly.

'I didn't say you looked ill. I said you'd changed. Your face is fuller. It suits you. Do you have something you want to tell me?'

Damn. *Should* she tell him? For a moment the temptation was overwhelming. She desperately needed to talk to someone, but her father would insist on blaming Luke...

In the end she said only, 'Maybe I have put on a little weight.'

'Hmm.' Joe eyed her assessingly, examined the tip of his cigar, then laid it carefully in the antique ashtray.

Ominous, Olivia thought gloomily. She twisted round to stare into the fire.

'You're having a baby, aren't you?' Joe spoke in his boardroom voice, as if he were asking for a report from a subordinate. 'Your mother looked exactly like that when she was expecting you and Raymond.'

Her father's words, spoken without heat, hammered into her brain in short, stunning blows. She might have known he would guess. Joe Franklyn was an expert at reading the signals of unspoken communication.

'I may be,' she said, not looking at him.

There was no 'maybe' about it. Her new young doctor had confirmed the results of her home pregnancy test only yesterday.

Joe strummed his fingers on the smooth leather arms of his chair. 'It's Luke's, of course,' he said, as if there could be no doubt about it. 'Good thing you didn't get that divorce.'

He didn't sound upset. Merely brisk and practical. Olivia watched a small blue flame inch its way along the top of a log. Should she tell him the whole story and risk his telling Luke? Or think up some lie to distract him from the scent?

No, she couldn't do that. It would hurt him too much. Like most fathers, Joe Harriman preferred to think of his daughter as a model of old-fashioned virtue.

'We – I went to his apartment just once,' she said. 'To fetch the Starsky's dog.'

'That's not an answer.' Joe leaned forward, put two fingers on her chin and made her face him. 'But I assume it counts as a "yes"…?'

In spite of the fire, his touch felt cold against her skin. She jumped, and he dropped his hand at once. Custard, rudely awakened from sleep, gave a meow of protest and dug his claws into Olivia's knees through the soft cloth of her blue velvet slacks. Oblivious to the pain, she stroked his yellow fur with rhythmic concentration.

'If I told you it *was* Luke's – would you tell him?'

Joe's narrow mouth flattened. 'No. You would.'

Olivia shook her head. 'I can't, Dad. I don't want him to know. He doesn't love me, and I couldn't bear for him to come back to me the way he did the last time – only because he felt responsible for the baby.'

'Why not? You had no such scruples before. And he damn well ought to feel responsible.'

'Yes, but...you see, I thought then he *would* grow to love me. I meant him to. Now I know he won't. It's not his fault...'

'Don't you think he has a right to know?' Her father sat back, linking his hands on his stomach as if he'd made a judgement and expected it to be the end of the matter.

Olivia's laugh had a bitter ring to it. 'I'm not even sure he'd believe me.'

'He'd have to in a few months, wouldn't he?' Joe reached for his cigar and took a couple of short, expressive puffs.

'There's a good chance he might think it was somebody else's. You see he *was* careful. At least, I think he was. The fact is that I really don't know how it happened, but it did.'

Joe grunted and cleared his throat. 'What are you going to do, Olivia? That's the point.'

'I'm going to spend the night here. And in about seven months' time I'm going to have a baby.' Olivia stood up and made for the door. 'After that – I don't know. I suppose I'll be a mother.'

Impossible idea. She couldn't believe it herself, wasn't sure she wanted to believe it.

'Do you *like* children?' Her father sounded wary all of a sudden, out of his depth.

Olivia dropped her forehead against the smooth oak of the door. 'Not particularly. But this one will be mine.'

'And Luke's,' her father pointed out heavily. 'You have to tell him, Olivia.'

Oh no! Olivia spun round, searching for words that might convince him. '*You're* not to tell him,' she cried. '*You're not*. If you do I'll...I'll put the baby up for adoption.' She wouldn't, but it was the only threat she could think of that had a chance of making her father hold his tongue.

'Don't be ridiculous,' Joe waved his hand, dismissing her outburst as if she were a child stamping her feet in a tantrum.

'I'm not being ridiculous. I mean it.'

'Do you?' Joe raised a hand, smoothed it across his balding head. All at once he looked old and confused. 'Very well, I won't tell him. But I think you're making a very grave mistake.'

'I'm *not*,' Olivia insisted, willing him to understand. 'Don't you see? I can't live with a man who doesn't want me – who stays with me only because his conscience won't let him leave. I...I couldn't bear it. Really I couldn't.'

Joe opened his mouth, but before he could say anything, Olivia had scooped up Custard and hurried out of the room. As she was closing the door, she looked back.

Her father was staring after her, bleak-eyed, like one of those statues guarding the family vault. Olivia shivered. He had looked like that the day Raymond died. But she *couldn't* tell Luke. Her father's concern was for her. He didn't understand that she had no right to shatter Luke's life a second time; that the man who had been her husband must be allowed to live the rest of his life in peace.

Olivia made a soft, anguished sound in her throat and stumbled up the stairs to the room that had been her refuge since childhood.

Custard wriggled irritably, and she dropped him on to the bed before crossing to the window. The garden was dark, yet in her memory it was bright with flowers and laughter – the way it had been the day she married Luke.

She made herself look down at her waist.

Flat as a pancake. It didn't seem possible that down there somewhere cells were dividing and a baby was starting to grow...

Olivia lifted her hand and, with a slow kind of wonder, stroked the blue velvet covering her stomach.

'Merry Christmas, Luke's baby,' she whispered. 'Merry Christmas.'

Olivia was six months pregnant when Joe called one

evening to ask her to be his hostess at the Franklyn Foundation's annual ball.

She refused at first, pleading her size. But her father said her size didn't matter. When he explained that the assistant who'd filled the bill in previous years had recently retired, she reluctantly agreed to do as he asked.

The Franklyn Foundation, which doled out money to needy groups connected with the arts, was one of her father's favourite tax write-offs. The annual ball attracted press as well as donations.

'I don't want my picture in the papers,' she warned him.

Luke read the papers. He would probably assume the child was someone else's, but she wasn't ready to take that chance. Not yet.

'I'll make it clear to them you're not to be photographed,' Joe agreed. 'I need you, Olivia.'

Olivia sighed. 'Yes, all right. I've said I'll do it. But only if you promise not to make me dance. I feel clumsy enough as it is.'

'It's a deal. You can plead your delicate condition.' His voice deepened, became less flippant. 'How are you, Moonbeam?'

'Great,' Olivia replied truthfully. 'What with Hopeville, and getting ready for the baby, I haven't had time to be delicate.'

'That's good, that's good.' Joe hung up before she could change her mind and told his secretary to add a new name to the guest list.

chapter fourteen

Luke's immediate instinct on receiving an invitation to the Franklyn Foundation's annual ball was to throw it out. But as the day wore on, the white square with its silver lettering seemed to jeer up at him from his waste basket, taunting him, accusing him of avoiding the ball purely because it was connected with the Franklyns. Eventually, he jerked the invitation from its resting place and read it over, this time with care.

He didn't particularly like dancing, but he'd been told by an outspoken ex-girlfriend that he danced passably, by current standards at least, provided he stayed in one spot, moved his hips and didn't attempt to lead his partner around the floor. It was a doubtful compliment which had amused him at the time.

The real question, of course, was whether he would have attended this society fling if he hadn't suspected that the invitation came from Olivia.

He might, he supposed. Not exactly his scene, but it didn't hurt business to be seen in the company of the tax-shelter crowd now and then.

He stared down at the shiny silver lettering. Dammit, he was not going to let Olivia continue to influence his choices. She had once told him she rarely attended the annual event, but on the off-chance that this was another set-up, he would take a partner. That way no one could think he was unattached.

He reached for the phone to call Georgina, a recent divorcée whose brother was an old friend.

It was no surprise to Luke that Joe Franklyn had chosen the

oldest and most sedately elegant hotel in Vancouver as the setting for his ball. Pausing in the lobby to look around, he noted high ceilings, gilded white walls, and a lot of brocade and mahogany. In the ballroom the lights fell on gleaming white tablecloths and glinted off crystal and ice behind the bar. An assembly of Vancouver's famous and philanthropic stood about bathed in the soft glow from chandeliers, while on a small stage at the back of the dance floor, a soberly-dressed band was running through a medley of tunes more old than new.

Luke glanced down at the woman who was clinging to his arm with flattering tenacity. Her wavy blonde head barely reached his shoulder. She was a pretty thing – small, lithe and with curves in all the right places. Would tonight be the night? The night he finally left the memory of Olivia behind?

Georgina, becoming aware of his scrutiny, flipped back her hair and gave him a seductive smile, which he returned with an appreciative grin before putting his palm on her bare back to urge her in the direction of a table where a group of his business associates sat waiting for the dancing to begin.

Luke ordered drinks for himself and Georgina and sat back to take an unobtrusive survey of the room.

Joe Franklyn was there with a pregnant woman in a long-sleeved, midnight blue dress. He couldn't see her face, but he could hardly miss her belly. The Crumps were there too. He could hear Mrs Crump greeting an acquaintance.

There was no sign of Olivia.

Good. With a feeling that he told himself was pure relief, he tilted his chair back, rested an ankle on his knee and turned his attention to Georgina.

Half-an-hour later, after Joe Franklyn had made a brief speech of welcome, she dragged him on to the dance floor. Resignedly at first, Luke began to move his hips in time with the music.

Georgina moistened her lips and shimmied around him with a sexy swish of black satin.

Luke smiled encouragingly and placed his hands on her hips.

Georgina shimmied closer, rubbing herself against him like a sleek, blonde cat waiting to be fed. The band chose that moment to start up a boisterous rendition of *'Don't Be Cruel.'*

Georgina laughed. 'Maybe later,' she said. 'Come on, let's sit this one out.'

He took her back to their table, after which she turned her back on him and began an animated conversation with a young stockbroker who had come alone to the dance.

Luke left her to it, and went to pay his respects to the host who, for the time being at least, was still his wife's father.

He found Joe standing near the band, looking pained as he tried to carry on a conversation with a gaunt-faced man in a kilt over the strains of *'Rock Around the Clock.'*

Luke held out his hand and shouted, 'Good evening, sir.'

Joe took it and said something that might have been 'Harrumph.' After a few moments of stilted conversation, Luke concluded his presence wasn't welcome.

He was about to make his way back to Georgina, when his path was blocked by a large expanse of blue silk. Without looking up, he started to make his way around it – until a familiar scent gave him pause.

With curious reluctance, he allowed his gaze to be drawn upwards to the face above the dress.

No! She *couldn't* be. He was seeing things. Luke rubbed his eyes and focused on the swelling protrusion of a stomach draped in blue. Dammit, he hadn't had all *that* much to drink.

Taking a long breath, Luke held out his hand and said as evenly as he could, 'Good evening, Olivia. How are you?'

'Hello, Luke,' she replied, in a voice that wasn't as assured as he remembered. 'This is a surprise.'

A surprise? She called it a *surprise*? Luke reached for support that wasn't there as something pointed and painful twisted in his chest. He wasn't imagining things. Olivia was most definitely pregnant. He took a step forward, still half-expecting she would vanish the way illusions were meant to do. But she remained poised in front of him, solidly pregnant, and yet somehow luminous in the soft ballroom light.

She was not some spectre conjured up by heat and whisky.

Luke shook his head in an attempt to make sense out of absurdity, and Olivia's troubled dark eyes met his with what looked like consternation. For a few seconds he felt as if the floor had been sucked out from underneath his feet.

'Olivia?' he said at last, as the ballroom and her blue, swollen body came sharply back into focus. 'Olivia? You're...'

'Yes,' she agreed. 'I'm pregnant. It happens sometimes.'

'Not to you.' Anger, flaming and unstoppable, surged up from some dark place in his soul and made him want to hurt her...to wound her as she had wounded him. How *could* she be pregnant by some other man?

When Olivia gave a small, quickly suppressed gasp, he knew he'd struck home.

Immediately he wanted to comfort her, would perhaps have done so if at that moment her lips hadn't parted in a small, bitter smile.

'As you can see,' she said acidly. 'Even to me.'

'How...I mean when...?' Damn. Why did his mouth feel as if it were coated with sand? And why should he care that she had found release in someone else's arms? He was about to do the same thing himself.

'I'm due in about two months,' Olivia replied, as if she were saying it would probably rain next week. When he didn't answer, she murmured, 'Enjoy the rest of your evening,' and turned away.

Instinctively, Luke put a hand on her arm to detain her. 'Wait. We have to talk.'

'No. We don't. We've already said everything we need to say.'

From behind him, Luke heard Joe's voice shout above the pounding of the music, 'Don't be a fool, Olivia. Talk to him.'

Olivia shrugged and turned sideways so that all Luke could see of her was the size of her belly.

'What's the point?' she asked.

'The point?' Luke answered for Joe, making himself speak slowly and calmly. 'For one thing, you are, so far as I know, still my wife. And you appear to be having a baby.' The coolness of his words had no connection with the heat he felt inside, but he knew better than to let her think he cared. Hell, he *didn't* care.

After a pause, she said, 'All right. We can talk in the lobby if you like,' and turned her back on him without waiting for his reply.

Feeling as if he'd been hit on the head by a plank with very big nails, Luke followed her around the edge of the room. Her dark blue dress billowed around her hips like a small tent, and although she still walked as if she owned the world, it was more the walk of a miniature tank on the move than the seductive motion he was used to.

Luke swallowed an unusual thickness in his throat. Even disguised as a tank, she had the power to move him. There was something poignant and courageous about this new Olivia. This Olivia who, last year, had saved a woman's life and now was about to give birth to a child. He felt the need to protect her...from what he didn't know. From himself perhaps.

He wasn't used to feeling protective about Olivia.

Muttering, 'Excuse me,' he dodged around two waiters carrying trays of *hors d'oeuvres,* and grabbed her by the elbow.

She glanced up at him doubtfully, but said nothing.

They had almost reached the big gilt doors when an indignant voice exclaimed from the dance floor, 'Oh! But I thought...are you telling me that's his *wife*?'

Luke glanced over his shoulder, just in time to see Georgina waltz past in the arms of the stockbroker, her pretty mouth wide with shock and disapproval.

So much for tonight being 'the night.'

Yet, as he led Olivia out into the lobby, he was surprised to realise he didn't give a damn.

They paused by the reception desk. 'Over there will do.' Luke jerked his head at a group of red damask chairs in a corner near the velvet-draped windows.

Olivia nodded and allowed him to steer her to the most comfortable seat, an overstuffed armchair with a well-padded back. She sank down without a word, and folded her hands in what had once been her lap.

Now that he had her where he wanted her, Luke discovered he had no idea what he planned to say. And obviously she wasn't going to help him. The knowledge did nothing to improve his temper, particularly as he was aware that, this time, he had no real cause for complaint.

'You didn't waste any time,' he said finally.

Why had he insisted on this conversation? Why hadn't he had the sense to turn his back on her, and leave her to the tender mercies of whoever had put her in this state?

'Doing what?' She ran a finger around the low neckline of her dress, as if she felt too warm.

He jerked a thumb at her stomach. 'Turning the lie you told me into somebody else's truth.'

Olivia moved her hands protectively over her swollen belly. 'Oh, I see,' she said dully. 'That's what you meant.'

Luke tried not to grind his teeth. 'Are you going to marry him once the divorce is final?'

Olivia examined her foot in its blue satin shoe. 'That's not very likely.'

'Hmm. Just toying with him, were you?'

She released a faint sigh, and went on examining the shoe. 'No, nothing like that.'

'I see.'

Olivia half-rose from her chair, then thought better of it. What was the sense in being angry? Luke *didn't* see, of course. She'd been fairly sure he wouldn't. The timing was right, but he'd been careful. So, why should he suspect that *he* was the author of her condition?

All the same...there was something wrong with this scene.

Luke was glowering at her as if she'd committed some heinous crime – as if he *really* minded her being pregnant. But why should he? He didn't care about her; couldn't wait to be free of her, so why...

'Do I know him?' Luke asked, breaking in on the chaos rattling around her head.

What incredible irony! Olivia's lips twitched in what she hoped was a smile. 'I doubt it.'

Luke frowned and leaned towards her as though he read something in her face he wasn't meant to see. 'You're not going to tell me it's mine?'

Olivia dug her nails into the red damask arms of her chair. 'Have you heard me tell you that?'

He shook his head, still frowning. 'No – and I find that surprising. You say the man's not going to marry you. I'd have thought that made me a prime target. You can't have forgotten I fell for it once. At least *this* time you have irrefutable evidence.'

Did he *have* to sound so bitter? She'd known it was a mistake to talk to him, known she should escape while she had the chance – yet, in the end, she hadn't been able to pass up the opportunity to be with him, if only for a few snatched, unhappy moments in the lobby.

'Not irrefutable,' she said. 'And even if it was, I wouldn't go back on my word. I promised you your freedom, Luke. Remember?'

'Sure. I remember. I'm just surprised you do.'

She choked back a small, wounded gasp. Why, oh why hadn't she left the ballroom the moment she saw Luke with her father, instead of standing frozen to the floor until he noticed her? But his back had looked so endearingly familiar, so strong and upright, that she hadn't been able to tear her eyes away.

And now...?

Supposing she told him the truth? That would wipe the small, hard smile off his lips. He might even believe her.

For a few seconds Olivia was tempted. Then she looked at him sitting across from her in his evening clothes, all masculine and beautiful and unreasonable – and she couldn't do it. It wasn't fair he should be burdened with a family he didn't want.

She put a hand on her stomach, and felt a hearty kick that made her smile inside. That kick made up for a lot.

Luke must have noticed the change in her expression, because he stopped looking like judge and jury combined, and asked quite kindly, 'What are you going to do then? Without a husband?'

Behind them, a man with a loud voice started an argument with the desk clerk about a key. Olivia waited until he quietened down before replying, 'Exactly what I'd do if I had one. I'm going to be a mother.'

'I can see that.' His smile was now irritatingly patient. 'I meant how are you going to look after it?'

'The same way everyone else does, I suppose.'

A spark flashed in Luke's eyes, and he moved to grasp her wrist. 'Olivia, how could...' He stopped, wiped the back of his free hand across his forehead and shook his head as if he had just awoken from a dream.

'Sorry,' he muttered, and dropped her arm as abruptly as he'd grabbed it.

Olivia rubbed her wrist and stood up. There was nothing to be gained by prolonging this conversation. 'I have to get back to our guests,' she explained.

Luke nodded, and she had a feeling he was relieved. 'Of course. I didn't mean to distract you from your duty.'

'Duty?' Olivia tried to smile. 'It's not that onerous.'

'Good.' His gaze shifted to a discarded evening paper lying on the table beside his chair. 'Take care of yourself. I hope...everything...goes well.' He picked up the paper and began to scan the front page.

'Thank you.' Olivia touched a hand to her forehead, wondering why she suddenly felt dizzy. Ought she to say goodbye?

She decided she couldn't summon the energy.

Turning her back on him, she edged her bulky body through the obstacle course of chairs and tables, holding on to each sturdy wooden back as she passed. When she reached the reception desk the smell of polish on mahogany made her sneeze.

She knew she ought to keep walking, but for the moment she was too tired to move.

Luke was watching her. She could feel his eyes on her back...

Slowly, not wanting to, she turned around.

He was sitting where she had left him, his dark clothes in dramatic contrast to the wine-red fabric of the chair.

Oh how much, how very much, she loved him. Olivia closed her eyes, unable to look at him any more. *Should* she tell him? *Did* he have the right to know, as her father said?

She opened her eyes, took a half-step towards him – and at that moment he lifted his hand in a gesture of farewell.

She stopped. He was dismissing her. Of course he

wouldn't want to know that he was forever bound by the ties of fatherhood to a woman he despised.

Their eyes met briefly, and she nodded her acceptance of his dismissal before stumbling across the lobby, dodging tourists and party-goers until she came to the entrance to the ballroom.

At first she couldn't see her father, and as she leaned against the wall scanning the crowd for a glimpse of his bald head, a woman's voice bellowed in her ear, 'Ah, there you are, Olivia. I've been looking for you.'

Oh no. Not Mrs Crump! Olivia pressed both hands against the wall. Please, not now, when her heart was breaking. The throbbing in her head intensified as Dora Crump's persistent voice shouted, 'Olivia! I said I've been looking for you.'

'Yes, I heard you, Mrs Crump,' Olivia replied tiredly. 'Are you enjoying yourself?'

'Always too noisy, these affairs.' Mrs Crump continued to bellow. 'I want to talk to you about that baby, Olivia. Your father tells me you and Luke have separated. Is that why he's here with another woman?' The band had come to the end of a set, and her voice thundered to the farthest reaches of the room.

Gasps of shock and excitement rose from the throats of the assembled guests.

Finding no secure grip on the wall, Olivia reached for the back of the nearest chair as all heads swivelled in her direction. One head in particular, she noticed. It belonged to a blonde young woman whose face had turned the colour of old brick.

Olivia edged round the chair and sat down. She wondered if Luke had heard Mrs Crump's announcement, and a small, malicious part of her hoped he had.

'Ah. Olivia.' Joe swept up to them as if he hadn't heard a word of the exchange. His eyes were a little bluer than usual, the colour of his cheeks more waxlike, but apart from that no one who didn't know him would have sensed his outrage.

'Good evening, Dora,' he said to Mrs Crump. 'Olivia, are you sure you're quite well? You look pale.'

'*So do you*', Olivia thought. But all she said was, 'I'm fine. Just a bit tired.'

Mrs Crump started to say, 'Joseph, I really think...' but was cut off in mid-sentence when Joe held out his hand to Olivia and said, 'If you don't mind, Dora, I'd like to talk to my daughter. In private.'

'Oh well, of course,' Mrs Crump said huffily. 'I wouldn't want to intrude.'

'I'm sure you wouldn't.'

Joe's lips were white and flat as he took Olivia by the hand and led her to a small office off the ballroom which was as far from the band as they could get.

'I'm sorry, Moonbeam,' he said. 'Dora's been a friend of the family's for many years, but there are times when I'd like to kick her fat posterior from here to Hades.'

At any other time, Olivia would have laughed. Now she was aware of nothing but the need for escape. Bowing her head, she let her long hair fall across her face. 'It's all right,' she said. 'I'm used to her.'

Joe put a finger under her chin. 'You look exhausted. I'll get the limo to take you home at once.'

Olivia shook her head. 'Our guests...'

'Are doing nicely without us.'

Olivia pushed back her hair and went to the door of the office. The band was returning from a break, dancers were drifting on to the floor, and those at the tables were concentrating on drinks and *hors d'oeuvres*. As her father said, the guests were doing nicely without them.

It was the same every year. Once the speeches and introductions were over, everyone got on with the serious business of drinking, eating and dancing.

'Did you talk me into coming because you'd invited Luke?' she asked, voicing a suspicion that had been growing in her from the moment she'd laid eyes on her husband. It wasn't a question, nor yet an accusation. She was too stunned, too bruised by the events of the evening to be angry.

Joe cleared his throat, reached into his pocket for a cigar that wasn't there, and said, 'He was included in the list of possible guests.'

Olivia nodded tiredly. It was too late to remonstrate with her father, whose eyes had narrowed suddenly.

'You look like hell, Moonbeam,' he said. 'I'll get the limo.'

'No, I don't need...' She stopped, put a hand to her head and let the thought go – because all of a sudden she *did* need, very badly, to get out of this hot, stuffy, room and into the cool summer fragrance of the night.

'Come with me.' Joe put a masterful arm around her shoulders and half carried, half dragged her out of the ballroom. She heard the curious murmurs behind her and didn't care.

The next thing she knew, her father was helping her into a limo and telling the driver to take her directly to The Cedars. 'I'll call Mrs Cavendish,' he said. 'She'll be waiting for you. And make sure you get right into bed.'

Olivia nodded, too weary and too desolate to argue.

Luke, on his way across the lobby, saw her leave.

He watched as the door of the limo closed, glimpsed her white face through the window and went back into the ballroom to find Georgina.

chapter fifteen

She came at him practically spitting, the svelte young woman who, earlier that evening, had welcomed him with a smile.

Luke held up a hand to fend her off, his mouth twisting in weary self-derision. 'Hold it,' he ordered. 'I've been brought up not to fight back.'

Georgina came to a halt with the young stockbroker hot on her heels. 'How could you?' she cried. 'If I'd known your wife was expecting a baby…'

'I didn't know either,' Luke interrupted. 'We're getting divorced. But I'm sorry you think that I misled you.'

Georgina glared. 'Are you telling me you're deserting her *and* the baby?' Her satin dress rustled with indignation.

'That's between me and my wife,' Luke replied.

'Georgina…' The young stockbroker shuffled uncomfortably behind her. 'Would you like to dance?'

'She'd love to,' Luke said quickly. 'Wouldn't you, Georgina? And perhaps your friend won't mind seeing you home?' He raised a questioning eyebrow, and the young man nodded eagerly.

'Good. That's settled. Goodnight, Georgina. I apologise sincerely for the confusion.' Luke swung away before she had a chance to aim further shafts his way.

So much for Georgina. He didn't mind, but he did regret causing her distress. Accepting this invitation had been a monumental mistake. What, in God's name, had possessed him? Latent masochism? Or an insane desire to lay himself open, yet again, to the grief only Olivia's machinations could bring.

If that was the case, he was definitely out of his mind. Not even the world's most dim-witted blockhead would allow Olivia Franklyn to get her claws on him more than twice.

Luke's mind was on the past as he strode into the lobby, and he didn't, at first, notice the man standing in his way. By the time he did, it was too late to avoid him.

'I hope you're pleased with yourself, young man.'

Damn. The last thing he was in the mood for now was a confrontation with Joe Franklyn.

'Not particularly,' he admitted, making an effort to keep his tone civil.

Joe didn't blink. 'Do you have even the slightest idea what you've done to Olivia?'

Luke frowned and shook his head. 'I haven't done anything to her, to my knowledge. Presumably that honour went to the father of her child.'

'Don't be a jackass,' Joe snapped. 'You *must* know...' He stopped, made a noise that was a cross between a snort and a sneeze, and developed a sudden interest in his patent leather shoes.

'Must know what?' Luke's frown deepened. He could understand Joe's concern for his daughter, but her pregnancy had nothing to do with *him*. Even Olivia hadn't suggested that.

Joe cleared his throat. 'Never mind. Ask Olivia,' he replied, and spun round to talk to a passing dowager whose teeth kept clicking out.

Luke stared at the back of Joe's head. Had everyone, including himself, gone completely crazy? It was beginning to look that way. He'd better remove himself from the danger zone before he fell victim to further contagion.

Five minutes later, in the hotel's cavernous underground car park, he folded himself into the front seat of his new Corvette and attempted to put the events of the evening into perspective.

Something had happened to him tonight. Something that left him feeling hollow, stunned, as if he'd lost a prized possession he knew he would never see again. He had felt that way once as a child when he'd dropped his whole week's allowance down a drain.

The difference was that this time he wasn't sure what he'd lost.

A giggle came from behind the nearest concrete pillar, and a flash of red skirt caught his eye. Distracted, he glanced through the window and saw a man's hand slide purposefully up a nylon-sheathed thigh.

Sweat beaded on Luke's neck and brow. With a muttered curse, he laid his arms on the wheel and rested his forehead on his hands.

Red was Olivia's colour of choice for seduction. And it worked. Lord, did it work! He remembered the feel of her limbs wrapped around his – warm, silky and numbingly sweet...

At the climactic moment she had always cried his name.

Luke gripped the wheel, and when his body hardened, responding automatically to the nature of his thoughts, he groaned out loud.

'Dammit, Olivia, *why*...?'

Hearing the sound of his own voice reverberating in the confined space, he resolutely pushed himself upright.

What was it Joe had said? Something about him being pleased with himself for what he'd done to Olivia? His mouth flattened. *He* hadn't done anything to Olivia. She...

Hold on. Wait a minute. Joe had started to say he must know...must know what? Luke pressed the bridge of his nose between forefinger and thumb as a memory, fleeting but startlingly vivid, caught at his mind and refused to let go.

Olivia hadn't actually *said* he was responsible for her baby, and had more or less indicated the opposite. But in those last few seconds in the lobby, when she had stopped by the desk and turned around, there *had* been something – a hesitation, no more, as if there was still unfinished business between them. She had looked sad and vulnerable in that moment, and he had wanted desperately to go to her...

Yet he had waved her away. He remembered quite clearly now. Her shoulders had drooped, she had nodded slightly as if accepting some sort of decision – then hurried out of the lobby. He had been surprised that a woman in her condition could move so fast...

'You're a fool, Harriman!' Luke exclaimed. 'A first-class, prize-winning jackass.' He sat bolt upright and slammed his fist on to the dashboard.

A couple of men in suits passed by, glanced at him askance and changed direction.

Luke threw back his head and let out a sound that was meant to be a laugh but came out sounding more like a howl of remorse.

He stared blankly at his throbbing fist. Then shook his head and started up the car.

At precisely seven o'clock in the morning Luke, unshaven, unrested and wearing only a rumpled T-shirt and jeans, stood on the front steps of The Cedars pressing a demanding finger to the luminous white disk of the bell.

Last night, when he had discovered Olivia wasn't home, his first thought had been to drive at once to see her. Then it occurred to him that no one would answer the door at this hour, and he had no choice but to leave it till morning.

A shuffling sound came from inside the house, followed by silence as, no doubt, he was thoroughly inspected through a peephole. After that a bolt clicked back and the door was slowly dragged open.

Mrs Cavendish, dressed all in black, regarded him without favour.

'Good morning. I've come to see Olivia,' Luke said.

'She isn't here, Mr Harriman.'

'She...' Luke choked back an impatient retort. 'Mr Franklyn then. I'd like to speak to him, please.'

'Mr Franklyn has gone to the hospital,' the housekeeper said stiffly.

'Hospital?' Luke's stomach took a nosedive to his knees. 'Olivia?'

'Naturally.' The Cavendish nostrils twitched in a way Luke found particularly maddening.

Alarm bells clanged in his head. Fear stroked his skin with cold fingers. He made himself brush them off. 'Which hospital?' he asked.

She told him, and he said 'Thank you,' and seconds later was skidding down the driveway on two wheels.

He had only driven a block when the ear-splitting shriek of an ambulance forced him to pull to a stop. As he waited impatiently for the emergency vehicles to pass, it occurred to him that only once before had he experienced such a feeling of urgency. On that occasion he had more or less fallen down a mountain to get to Rosemary.

This was different. This was Olivia, who was almost certainly having his child. He had to get to her, had to be with her...premature births could be dangerous.

'Dear God,' he prayed, his knuckles white on the wheel, 'Take care of her. Please. Don't let anything happen...'

Two ambulances flashed by, and at once he shot into the traffic and changed lanes to avoid a slow-moving truck. The car behind him honked its owner's outrage.

Luke didn't care. 'Don't let it be too late,' he pleaded, to a Deity he'd paid little attention to over the years. 'Let her come through this and I swear I'll make things right.'

It was his fault she had gone to the hospital with only her father to support her. He had taken his pleasure and left her to bear the consequences alone.

Oh, he hadn't known, hadn't believed the baby could be

his. But he should have known. She had told him long ago that she'd changed – and the evidence – her dedication to Hopeville, had been there for anyone to see.

But the most telling evidence, the truth he could no longer escape, was that she had chosen to have this baby of his. The old Olivia would have put her own convenience first.

'You're a jerk, Harriman,' he muttered, as he pulled into the hospital lot. 'Too damn stupid to see what you had. And now it could be too late.'

He swung himself on to the pavement, and a small, grey-haired lady with an umbrella told him to watch where he was putting his big feet.

With a murmured apology he hurtled through the big double doors and slammed to a stop at the reception desk.

'Franklyn?' the receptionist murmured, casting a languid eye over her computer screen.

'That's what I said.' Luke tried, unsuccessfully, to hide his impatience.

The woman punched a couple of keys. 'There's a Franklyn on the third floor,' she said. 'But...'

Luke was already halfway across the lobby. 'Only family are allowed,' the receptionist called after him.

'I am family,' he shouted, shouldering his way on to a crowded elevator.

'No consideration for other people,' a prissy little voice murmured behind him.

Luke paid no attention. When the doors slid open he was first off. The nursing station was to his right, and he stepped briskly towards it. Then all at once, the walls of the sea-green hospital corridor seemed to blur, shimmering and billowing like the Northern Lights until, in desperation, he closed his eyes.

He was dreaming on his feet. Lack of sleep had made him delirious. Luke reached blindly for the railing along the wall.

Further down the ward wheels squeaked, and a man's loud voice said, 'Not in here, Mr Ajanian. Come along, I'll take you to your room.'

Luke made himself open his eyes.

He wasn't dreaming.

Plodding towards him was a dark-haired, very pregnant woman wearing black slacks and a red maternity smock.

Olivia's first thought was that the disreputable-looking character standing in her way was one of the hospital's regular deadbeats. Because he couldn't be Luke.

Then he said, 'Olivia,' in a hoarse, totally unnatural voice – and she knew he was.

She moved her lips in what she hoped was a smile, held out her hand and said as casually as she could, 'Hello, Luke. What are you doing here?'

He didn't take the proffered hand, and now that she had a chance to examine him closely, Olivia saw that her initial impression of his condition had been nothing compared to the reality. She swallowed a gasp of dismay.

What had happened to him? He looked terrible, as if nothing but sheer willpower was keeping him on his feet. With his face unshaven, his clothes wrinkled and his eyes dark with fatigue, he might have spent the night on the floor of some seedy bar. She could detect no resemblance to the suave, urbane businessman who had attended her father's ball last night.

Oh, if only she could take him in her arms, grunge and all, and kiss away the lines of care and stress. Was *she* responsible for those lines?

Olivia went on staring at him with a hunger she could no longer conceal. Appalled as she was by his appearance, he was still the only man who could touch her heart.

His skin, so tanned and healthy-looking last night, was a dull beige, his eyes glazed and seemingly unfocused.

Unable to stop herself, she reached up to touch his shattered face. There had to be something she could do...

Luke reacted to her to her touch as if he'd been struck by lightning.

Colour returned to his skin in an angry rush, and he shot out a hand and seized her arm.

Olivia blinked. Did he think she would try to run away? It had been months since she'd been able to run.

Seconds later she was not so much running as flying, as Luke towed her down the corridor with no regard for her ability to keep up.

'Luke, slow down,' she cried. 'I can't...'

He stopped so fast she almost ran into him.

'Sorry,' he said, as though perhaps he meant it. 'Where can we talk.'

'Right there.' She pointed to an empty sunroom with padded orange chairs arranged in a circle around a square table piled high with tattered magazines.

'Fine.' He steered her through the door. 'Now sit.' He spoke as if he expected to be obeyed.

Olivia sat.

'All right, now explain.' He stood over her, hands on hips, like some gaunt-faced inquisitor extracting a confession – an inquisitor who could definitely do with a shave.

'Explain? What are you talking about?' Olivia wondered if she looked as blank as she felt.

Luke took a deep breath. 'Why are you here? I thought you were having the baby.'

Olivia's heart, which had been beating much too fast, slowed down as if it meant to stop. If she hadn't known better, she would have sworn he had actually cared that she was about to give birth.

'No, there's nothing the matter with *me*,' she hastened to assure him. 'I'm here because of my father.'

Luke sank on to one of the orange chairs with the sinuous grace that, even under stress, came to him so naturally.

'Your father?' he exclaimed. 'What...? Oh. Yes. Mrs Cavendish did say he was at the hospital. I thought he'd come to be with you.'

'Because I'd gone into labour?' Olivia pleated the hem of her red smock.

'Yes. Of course.'

'But I haven't.'

'I can see that.' Luke's long frame seemed to relax. Marginally. 'I thought I was losing my mind when I saw you waddling along the corridor out there.'

'I wasn't "waddling".'

'Oh yes, you were!' The mask that was Luke's face cracked a little, and he stretched out his legs and hooked his arms over the back of his chair. 'I think you're supposed to.'

Olivia attempted a smile, but in the end she didn't feel up to it. The night had been long and frightening and now that it was over, this sudden confrontation with Luke was almost more than she could handle.

'My father had a heart attack,' she said releasing the dreadful words in a rush. 'Last night, after he came home from the ball. I was in bed, but I heard him call out.'

Luke's head jerked up. 'Is he all right?'

'They think he will be. He's sleeping now, and the doctor says if he's careful about his lifestyle, there's no reason he shouldn't live a normal life.'

Luke passed a hand across his forehead. 'I'm glad. And you...you spent the night here?'

'Mm. We weren't sure he was going to make it at first.' Again she tried to smile, this time to blot out the awfulness of finding her grey-faced father seated on the edge of his bed groaning in pain.

'You've had quite a night, haven't you?' Luke studied her with what looked like concern. 'Have you eaten?'

She shook her head. 'I was just on my way to the cafeteria.'

Luke stood up at once. 'Of course. You must be starving. I shouldn't have kept you here talking...'

'It's all right. Do you...have *you* had breakfast?' Why were they sitting here discussing food when there were so many more important issues to be resolved?

A tapping sound drew Olivia's gaze to the door. An old lady in a pink dressing gown was advancing unsteadily into the sun-room with the aid of a stick.

'Isn't it a lovely day?' she said, shuffling sideways like an elderly crab, and settling herself in a chair near the window. She reached into her pocket and fished out a battered pack of cigarettes.

Was it a lovely day? Olivia hadn't noticed.

'Yes, beautiful,' she agreed.

The old lady threw a shifty look at the door and clamped a cigarette between her gums. 'Better not let the nurses catch me lighting up,' she said, grinning with what was left of her teeth.

Luke stuck his head out the door and assured her there wasn't a nurse in sight. 'Let's go get you some breakfast,' he said to Olivia, holding out his hand.

She accepted it with the uncertainty of a teenager on her very first date. It felt warm and strong and reassuring. As he drew her to her feet, she gave him a cautious smile.

'Better watch out,' the old lady called after them. 'That baby will be popping out any day now. I know. Had six of the little devils myself. And not one of 'em the worse for a bit of smoke.'

Olivia shuddered, and Luke smothered a grin. 'Not your idea of a good time?' he asked mildly.

'What, six kids? Or cigarettes?'

'Both. Either. Though I'd hate to see you smoking around our baby.'

Olivia tightened her grip on his hand. 'Our baby?' she repeated, in a voice that refused to rise above a whisper.

The elevator arrived, miraculously empty, and Luke took her arm and hustled her inside.

'It is our baby, isn't it?' The doors closed with a disconcerting thud.

Olivia closed her eyes and sank against the wall. He knew. And he believed. But she hadn't meant him to know. Luke didn't *want* this baby. What if...?

Her thoughts skidded to a stop as the elevator arrived on the ground floor. Immediately Luke took charge of her arm again and marched her along to the cafeteria.

'Wait here,' he said, depositing her at a green table in a corner. I'll fetch your breakfast. Scrambled eggs, apple juice and tea?'

He'd remembered. 'Yes, thank you,' she said faintly. Funny, she hadn't realised how weak she felt until she sat down.

Hers weren't the only eyes that followed Luke as he walked with long, unhurried strides towards the counter. In spite of his unkempt appearance, Olivia felt a foolish glow of pride. She had noticed last night that his hair was a little longer than usual. It looked nice that way. And hadn't he lost weight? The T-shirt and jeans clung so snugly to his frame it was hard to tell. Maybe he only *looked* leaner. Either way his effect on her was devastating. She might be seven months pregnant, but one glimpse of Luke was still all it took to turn her thoughts to bed.

Stop it, Olivia. You're a long way from bed. She put up a hand to prevent the words from spurting out of her mouth. *First you have to figure out how to explain to that gorgeous, dishevelled and quite probably angry man over there why you neglected to tell him he was about to become a father.*

It didn't bear thinking about. Yet think about it she must – because he was already on his way back to the table bearing a tray piled high with plates of toast and egg.

Luke unloaded the tray and sat down. 'Eat up,' he said, setting an example by biting crisply into his toast.

Olivia breathed in the smell of melted butter and began to eat.

'Mm. That was good,' she told him ten minutes later, after she had tucked away the last mouthful of egg. 'Thank you.'

Luke nodded and put down his knife and fork. 'Right. Do you plan to explain yourself?' He spoke with a mildness she was sure was deceptive.

A young woman in a blue overall arrived to clear away their plates. Olivia sent up a prayer of thanks for the extra few seconds to collect her thoughts.

In the end though, the delay made no difference. She still had no idea what to say. To make matters worse, the standard cafeteria smell of coffee and frying was growing stronger as the morning progressed. These had become her two least favourite smells since she'd been pregnant.

'Explain myself?' she repeated weakly, still stalling for time. What did Luke expect her to say?

Irritation flared in his eyes and was immediately brought under control. 'The baby *is* mine, isn't it? I want the truth this time.'

He didn't sound angry. But how could he not be?

Olivia nodded, glad, in a way, that there was no longer any reason for concealment. 'Yes,' she admitted. 'But I didn't think you'd believe me if I told you.'

'Can you think of one single reason why I should?'

'No. But you do. You just said so.'

Crockery clattered behind the counter, and Luke ran a hand across his forehead. He looked incredibly tired. 'Yes,' he agreed. 'I do. Your father said something that made me think. And I remembered the way you'd looked at me last night. So sad and yet so – I don't know. In any case I knew you weren't acting.'

Olivia refilled her teacup from the small metal pot and carefully added milk. 'No. I wasn't acting. I don't much any more.'

She put the pot down, and Luke leaned over the table to take her hand. 'Look at me, Olivia.'

Olivia looked up with silent resignation. This wasn't going well. In her fantasies, Luke had always melted to marshmallow the moment he learned the burden she was carrying was his.

He wasn't melting now. He was smouldering.

'Why didn't you tell me?' He spoke hoarsely, as if he had to force the words past an obstruction in his throat.

Olivia attempted to pull her hand away.

Luke maintained his grip briefly, then muttered something she didn't catch, and let go. 'Why?' he repeated.

Damn. She'd hurt him again. She hadn't meant to.

Olivia swallowed a mouthful of tea she couldn't taste. 'Because I knew, if you believed me, you'd feel obliged to come back to me,' she said. 'To look after us when you didn't really want to.'

He gave a dry laugh. 'That didn't bother you before.'

'No, it didn't. I wanted you at any price then.'

Luke moved his head from side to side, slowly, as if he couldn't believe what he was hearing. 'And now?'

'Now?' Olivia, who had been staring unproductively into her tea, raised her eyes as far as the T-shirt stretched across his chest. 'Now I find the price is too high.'

'You don't want to be married to me? Is that it?'

Oh dear God. Were all men so terminally dense? Didn't he understand that the only reason she hadn't told him the truth was that she loved him – loved him far too much to hold him against his will?

'Olivia? I need an answer.'

With an effort, she shifted her gaze up to his jaw. It looked very square and grim.

'I...it doesn't matter what I want, does it?' she said despairingly. 'You don't want to be married to *me*.'

From the corner of her eye she noticed two hospital aides craning their necks to hear more. Behind the counter, someone dropped a tray. The smell of frying was curdling her stomach.

Luke sat unmoving across the table.

'Luke?' At last she found the courage to meet his eyes.

What she saw there confused her. She had expected condemnation, even outright rejection. She saw no sign of either. Yet nor could she detect any indication that he looked on her as more than a burden he had borne once, and perhaps would again.

'It's all right,' she said dully. 'The divorce will be final soon. And you needn't worry that I won't be a good mother. Of course you can see the baby any time you want...'

'Olivia!' Without warning, Luke pushed back his chair and stood up. 'Shut up. I...Oh, hell!.' He gripped the back of his chair until his knuckles turned white. 'OK, let's start again. I'm sorry. I meant, don't be an idiot. And you'd better believe I'll see that baby any time I want. Why do you think I'm here?'

'I don't know. I suppose you feel guilty. But you needn't...'

'Olivia!' This time Luke roared so loudly that every head in the cafeteria turned his way. 'Don't you get it? I'm telling you there's no way you're going through with that divorce. You're my wife, dammit.'

What was he saying? He couldn't mean... Olivia put a hand to her head, resolutely repressing any inclination to stand up and melt into his arms.

'It's not entirely up to you,' she pointed out, in a voice so low she could scarcely hear it herself.

Luke removed his hands from the chair and planted his fists on the table. 'You're right. It isn't. Let me make myself clear. I don't want a divorce because I want to stay married to you, Olivia Franklyn. For better, for worse and...'

'For your baby,' Olivia finished, gazing into her cold tea and wishing she could drown in its clouded depths.

Not a sound came from behind the counter. The room was so quiet she could hear the couple at the next table breathing. Then Luke bent down, took both her hands in his and pulled her gently but firmly to her feet.

'What are you talking about? Olivia, I'm trying to tell you...I want you to be my wife. Not just the mother of my child. My...' He stopped, and the silence grew so loud he finally took note of the gaping mouths and the eager ears straining to hear.

He glanced briefly around the room and his lips tipped up with just a hint of malice. Taking Olivia's arm, he drew her to his side. 'OK, ladies and gentlemen,' he said, in what Olivia called his Chairman-of-the-Board voice. 'Let me introduce you to my wife. I'm about to propose to her. For the first time.' As all the jaws dropped lower, he turned to Olivia and whispered, 'I'd go down on one knee, but I doubt you'd be able to see me over that bulge that used to be your stomach. So here goes.' He raised his voice again so everyone could hear. 'Will you marry me, Olivia Franklyn? This time for always?'

Olivia ran her tongue across unusually dry lips. 'For always? You mean...'

'I mean for always.' Luke's arm tightened on her non-existent waist.

She tried to say, 'Yes,' but the word that emerged was, 'Why?'

A giggle erupted from behind the counter. Closer to hand, a chair scraped on the floor.

Luke gazed blankly at the top of Olivia's head, which was all he could see of her since her attention seemed riveted on her stomach.

Why? She was asking him *why* he wanted to marry her? The question crashed in on him with a blinding sense of shock.

If she had asked him that yesterday he wouldn't have known how to answer. But he knew now why he had accepted the invitation to Joe's ball, why he had made no effort to instigate divorce proceedings himself. He had felt the first glimmerings of understanding last night. Later, the knowledge of what this impossible woman had come to mean to him had gone unheeded in the need for action. Then he had stepped out of an elevator and seen her walking towards him, cool as a cucumber, the picture of healthy expectant motherhood. In that moment, the depth of his relief had been so profound it had exploded into anger. Yet still he hadn't accepted or acknowledged what any teenage fool would have known at once.

He would remedy that omission now.

'Because I love you,' he said.

He heard the quick hiss of indrawn breath, the suspended hum as their audience waited to hear what she would answer. Then Olivia raised her head and gave him a smile of such radiance that the muscles in his throat contracted and, just for a second, he couldn't breathe.

The moment the air rushed back into his lungs, he responded the only way he knew.

The cafeteria's entranced customers broke into cheers of approval as he placed both hands on his wife's shoulders and kissed her with serious intent.

The remembered sweetness slid like honey across his palate and down his throat, and he gave himself up to an enchantment that, only days ago, he would have sworn he would never know again. And Olivia, his Olivia, responded as she always had – with eagerness, intimacy and passion.

When at last Luke released her, the entire cafeteria burst into a round of spontaneous applause.

'I think,' Luke murmured into Olivia's ear, 'that this is where I'm supposed to pick you up and carry you out in triumph, to the accompaniment of a lot of loud and soaring music.'

She giggled. 'I don't think you can.'

'You don't?' He took a step backwards, studied her expanded figure with sober concentration, and finally shook his head. 'I do believe you're right. Will you settle for an arm around what passes for your waist?'

'As long as it's *your* arm.' Olivia laughed, but there were tears in her eyes.

Luke brushed them away. 'We'd better check on your father,' he said. 'After that you and I are going home.'

Olivia sniffed and managed a smile. 'Whose home? Yours or mine.'

'Ours, in either case. But since the penthouse is further away, let's go to yours, and give the neighbours something to talk about.'

Olivia nodded, and Luke draped his arm over her shoulder and led her out into the hall. Behind them, the cafeteria's customers rose as one and broke into a further round of thunderous applause.

'Shall we give them an encore?' Luke whispered.

'I think we should.' Olivia nodded gravely and lifted her face for his kiss.

epilogue

Luke lay on his side in the big bed gazing at his wife's sleeping face. Was it possible for a heart to burst with love and pride?

Two months ago, Olivia had presented him with two perfect twin daughters. Sarah, serious and sweet, and Michelle, already a busy, gregarious charmer. To Luke they were both small miracles, and the baby smell of powder and milk had quickly gained the power to twist his heart.

Olivia's instant adaptation to motherhood was another miracle. She adored the babies as much as he did.

They had waited until today to have them christened, in order to give their doting grandfather time to recover his strength, and their equally doting aunt time to return from her honeymoon in Hawaii. Now the christening was over and his daughters safely tucked in to their cribs in the house they had bought not far from Olivia's old home. It wasn't as large as the mansion she'd grown up in, but it had a view of the water through the trees, room for Luke's books – including a particularly fine Darwin first edition – and they both agreed it was the right place to raise a family.

Luke touched a finger to Olivia's nose, and she opened her eyes and smiled sleepily.

'It went well today, didn't it?' she murmured. 'The babies didn't cry and Mrs Bayliff and Mrs Dumont didn't come to blows.'

'No, they came to sherry, and had to be taken home,' Luke said dryly. 'Perhaps we should count ourselves lucky.'

'I do,' Olivia said simply. 'Very, very lucky. Luke ...?'

'Mm?'

'Are you happy?'

'Yes,' he said. 'Happier than I ever dreamed possible.'

'I'm glad.' With a contented sigh, Olivia turned on her side and laid her palm on his naked chest.

Luke placed his hand over hers.

They stayed like that for some time, tired, at peace, but not yet ready to take leave of the day.

Eventually Olivia said, 'Luke, now that we've got through the christening – do you think it's time we thought about...'

'Yes,' Luke said, trailing his fingers lightly down her side. 'I do.'

'No, I meant...well, a while ago you said something about raising a football team. What do you think? Not just yet, but maybe in a couple of years...'

'What?' Luke propped himself up on one elbow. 'You want a football team? *You*, Olivia?' His voice held a note of teasing disbelief. 'Do you know how many players there are on a football team?'

'No...'

'I didn't think so.' Without warning, he hooked an arm over her hips and pulled her to him. 'Never mind. If you're sure that's what you want, we'd better get started right away. Because it's going to take us a while to make a team.' He smoothed his palm possessively over her hip.

'A very *long* while, please.' Olivia gasped, as his fingers wrought their inevitable magic on her libido. 'I do love you, Luke.'

'I know.' He kissed the base of her throat. 'And you know what? To my eternal amazement, I love you. More than...' He stopped abruptly as something soft brushed across his cheek.

Custard, seated on Olivia's pillow, was washing his face.

'On the other hand,' Luke continued through his teeth, 'I am not, at this moment, especially crazy about your cat.'

Olivia giggled and deposited a bristling Custard on the floor. 'Better?' she asked.

'Much.' Wasting no further time, Luke pulled her back into his arms and got on with the business of making love to his wife.

Custard sneezed, raised his tail and stalked across the carpet to the window, where he sat contemplating the lovers' moon with baleful eyes. Only when the noises from the bed had subsided into the sound of contented breathing did he return to Olivia's pillow to complete his interrupted ablutions.

Oblivious, Olivia smiled in her sleep, snuggled into Luke's shoulder and dreamt that a team of little Harrimans, were playing football on the moon.

We're sure you've enjoyed this month's selection from Heartline. We can offer you even more exciting stories by our talented authors over the coming months. Heartline will be featuring books set in the ever popular and glamorous world of TV - novels with a dash of mystery - a romance featuring two dishy doctors – and just some of the authors we shall be showcasing are Margaret Callaghan, Angela Drake and Kathryn Grant.

If you've enjoyed these books why not tell all your friends and relatives that they, too, can Start a New Romance with Heartline Books today, by applying for their own, **ABSOLUTELY FREE**, copy of Natalie Fox's LOVE IS FOREVER. To obtain their free book, they can:

- visit our website @www.heartlinebooks.com
- *or* telephone the Heartline Hotline on 0845 6000504
- *or* enter their details on the form overleaf, tear off the whole page, and send it to:
  Heartline Books, PO Box 400, Swindon SN2 6EJ

And, like you, they can discover the joys of belonging to Heartline Books Direct™ including:

- ♥ A wide range of quality romantic fiction delivered to their door each month
- ♥ Celebrity interviews
- ♥ A monthly newsletter packed with special offers and competitions
- ♥ Author features
- ♥ A bright, fresh new website created just for our readers

Please send me my free copy of *Love is Forever*:

Name (IN BLOCK CAPITALS)

_____

Address (IN BLOCK CAPITALS)

_____

_____

_____

_____ Postcode _____

If you do not wish to receive selected offers
from other companies, please tick the box ☐

Heartline Books...
Romance at its best